FOR WHEN IT RAINS

Marvin Day

The First Fragment

First Edition

Edited by Jessica Julien at Desert Ink Editorial (@desertinkeditorial) and Liv Bertange

Original oil painting and cover design by Adam Solid (@solidadam)

Cover Typography by Michelle Spivak

Formatted by Jessica Julien at Desert Ink Editorial (@desertinkeditorial)

To my mother

CONTENTS

A Carol After Midnight

"Fucking Christians . . ." Todd muttered under his breath. *Where did we go wrong?* he thought to himself as he pulled his black jacket tighter and tucked his black scarf against his chin. It was pitch dark out and colder than death. And Christmas Eve.

Carolers stood on the wide concrete steps of St. Paul's cathedral that Todd walked past. A total of ten fat American Christians, all white. He did his best to ignore their presence and their flat melody. *It didn't used to be this way,* he thought. The streetlights cast a dim yellow haze on the snowy street and sidewalk. It was that new, pure snow—fresh and hadn't yet turned into the shitty blocks of ice that would last till March.

Todd hated this part of the world.

Not more than two years ago, he had been in sunny southern France. Life had been good. Life had been different. Life had been the way he had spent hundreds of years grooming it to be. But then everything got fucked. He got greedy. And, worst of all, he got caught.

He'd ran. And through a series of fleeing for his life, hiding, and plain trying to survive, he'd ended up in eastern Pennsylvania. And, of all places, Bethlehem, Pennsylvania. Ironic indeed, because back in old Bethlehem was where Todd's antithesis had been born. *The good ol' son of God his damn self,* Todd thought as he huffed along the snowy sidewalk.

He glanced over his left shoulder; the carolers were balls deep into "O' Holy Night" and weren't doing the old song any favors. He winced again at the thought of them continuing their chosen catalog. He then thought about crossing the southern border; warm, white-sand beaches, big-titted Mexican redheads, and lots of homeless people. The homeless were, after all, the easiest to eat. But the Vatican still had his scent. If he tried to leave the US, he would get snagged fast as shit. No. He had to lie low for a while. Maybe snake his way down to west Texas soonish and perhaps find a way to sneak across the border. If he could get to Mexico, he might be able to get into his Swedish savings account . . . unless the Vatican had done its homework. But he figured they hadn't. Sure, they were deadly and known for excessive violence, but they were scatterbrained and unorganized. Otherwise, his self-exile to North America would have been much more difficult. By the time they had realized what he had been doing, he'd already been long gone. He had killed twelve of their agents when they'd ambushed his little French bungalow, but Todd was fast. Real fast. Sure, they'd been armed to the fangs with high-caliber weapons and fancy techno gadgets, but none of it meant much when Todd was mad. It had been a few centuries since he'd had a bloodbath like that on his hands. As he stood there, breathing hard on a pile of dead and dying bodies, he'd known he had to run.

But now, somehow, they had found out he'd ended up in the States, so now he was stuck.

It was a strange place. He had never seen so many steak sandwiches and sweat-pants before. He never cared for the States, even before they were states, back when good ol' Vineland was an excuse for Vikings to take a holiday from their families.

Todd wasn't happy, and the onset of the cold and Christmas made it worse.

Next to the church was a graveyard by the name of Pinewood Cemetery and beyond that a small park. He huffed toward the bus stop at the far end of the park when he spotted an old man sitting alone on a green park bench.

"Excuse me, sir? Perhaps I could bother you for a light?" the old man said.

Todd stopped dead in his tracks. He'd intended to walk past the senior and ignore him, but for whatever reason, he stopped.

"... Uh. Yeah. Here ya go," Todd said.

Pulling a silver Zippo from his dark gray chinos. He handed the lighter over. The old man took it with stubby, wood-like fingers. His other hand already held a sturdy-looking wooden and ivory pipe. The antique was packed with moist tobacco. A minute later, it was a blazing pot of embers. It smelled good. The aroma put Todd at ease, and as the old man handed the now warmed Zippo back, Todd fetched a smoke of his own. Hand rolled, of course. None of that shitty factory-rolled crap. He paused and lit his too.

"Might as well set a spell. Got almost an hour before the 99 stops by," the old man said, letting out a billow of thick smoke.

Todd was caught off guard. "How do you know I'm waiting for the bus?" he asked.

"Why else would you be out here in this frozen hell?"

Todd smirked and jutted his chin back at the church and its humdrum choir. "Maybe I'm just here catching the midnight show."

"They're goddamn horrible. Not supposed to be out this late, even if they had an ounce of talent. Giving the holiday a bad taste, if you ask me."

This made Todd grin. He took a sharp drag, looked at his watch, and realized he would indeed have to wait a spell. He exhaled and took the seat next to the old man.

"You waiting on the bus too?"

"Nah. My loving wife doesn't care for me smoking. So, I like to take a nice long walk at night," he said, taking a slow puff on his pipe.

"Real ball buster, huh?" Todd asked, trying not to smile.

"Aye," he said as he fished around in his overcoat pocket. He pulled out an antique flask and handed it over to Todd. "She don't care for me drinking none neither."

Todd took the flask. Despite his grumpy disposition, he couldn't help but enjoy being caught off guard. Maybe this stretch of the world had a few redeeming attributes after all. He took a shallow swig from the flask. A sweet burn rinsed his mouth; brandy, and an expensive one at that. The old man had taste. He handed the flask back, and the man followed suit.

"How's your Christmas suiting you thus far?" the man asked while tending to his pipe.

Todd pondered the question. He hadn't had the time to acclimate himself enough to even consider the notion of the made-up holiday Americans were so obsessed with.

"You know, just the usual . . . tree, lights, and the whole turkey dinner with the in-laws. I suppose business as usual."

The old man took a long and slow pull. "Wife, huh? Didn't reckon you the type to keep a significant other." He passed the flask back to Todd, who took it without question.

He sipped and replied, "You say that like you know me, old man."

His rebuttal had fangs. Todd snapped out of his temporary comfort, dragged hard on his own smoke, and straightened. A firm contradiction to the old man, who stayed relaxed and glued to the bench.

"You're not that hard to read to anyone paying attention. Matter of fact, had a hunch you'd be out here this very night," the old man said, staring out at nothing in particular.

Todd felt something inside. Something he thought he was no longer capable of feeling: shock. Almost all his human emotions had all but dulled away over the centuries since he'd stopped being, well, human. But the old man had floored him. And another old emotion reared its head: curiosity.

"You some sort of mind reader? Maybe a fortune teller?" he asked, befuddled.

"Not much for fortunes. But I do have a niece out west. Reads a mean deck of tarot. Now, *she* could read your fortune. I bet she'd love to set a spell with the likes of you. Name's Janis if you ever make it out to Wyoming."

Todd sat, stumped and flat-out confused by the little old man beside him.

"I don't plan on sticking around the great U.S. of A for all that long. I'm sure your niece is a knockout, but I have business elsewhere," Todd said, lighting another smoke and reaching his hand out for the flask. The old man passed it along.

"Well, that's a shame. Not a fan of Scrapple, I take it? Not bad with some apple butter or real maple syrup. But maybe your tastes lay elsewhere," he said as Todd took another swig of cold brandy.

He wiped his lips with the back of his hand. "You're strange, old man. If I didn't know better, I'd say you were hinting at something."

"Ye see, the problem is . . . I can only assume. Now, I know it's rude to do such, but, in my years, I've gotten pretty good at it," the old man said, also extending a hand, ready for the flask.

"Well, you got my attention. So, what would you so boldly assume of me if you were to do such a thing?" He smoked more.

The old man rolled the question around, took a small sip of brandy, and continued, "My mother said I was touched." He handed the flask over. "When I was just a boy, near the turn of the century, I had certain premonitions . . ." he trailed off, worlds away, lost in thought. He took a loose puff on his pipe and continued, "I would have certain visions. I would see certain . . . auras surrounding people. I could see who they were deep down inside. My mother said I could see their souls. Not sure if I ever agreed with her, but it was an easy way to sum up what I was capable of." The old man trailed off again as he put the pipe to his lips.

It seemed to Todd that it was the first time he had said any of this out loud. It was in this moment that he noticed new snow was falling. He looked out at the empty street, lit by a dim yellow streetlight. "I haven't met many of you in my years. And the few of you I have met have most certainly left a deep impression," Todd said with a mellow tone as he turned toward the old man. Fresh flakes were gathering on his fur collar and twill hat. "So, you know what I am?" he asked.

"Well. Like I said, I'm not one to assume, but I've been watching you for a few weeks now. You've been traversing these streets, and I've nothing but time to watch people, and, well, you caught my eye."

Todd lit yet another cigarette off his old one. "So, tell me. What does my aura tell you?"

The old man sat up straight and looked out into the new falling snow. "My grandson asked me how old I was on my last birthday. I told him I was every bit of eighty-two years old. Now, my grandson was nine, and when I told him this, he got this lost look in his eye, like he was trying his damnedest to fathom what that meant. Now, judging from the way I see you, I would guess I would get a similar look in my eye if I were to ask you how old you were."

They both sat in silence. It was out there now, the truth. Or at least the truth in a dark room, stumbling around looking for the switch.

"In my defense, I'm not the only freak sitting out in this frozen hell tonight. I meant what I said. I haven't met many of your type. So, we are both in rare company tonight, I suppose," Todd said.

Both men sat. Bare souls and nothing to hide. Sharing a bench in the dead of night on Christmas Eve. The snow fell with little care, and the world kept spinning. Two men; drinking, smoking, all but alone if not for this encounter.

"I need you to kill me," the old man said.

Todd turned. He could see the man was still staring out at nothing, wearing an almost stoic expression. It wasn't a question or some sort of sad joke.

"Why would I do that?" Todd asked.

"I'm dying. Terminal cancer. It's spread to all my organs," the old man replied.

He didn't offer any more details. He didn't need to. That's when Todd saw it in the old man's eyes; he was tired. His face gaunt and hollow. His eyes world-weary and sad.

"I think I'll walk, thanks for the brandy." Todd stood and turned to leave.

"Wait," the frail man ordered.

And for some reason, Todd did. He turned back to the still-seated man.

"I've never been the begging type, and I ain't gonna start tonight. I know what you are, and I ain't judging you, neither. The way I figure it, everything on this weird planet has a place and a purpose, and most of it is beyond me. But I know my place. And *my* purpose. And to both ends, I've accomplished what I've needed to do. I was a faithful husband, a caring father, and a provider. I served my country in WWII, and I did better financially than my folks before me." He drifted off for a second, going to that other place. "Then the doctors found dark spots in an X-ray of my lungs . . ."

Todd, stock still in his tracks, stared at the fragile husk in front of him. ". . . I'm sorry to hear that." He was feeling another ancient emotion, pity.

"Don't fucking patronize me," the old man snapped at the gesture.

Todd didn't know what to say but blurted out words, regardless. "Hey, I'm being nice, Captain, relax," he said with a raised hand.

"You wanna be nice? Then do what I ask. Do me the kindness no one else will. I tried to do it myself. Hell, I sat in my rec room for an hour with a barrel in my mouth, but I couldn't pull the trigger. I was too chickenshit. I gave up. Unloaded my revolver and went about my day like nothing had conspired."

Todd was becoming aggravated. "But why? Why not just live out the rest of your days surrounded by loved ones and drinking all the brandy you can get your hands on?"

The old man re-gripped his pipe and twisted the warm bowl in his hand. "Because it's my right to choose."

"Wait. Come again?"

"See? That's the problem with your type. You're already dead. And it's probably been an eon since you felt the real threat of mortality. Tell me, do you remember life before you turned?"

"I don't know what you're talking about." Todd wasn't comfortable admitting anything. Not here. Not this night.

"Piss right off with you, then. You know what I'm saying, play coy with me if you choose, but believe it or not, I'm on your side."

"Oh yeah? And how's that?" Todd asked, lighting a cigarette.

"Cause you and I are above the food chain. Apex alphas, as it were. Main difference is you're the immortal type, is all. I'm not like the normal sheep you're used to dealing with. Most of these fools need to die. We got too many idiots roaming around already. I'm okay with you thinning the herd." He paused to tap out the ashes of his well-worn pipe. "You could consider me a trophy kill. How many of my type have you met, let alone had the pleasure of dispatching?"

"None, I suppose. Some time ago, if I recall, your type was called Seers."

Frailty be damned as Todd saw a spark of passion light up in the old man's eyes.

"Seers, huh?" he asked, more to himself. "That's a new one. Kinda think I'm fond of it. And what did they call you back in the day?"

"You know already, old man. Hell, I'm sure you could look into my head and tell me all sorts of horror stories."

"Nah, not with you. Might shit myself if I dug deep enough."

Todd chuckled. He liked the old man. Despite himself, he realized this was by far the most interesting conversation he'd had in too long to count. "Look. I'm not here on a vacation. I'm trying to lie low, and murdering an old man on Christmas Eve is gonna bring way too much attention to your quaint little town, and me."

The old man heard the words, but he didn't respond. He stared out across the snowy graveyard. Faint and rhythmic streams of breath were visible as he thought to himself. Todd felt a pang of pity in his gut. Somehow, this old coot got to him. This was an interesting lesson in irony, because Todd was, and had been for centuries, a monster. And not the forlorn storybook type of monster that still had a heart of gold somewhere deep down. No. He liked being a monster. The kind that killed and liked doing it. He killed for sport and sustenance and, on more occasions than he could count, he killed for fun. Pure evil enjoyment. For a time, back in Cairo, he would turn newborn babies just to watch the city's reaction. During the Black Plague, he would drain aristocrats to near death to watch doctors declare them victims of the crawling death. They would be stripped of their stations and cast to the slums of London, where they would contract the plague for real and die slow, morbid deaths. Back when Atlantis was still a hot tourist spot, he enjoyed the local virgins so much that the entire island underwent a self-imposed Martial Law as the locals patrolled the streets, torches in hand, looking for the Maiden Killer of Atlantis. Yet despite the depths of carnage and chaos Todd had either experienced or even flat-out caused, he was floored by this tiny old man who was asking him to do what had become second nature to him.

Todd cracked his neck and spoke up. "Tell you what, think it over, really mull it over. I'll meet you back here in a week. And if you're still absolutely sure, I'll do what you're asking."

"I need it done now. Right now," the old man said.

"You're not in the position to make demands. That's my offer. Take it or leave it."

The old man's free hand reached into the folds of his layers of jacket and sweaters and pulled out a small caliber pistol, which he aimed in Todd's direction.

"Kill me, or I start shooting."

The night was shaping into an interesting series of events, Todd thought. "I know you ain't that dumb. Those slugs aren't doing anything other than ruining my clothes."

"Silver slugs. Even dipped them in holy water last Sunday mass when the misses weren't looking. Now, I'm done pussy footin' around. Let's do this." The old man, pistol still drawn, rose to his feet.

He was all of five feet and just layers of clothes. As the light shifted through the snow, Todd could see how gaunt the old man's face was. He was sick. Very sick.

"Hey, I like movies too, but that silver shit isn't gonna work either," Todd bluffed. Truth was, it did work. It hurt like hell, and if he didn't dig the rounds out of his flesh within a day or so. His flesh would heal around it, and he would eventually lose his strength and risk slipping into a coma.

"Bullshit. Last and only ghoul I killed back in Japan would beg to differ." The old man looked frail, but his pistol didn't waiver. It stayed on its target: Todd's chest.

"That's such an ugly word. That's basically our N-word," Todd said. He was getting mad now.

"Then do something about it, you godless sack of shit," the old man said, taking a single step forward.

"Now, hold on, you need to calm down right now before you make a scene."

The old man thumbed the hammer of the revolver and half-stepped a little closer. Todd backed up. As he did, his heel caught the edge of the snowbank, and he fell back onto the frozen mound. As he floundered, the old man closed the gap and looked down on him, gun still on target.

"You got till the count of three. I didn't want it to go this way, I really didn't. I was hoping we could settle this like gentlemen. One old soul doing another a simple favor. That's one . . ." he said, leveling the revolver with Todd's heart.

"Don't do this. You're starting to piss me off," Todd said, pushing up against the cold ground.

"Then so be it. That's two . . ."

Todd made it to his feet as he brushed off his pea coat. "Listen here, you old fuck! I've had enough of your shit!" Todd reached out for the pistol.

"Three!"

The old man exploded as hundreds of rounds ripped away at his fragile body. Most of them went through the old man and pelted off Todd; hot slugs of lead scattering and spinning across the frozen landscape. The sound was deafening. High-caliber rifles emptying magazines, destroying the old man. Todd wiped at his face; fresh blood, and lots of it, sprayed in chaotic arches across his body. As the body of the old man fell to the ground, Todd strained to look past him. Thirty feet away stood the carolers. All armed with assault rifles that were smoking. All ten were scrambling to reload their weapons as they shouted and huffed. Todd squinted hard and realized that the plump choir wasn't out that night to share in the holiday spirit. They were with the Vatican. They'd found him. He looked down at the crumpled old man. He lay face down in a pool of his own slowly freezing blood. His face was a mash of raw and pulped flesh. Todd couldn't help but feel a lump in his throat. He'd had a personal moment with a human—a genuine moment. Something real.

He heard rifles racking. The soldiers of God were leveling their weapons, ready for another assault. This made Todd mad . . .

Seconds later, every caroler was in pieces, steaming and bloody on the ground. Todd was soaked in red as he huffed, catching his breath. The scene was a chaos of crimson. Flesh, entrails, empty ammo shells, and oozing ichor everywhere. Some fucking Christmas this was turning into.

Todd gathered his coat up under his chin and marched away from the scene as the sound of sirens roared in the distance, mumbling to himself, "Fucking Christians."

A GHOST TOUR

Jennifer pulled her coat tighter as she traversed the dark sidewalk. Up ahead, she could see the group gathered for a tour. A mishmash batch of ages, some broken off and conversing together, while others stood quiet, staring off towards the vacant streets running by the intersection. She assumed this was the place. Pulling the invitation from her pocket, she read the small print:

A GHOST TOUR

6TH ST. & COFFEEKENNY

COURTESY OF THE STANDARD 99

The streetlamp on the corner illuminated the brass plated street signs, confirming her suspicion. She watched the other tourists as they waited and talked; some shuffled their feet, maybe to stay warm. A single young woman stood on the outskirts of the group, her features striking. Jennifer couldn't help but stare, admiring her. Suddenly, the woman's eyes found hers, catching her watching. Startled, Jennifer tried to act natural as the young woman approached her.

"Hi, I'm Morgan. Are you here for the tour?"

Jennifer instantly liked this woman—her smile put her at ease. "Yes. I am."

"Do you have your ticket?"

Jennifer reached into her jacket, where she had just placed the ticket. It was gone. "Wait. I just had it." She fumbled in her other pocket, but it was empty as well. A flash of alarm lit Jennifer's face. "I swear I just had it; it must have fallen out." Panic seized her as her eyes quickly scanned the sidewalk behind her.

"It's okay."

Morgan's expression brightened, and she reached for Jennifer's hand. Jennifer locked eyes with the woman again, and warmth washed over her, urging her own smile to blossom.

"Okay. But I swear I had it."

Behind the women, the group stirred like a knowing flock of birds. A few shoved their hands in their pockets to keep warm, while others kept glancing in their direction. Jennifer noticed they seemed to regard Morgan fondly and, with a nod from the woman, the group began to move. Morgan glanced at Jennifer and rubbed her hands together in anticipation. "It's time! Whatever you do, don't get separated from us." She held out a hand, beckoning Jennifer to follow the group. Jennifer did as such.

"So, is this your tour?" Jennifer asked.

"I guess so. But I like to think of it as everyone's story. When are you from?"

"I'm from Oregon. A small town near Bend."

Morgan smiled. "Welcome."

The group shuffled to a stop in front of a stately and beautiful Victorian style home. It stood facing the street with a massive presence. From its perfect paint job—a mixture of dark colors—to its all-brass fixtures polished to a shine, its entire facade was in showcase condition. A small woman, dressed in what appeared to be a maid's outfit, broke away from the group and climbed to the estate's first landing, putting her well within view of the whole group with the house as a formidable backdrop. She took a moment to smooth out the pleats of her dress and cleared her throat.

"Mr. Blight was a rightful cunt," she declared, her voice small but steady.

The group muffled their laughter as some gasped at her curtness. The maid didn't seem to care and continued.

"Sure, everything was okay at first. There were six of them in total. Mr. Mathias Blight, his terrible wife Mrs. Bethany Blight, and their four children; Tobias, Robert, Peggy, and the youngest, Maddy. The kids were fine enough, polite even, but their parents were by far the worst people. Especially Mr. Blight."

Morgan and Jennifer eased toward the front of the group.

"They purchased this house in early March 1898 from a tobacco plantation owner who moved to Virginia. I don't recall the gentleman's name, but he was polite with a giant potbelly.

More stifled laughter from the crowd, but the maid did not pause.

"The first few years were just fine. Mr. and Mrs. Blight were assholes, but no more than the Lord or Lady of any other estate. They were the kind of assholes that were very tolerable, indeed. They did the usual obnoxious shit, but all the staff dealt with it. But one day, Mrs. B made eyes at one of the local carpenters' building bookcases in the basement. I don't blame her, really. He was a strapping man, big arms, a nice face—hell, I would have given him a go myself."

The crowd finally relaxed and let out a full laugh. Even Jennifer snickered, but she made sure that Morgan didn't see. A sideways glance showed her Morgan was also laughing and Jennifer's need for politeness melted away.

"But Mrs. B did make a go at the man. I think the carpenter's name was Ephrim or Ethan . . . I can't remember. Not that it matters. He never had any children on account of what happened, so there's no point in remembering." The Maid trailed off, staring, unblinking, down the dark street at nothing. "I never had kids either . . ."

The crowd lost what brevity it had accumulated. No one was laughing now. A cold breeze struck across the group and played with the maid's layered dress. She smoothed it out again. It must be more of a nervous repetition than an act of modesty. Once again, she cleared her throat and continued.

". . . Mrs. B was a bitch, but she wasn't a whore. Turns out Mr. B had gotten hooked on Chinese opium—unbeknownst to the family—and Mrs. B was dreadfully lonely. Seems that it had been this way for quite some time, maybe upwards of two years. So, her actions could have been more driven by loneliness than the desire for dick. Regardless, Mrs. B took the carpenter into the master bedroom many times. I won't debate the morality of her actions. It's not my place. Never was. I think our needs and desires can get complicated, and hers did just that. She loved her dick husband, but he didn't love her back. At least not in the way she needed. So, she found it elsewhere. But one night Mr. Blight came home early. He had been drinking. A lot. He found them naked in his very own bedchamber. There was a fight. Gunshots. Missy, the cook, ran to the bedroom. Upon opening the door, she was shot in the head. Mr. Blight had killed his wife and her lover. Multiple bullets in each. He was out of ammo, so he went to his office and fetched his shotgun. I'll never understand why the kids didn't run. Why didn't they fight for their lives and flee. Maybe it was such a surreal experience, seeing your blood splattered father toting a shotgun, that it might not even register as death incarnate. One by one, he shot all four of his kids and then sat in the vestibule behind me and took his own life."

The maid paused. Her audience, wide eyed and silent. After dropping into a quick curtsy, she straightened and stood stoic. Jennifer didn't realize she was holding her breath, but it felt like everyone else was too.

"Thank you so much for that story," Morgan said, her voice holding a musical lilt like bells in a breeze. "Now please, let's continue."

The maid joined the group, and they shuffled along.

Jennifer once again found herself at the back of the group. She pondered the story. The maid had been so straightforward but so personal at the same time. This seemed like a departure from what limited exposure she had in the form of historic tours. Had she been on a tour before? As she wondered, she felt Morgan beside her.

"Are all the stops on this tour as . . . colorful as that one?" Jennifer asked.

"All worthwhile stories are. But it also depends on who's telling it. Our maid companion has been through a lot." Morgan paused. Jennifer noticed the woman observing her. "Are you a good storyteller?" she asked after a moment.

"I am certainly no storyteller. You can ask all my college English professors that. So, it's a good thing I'm just a spectator," Jennifer said.

The small group crossed the street and turned left. This new street was narrower and crested from either side, with towering oak trees adding more shadows to the already dark night. As the street tapered, so did the sidewalk, forcing the congregation to walk in pairs. Soon they were at the next stop. It was a slim row home. The kind that shared a wall on either side with its neighbors. It was beautiful and just modest enough to keep it unassuming.

Jennifer watched the other tourists, most huddled together, whispering as if there were others around to disturb. But no one other than Morgan had approached her. None have even made awkward eye contact. She was used to the quiet life of a wallflower, but this was different. The urge to flee crept up her neck.

From the group stepped a modest man, broad and big—big hands, big, bearded face. For all the imposing stature instilled, his light hazel eyes bore a soft sadness that contrasted his onyx beard. He wore a simple fleece and jeans. Meandering at the stoop, he sat on the sixth step. Even seated, he was still taller than all the other tourists. As he wrung his hands together, Jennifer noticed the calluses through the gentle motion.

"My father died here." He jerked a thumb behind him towards the modest row home.

"It was a Sunday morning. He had me every weekend after my parents divorced. I didn't mind 'cause he let me stay up late and watch wrestling. And every Sunday morning we went to church."

Jennifer felt a lump in her throat. Why, though? She didn't know this man. Perhaps it the shared empathy of the group, or maybe it was his earnest delivery. As if noticing, Morgan wrapped an arm around her and gave her a reassuring squeeze. Jennifer offered Morgan a smile and continued to listen.

". . . I was young. Eleven. And that morning he asked if I wanted donuts. Of course I said, 'Heck yes.'"

The group offered a thin courtesy laugh.

"Well, he went to the donut shop while I got ready. A little short sleeve button-up shirt and a clip-on tie." The mountain of a man mimicked putting on the tie.

"And I sat there watching cartoons—I forget what was on. But that was another reason I liked staying with him. He'd let me watch pert'ner anything. Anyway, there I was on the living room floor watching the boob tube, and I noticed it was gettin' awful late. He had been gone too long."

The man wrung his hands together again.

"I started to worry. I got up and got something to drink . . ."

The man looked away, hiding his flushed cheeks, and continued as the group drew closer.

". . . and that's when it happened. The front door slammed open, and there he was. Holding his chest, covered in sweat. He was pale and breathing hard."

As he stood, everyone took a collective step back. He leaned against the stair railing and tried to gather himself. The group watched and waited.

Morgan leaned into Jennifer and whispered, "Sometimes the stories get harder. But that's why we tell them."

Jennifer furrowed her brow. "I don't understand."

"You will."

The man collected himself and resumed. "He came staggering in and fell on the floor. I was stunned. I didn't know what to do. I froze. Watching him on the floor. I tried to talk to him, but his head was somewhere else. His eyes . . . He was looking through me. I don't know if it was the pain or the shock of what happened, but he didn't see me."

He sat back down, and the tour group shifted closer.

"I had never felt so alone . . . I eventually realized I needed to call for an ambulance. Now, mind you, this was a long time ago; we didn't have 911 to call. I had to find the phone book and look up the number for the hospital. The whole while my dad's laying there going in and out. Muttering to God knows who. It was all a blur. My mom eventually found me, and we went to the hospital, but it was too late. Heart attack."

Someone in the group stifled a soft sob.

"He died in November. He had already bought me a few Christmas presents. So, a month later, I had to open them without him. It was hard on me and my mom. For years, we did our best. I couldn't have asked for a better mom, but that didn't mean it wasn't hard. The feeling of it all never left me. No matter what I did, it was always there in the back of my mind. If I had reacted faster, could I have saved him? In high school, I got mixed up with the kids on the wrong side of the tracks—that's what my mom called them. Lots of booze and drugs and obsessing over any woman who'd give me the time of day. Distractions. All distractions."

Jennifer watched the group. Every single person was fully absorbed. Even Morgan seemed drawn in.

"I went down the wrong path for decades. My mother disowned me. But she tried to help—tried for years—but I didn't want any of it. I wanted to be numb. I wanted to not feel. One night I got into a pretty bad tussle at a beer joint. Got shanked in the ribs. It was deep, and if I'm an honest man, I reckoned I deserved it. This girl had been giving me the eye all night. Pretty number. So, I made a move. Her boyfriend didn't like that. Next thing I know, I'm in the parking lot pulling a buck knife out of my ribs. I don't know how I did it, but I managed to drive here. I just wanted my dad. That's all I wanted. I parked right there."

He pointed through the crowd to the narrow street just on the other side of the sidewalk. No one turned to look. They watched the big man cry. He didn't hide it or play it off. He didn't even seem ashamed.

"And that's where I bled out. Right there in my car. Engine still running and everything. My mom found me the next morning. She cried for years." He dropped his head into his hands and sobbed.

The group stood motionless, avoiding eye contact, allowing the man a brief respite. Jennifer wiped away her own tears. She missed her mom, too.

"Thank you for your story. Please follow me this way," Morgan said, a voice like wind chimes.

Together, the group traveled on. It was full dark now. Coats pulled tighter, hats a little lower, but despite the cold, some tourists were smiling and laughing, conversing with whoever would listen. The flock turned right at the corner of King and Barron.

Jennifer followed behind; her pace had slowed. She was lost in her own thoughts. *What will my ghost story be? Maybe I won't have one? Not everyone should get one. What did he mean by bled out?* As she contemplated, she watched the other tourists. People watching always put her at ease. Watching how people talk and how they respond. How they stand or walk or maybe act when they think no one is watching.

"What do you think?"

Morgan was beside her as if she had been there all along.

"Certainly an interesting group."

"What do you see? When you look at these people? When you listen to their stories?"

Jennifer fidgeted, fighting for something to say. "This is morbid. But these are tragedies, and tragedies are usually morbid. I love a good horror movie or drama, but this is different. There are no happy endings here. Just *endings*."

She lowered her voice. "I feel like I don't really belong here."

"And why do you feel that way?" Morgan asked, also in a hushed tone.

"I don't know. I'm just feeling confused." She searched her memory for how she got to this area. Did she drive? Did she take the bus?

"That will pass. You're among friends. There's safety in numbers out here. It's important to let go and embrace everything. You might even have a good time." Morgan's brows lifted in delight.

Jennifer nodded. She could smell hot apple cider. Someone in the group had the foresight to bring a thermos full of something tasty. The scent made the group lively again as they embarked down a street of newer homes. The houses here were very modern and well designed, sleek and expensive.

"This is quite the departure," Jennifer said. But Morgan was gone. Startled, Jennifer glanced from side to side until she noticed Morgan was at the front of the group, talking to another tourist.

The group slid to a stop, everyone, Jennifer included, watching the conversation between Morgan and a lanky younger man with a shock of wily brown hair and a fierce glimmer in his eyes. He reminded Jennifer of a bird, each movement a jolt, bristling with energy and readiness. Morgan calmly addressed him, but he seemed to be hesitant; his shoulders drooping despite his height. She offered the young man a gentle hug. He took a deep breath and walked down the sidewalk of one of the upscale homes. The group followed, passing Morgan, and she joined Jennifer again at the back of the group, giving her a warm smile.

The home was sharp and angular. Mostly cement, smooth and monotone. There were copious windows, but they did little for the heavy tone of the home. Even the small front yard had minimal landscaping. The young man took to the porch and turned on his heels. His hands reached high above him as if to display the magnificence of the house. "Can you believe this absolute garbage?!" he yelled.

Shocked, the group drew closer.

"I mean, seriously! This was like living in one of those cement boxes you would bury a coffin in!" he exclaimed.

The tourists glanced at each other, unsure of how to react. Morgan leaned into Jennifer and whispered, "It's his first time. He's nervous."

"Don't get me wrong, I'm all for artistic expression; I performed in plays and musicals for twenty years, but what the fuck is this expressing?! But Joshua just had to have this overpriced box of depression! I know the architect was supposed to be some hotshot in his little bubble of the world, but honestly, I couldn't give two shits. Joshua and I argued for months about it. All I wanted was a cozy little home, maybe a fireplace with a mantle where I could show off all my awards. I had a lot of them, even a Tony, but I digress. Sure, I didn't like it, but I gave in—Joshua wanted it, so Joshua got it." He spun his hands, helping to deliver the point.

The crowd nodded, understanding the struggles of coexisting with a loved one.

"But when it came to decorating," the young man continued, "I had hoped I would at least have a say in the matter. But I did not." He dipped his chin to his chest. "That's when I should have left. They say hindsight is 20/20, but that doesn't deal with the remorse or rage or bitterness that comes with hindsight; summing it up like that doesn't deal with all the feelings left behind. I've never liked that expression." He wrapped his thin arms around his torso. "I'm rambling, I know. Morgan says it's good to share and talk through what happened. To talk about how we feel and get it all out in the open. I know she's right. I'm still upset, so this is very hard." He wiped away a stray tear. "Fine. Whatever. I'll talk. Things hadn't been great for a while. Well before we moved into this overpriced abortion. I was a bit older than Joshua, and I never really dealt with that. I knew he loved me, but sometimes I would see him talking to some young thing at the bar or at a club and, like an insecure asshole, I would get jealous sometimes. Ok, a lot of the time. I've had a lot of terrible relationships, and in hindsight, maybe I was the reason they always failed. There's that word again; hindsight. I'm sure it gets thrown around a lot here."

Jennifer glanced down the street while he talked, finding it difficult to watch him unravel before her. There weren't any cars, and she realized she hadn't seen a car, parked or otherwise, so far. Maybe there was construction nearby, and the streets were closed?

"Are you starting to get it?" Morgan asked.

Jennifer turned to Morgan; she leaned closely. Jennifer noticed a hint of juniper coming from her. It was mild and pleasant; the hair on her nape stood.

"I think so," Jennifer said, but really, she didn't. What was there to get? She shifted her attention back to the speaker.

"... we agreed on most of the big pieces—the couch and loveseats and such. We even agreed on the bedroom set. I really wanted the Shelby set by master Parisian designer J'adore, and Joshua did not say a peep! Shocking, I know. I really thought there would be pushback on that, but he just kissed me on the forehead and that was that."

The young man stopped suddenly, the change drastic. The fervor fueling his story seemed to extinguish. His hands felt around on his light jacket, looking for the pockets as he cleared his throat.

"But the bad stuff kept seeping in. So slowly that I didn't notice. Why would I? I wasn't looking for the signs. Even if they were right in front of me. Fucking hindsight. That word makes me feel so stupid. It's a slap across the face! It's like saying, hey dumbass, you deserve this cause you shoulda been paying attention!" He reached for his face, covering his tears.

"I loved that man. But he didn't love me. I don't know if he pushed the vase from the second-floor landing, but I do know he was trying to poison me. The vase that fell killed me, but I might have survived if I wasn't so weak from the constant microdosing of poison he had been slipping into my drinks. Even with murder he was dramatic—fucking poison! Who does that?!"

The group was truly lost now. Wide eyed and hanging on every word.

"I want to give him some sort of pass, some sort of way to admonish him from what he did ... I want to still love him ... But I don't know how to forgive him."

From the shadows of the porch, Morgan came forth and wrapped her arms around him as he sobbed. She smoothed his wild hair and kissed his head before addressing the group. "Let's go to our next stop. Left down Barron Street."

This meant Jennifer was now at the front of the group. As they continued, the homes shifted from modern to half built until they entered a neighborhood of uncompleted homes, empty lots, and stacks of building supplies. Shadows of building frames etched the sidewalk and street, the only parts near completion. Jennifer wondered how she would die. Hopefully in bed surrounded by loved ones. Not drowning to death. Flashes of darkness made her skip a step. She quickly righted herself and looked to make sure no one had seen. It was in her head. A flash of feeling. The weight of cold darkness. Her mouth full, unable to gasp for air. She kept walking, trying to blot out the intrusive thoughts . . . that ice-cold river . . . water rushing into the car as it sank.

It was dark and far too icy. She should not have driven that night, but she wanted to be home for Christmas. Her tires were bad, and she couldn't control the car as it slid off the old Pippen Bridge two miles from her parents' home.

She glanced behind her. All the tourists were talking or looking elsewhere. Maybe as lost in their own thoughts as she was.

The water was so cold and so sudden—so fast she couldn't react. Icy water flooded her mouth and nose, the frigid temperature numbing her eyes as she struggled against her seatbelt. Was she dead? Was *this* the afterlife? It was beyond freezing deep in that river, growing darker every second. Despite her chaotic fight, she couldn't free herself. With her lungs on fire as her muscles convulsed, her body took over and forced a deep inhale only to be filled with rushing water. A flood of feeling washed over Jennifer as she recalled her own death. The heavy mix of endorphins pumping into her blood as she started to pass. The sense of floating. Explosions of colors in her mind. The pressure. The numbness. She pulled her coat tighter and was suddenly happy to see her breath in the chilly air.

"Over here!" a clear voice called. Jennifer didn't need to guess who it was. Morgan's voice was like honey. The group turned and looked upon one of the dozens of vacant lots. There, near the front, was Morgan. She stood, hands clasped across her stomach. Her beautiful locks hung, framing her angelic features. The group huddled near her.

"This was the home of the Parson family. John and Mary Parson had two kids and by far too many cats." The group chuckled. It was needed.

"It was safe to say John wanted kids more than Mary did. Mary never cared for the idea of something growing inside her that wasn't her. But she loved her husband, and eventually she warmed up to the idea. What really sold her was all the fun prepping and shopping that came with the endeavor."

There were a few laughs from the crowd. Morgan's smile triggered a chain reaction of smiles.

"So soon, Mary and John had a baby boy, and things were good. His name was Timothy. We all called him Timmy. Mary had some struggles, but she managed. She ended up seeing a therapist, and she really did make strides, but postpartum depression can be daunting, crippling even. So many nights she stayed up crying in the shower, unbeknownst to John. Eventually she started drinking, and that led to neglect." Morgan stepped closer to the gathered crowd.

"We don't know what really happened. One day Timmy was playing in the backyard and Mary claimed he vanished. All the townspeople gathered, and with the local police, they canvassed the entire neighborhood. The final theory was that Timmy drowned in the creek behind that tree line." Morgan pointed over her shoulders at the forest. "There's a creek back there that leads to an underground lake. If he went down there . . ." Morgan's eyes drifted to the darkened woods before returning to the crowd.

"There's only so much that can be done in a situation like that. And slowly, people forgot about Timmy. But soon the Parsons had another child. A girl this time." Morgan brushed her hair back.

"Once again, Mary struggled. All those old demons came back, but worse. At first, the young girl's injuries were dismissed as accidents. A broken toe here, a black eye there. Each time, Mother Mary explained it all away as youthful blunders and clumsiness on my part. But after some time, John grew suspicious. Kids are certainly clumsy, but the wounds were serious. And try as he might, his daughter refused to talk and usually ended up in tears when pushed on the subject. John was a good dad. Or would have been. He tried, but in the end it wasn't enough. One day, he decided he had had enough and was going to leave and take his only child with him. I guess Mary had found the packed bags and figured out his plan because when he came home from work, he found Mary drowning his daughter in the bathtub."

The group didn't breathe, hanging on the word as she continued. "He was too late. Morgan Parson, age six, was dead. But it's not all a sad story. Mary Parson was sentenced to life in prison where she would be shanked to death. John remarried and ended up having six more kids. He got a chance to be a good father, after all." Morgan's eyes softened, full of affection as she nodded. The small group gave a muted applause thanks to the gloves and mittens everyone wore. Jennifer joined in.

"Thank you. You'll be happy to know our next stop is the waystation down the block. There's a cafe that offers coffee, ciders, and snacks."

This information gave a jolt of excitement to the group, each chirping about what snack they hoped for. They pushed on down the sidewalk, and Morgan and Jennifer followed.

"Wow. That was heavy. But you seem okay. Are you okay?" Jennifer asked.

Morgan smiled. "Yes. I'm okay. And you will be too."

"Ok, I'm starting to understand now. But there's one thing I don't get," Jennifer said, glancing over her shoulder at the lot Morgan stood at. "That house. It hasn't been built yet."

Morgan stared at the sidewalk with a grin. "You're right. And I haven't been born yet."

Don't Tell the Snow

Jeanette stirred her cold coffee. When she was a child, her father told her coffee would stunt her growth and make her pale; and as a child, she didn't question the logic of a parent. But now, as an adult, she wondered how she ever bought it. She stared out the window next to her booth into the thick, falling snow that surrounded the restaurant. Under normal circumstances, she would be gazing at another restaurant about three hundred yards away. However, the snow prevented that.

She sensed movement nearby. A few people gathered at the bar. The fat guy's lips were hard to read. Judging from his weight and sweaty, pallid complexion, he may have suffered from a stroke or heart attack some time ago, which would also explain the slurred speech.

One of the women, a thin, business-looking type, eyed Fat Guy. Jeanette could tell Businesswoman was used to speaking to a crowd. Her words were clear and pronounced, making it easier to read her lips. She was protesting Fat Guy leaving the building. The man with the tie, the manager of the restaurant, stood nearby listening to both sides of the debate, offering no input. Next to him was a city worker of some sort, garbed in a wrinkled work shirt dirtied by a hard day's work. Jeanette studied him for a long moment, taking in his strong jaw, tousled salt and pepper hair, and clear blue eyes; a man she may have fancied in a different situation.

Fat Guy threw up his arms and stormed off, disappearing around a corner. The three remaining exchanged nervous glances. Businesswoman twirled her long blonde hair and rotated her wedding ring with her thumb as she conserved with City Worker. Jeanette realized she wasn't the only one who fancied the man.

She watched the trio exchange words till Manager looked up and locked eyes with her. Startled, Jeanette forced a half grin and averted her gaze. She picked up her phone from the table and turned it on. Still no service; there hadn't been since it started snowing. She needed to get home and feed Lazy, her minx cat, who was without question pacing the kitchen floor in hunger. Jeanette had once read that Mark Twain had a cat named Lazy and thought it fitting for her own little cat, who did nothing but sleep and sleep some more during his kitten years. But how was she going to get home? After a long drive back, she stopped for her favorite meal at her favorite place. She had been visiting her family a few hours away but heeded the weatherman's warning of a sudden blizzard and had cut her visit short. But she hadn't planned on staying an additional ten hours at her favorite place.

At a nearby booth sat a family of four. Father and Mother exchanged words as two young boys slept, tucked into each other. Mother was muttering something about making a break for the car. Father's back was to Jeanette, but judging by Mother's eyes, Father wasn't agreeing. Jeanette watched Mother's lips, eyes, and hands; the three most telling features of a human. Her eyes were wide, with pitched eyebrows. Her left hand rubbed the side of her face, her lips drawn tight; she was terrified. But they all were.

A sudden shadow cast across Jeanette's table. She jumped and turned, looking straight into Fat Guy's gut. Glancing up, she could see that the rotund man was already deep into a monologue that would be forever lost on Jeanette. She smiled and waited for him to pause, looking for a response. With a hand and pointer finger, she gestured for him to wait a moment. She retrieved a pen and pad from her purse and wrote the simple, hurtful words she had written countless times for countless people. She turned the pad towards Fat Guy and watched him read them aloud "I'm deaf". Fat Guy blushed with embarrassment; his eyes darted around looking for an exit. Jeanette offered an easy smile and tried to comfort him. He feigned understanding and asked very meticulously if she could read lips. She smiled and nodded. Born deaf, she learned to adapt to a world centered on sound.

He exaggerated his words as he said, "Are you okay?" Again, she nodded. "Good, I am going to leave and try to find help." He stared at her as if wanting affirmation. Jeanette's eyes widened, and she scribbled on her pad, *just wait, too dangerous.* His thin lips tightened, and his hands found his hips, displaying the same opposition he offered to City Worker, Manager, and Businesswoman. After a moment he relaxed, realizing he couldn't explain himself to her as he had the others. He mouthed, "It has been too long. We cannot wait." She knew better than to argue. What could she say to a man who had already made up his mind? With her best voice, she pushed out the words, "Be careful." It must have been louder than she expected because Mother and Father at the nearby booth both turned to look. Fat Guy noticed and saw his way out of the awkward conversation. He nodded a gesture of finality to Jeanette and shuffled off to the family, surely offering them the same pitch that had tried to offer to her.

With a sigh of relief, Jeanette decided to shake the sleep out of her legs and refresh her coffee. She made her way to the bar where Manager was fussing with the phone, upset with the lack of a dial tone. As she approached, his professional side took over. He offered a grin and noticed her coffee cup. "A top-off?" Jeanette nodded, realizing how glad she was the power hadn't failed and that her impairment hadn't had to be explained to anyone else. Manager served her with a smile. With a full cup, she meandered her way around the establishment. On the other side of the dining room, about six people sat and talked or slept or fussed with their cell phones. She made her way to the front double doors, where she gazed out into the wall of drifting and falling snow. Her eyes settled on the gore about twenty yards from the front door. Ten hours ago, Punk Rocker had made his way to his car when the things in the snow got him. His body had been dragged away, but the wounds inflicted left his life force splattered everywhere. Deep ground snow was painted with blood, more than she thought possible, frozen in thick globs like a morbid snow cone. Her neck hairs stood alert. Things were watching, things were waiting; the snow had a presence reserved for a living being. She gazed past the carnage, wanting to see one of the things that mauled Punk Rocker. She sensed the snow staring back. Something awful waited out there. Were the people at the restaurant three hundred yards away experiencing the same quagmire? Was Lazy staring at strange things in the shifting snow from the kitchen window? It was too much to handle. She broke her concentration, feeling that she had given the snow enough.

Jeanette fell asleep at her booth, despite the copious amount of black coffee coursing through her veins; the need for slumber took its toll. When she came to, she noticed a commotion gathering at the front door. A glance at her phone declared it mid-morning, but the sky and snow out her booth window displayed no such thing. Still black. Still snowing. An easy two-foot of accumulation with no sign of the sun's hopeful rays. Turning her attention to the gathering mass at the front entry, she wiped the sleep from her eyes, smoothed her hair and blouse, and headed to the foyer.

Everyone was watching Fat Guy, who had one foot out the door. City Worker was at the back of the group pacing; Jeanette straightened her posture and pretended not to notice him. Manager was standing next to Fat Guy with one hand on the door handle, forbidding him from taking another step. Everyone was talking, too many mouths to concentrate on, but the general vibe was palpable. Fat Guy was leaving, and no one was stopping him. After a moment of protest, Manager, seemingly exhausted, backed away from the door, turning his back on the situation. Fat Guy was left alone at the door with most of the patrons watching and waiting and hoping. City Worker walked towards the bar with Manager following. Jeanette spied him whispering something to himself, even though she couldn't catch all the words, "dead" and "fool" were plain as day. Her heart sped up as the situation fell into her mind. She looked towards Fat Guy, his back to the crowd, gazing downward as if looking for the courage he might have dropped. After a long moment, he pushed the swinging door outward, allowing rogue flakes to find their way into the safe harbor of the restaurant. With shaky hands and feeble feet, he laid fresh prints in the virgin snow.

The moment slowed as the small, huddled group resumed their watch of Fat Guy, who was taking short steps into what would have been the parking lot on a normal mid-morning. It was obvious to Jeanette that Fat Guy steered clear of Punk Rocker's barely visible footprints as if to avoid the ill fate that had fallen onto his fellow patron. Ten feet . . . twenty feet . . . thirty. His stride grew as his confidence found its place. He circumnavigated Punk Rocker's remains wishing to not taint the tainted. With the dense snow falling hard, Fat Guy was almost out of view. Stopping next to a car he brushed away the loose snow clinging to everything as he pulled keys from his pocket. Jeanette's heart jumped; her car was nearby. The car door swung open with faint dome light giving presence in the now unknown. With a big smile, Fat Guy turned and mouthed loud words unheard by Jeanette. The crowd in front of her reveled, and she gathered that his speech was positive. The crowd conversed, and energy filled the foyer. As everyone exchanged what she assumed was pleasantries, she didn't take her eyes off Fat Guy. She was on her tippy toes with excitement when she noticed Fat Guy stop in his tracks, her grin fell to the wayside as she watched his throat open and a blanket of red pour down his chest. The crowd paused as they realized what was happening. Fat Guy's head tilted back unnaturally, his crown meeting his upper back. An instant later, his knees found the pavement as his large gut zipped open, letting loose his heavy innards. Thick steam poured off his entrails and neck stump as the snow creatures pulled him apart. Mother was quick to cover the eyes of her shocked children. People cried, shouted obscenities, and gagged on their own tongues. Jeanette felt the color leave her cheeks and grew weak in the knees. In an instant, Fat Guy was gone. The glowing dome light of his car showcasing the pints of life force left behind in the snow. Shocked, the patrons sat in silence as hope of escape fled the small foyer. Jeanette turned away, holding her face, tears welling up fell freely; another gone by way of the snow. She brushed her tears aside and found that City Worker had been watching her; his face was a solemn mask, his hands said he wanted to comfort her, but he didn't. His gaze found the ground, and he turned back to the bar, offering words to Manager, who nodded in agreement and reached for a bottle of whiskey from the bar's rack of liquor. The crowd dispersed from the foyer, returning to their seats.

Jeanette retreated to her booth, clutching her purse. She wanted to crawl onto the padded bench and disappear. Back at her parents' house, she was surrounded by her perfect siblings—her brother and sisters—with their significant others and offspring, a full house with proud grandparents. She was used to being the black sheep, the almost child that her parents loved but wished better for. Her handicap left Jeanette stifled and paralyzed when it came to finding a mate. Coming from an Italian family, it was important. Back there she knew her lot in life; a clerical error, an oversight written off by her parents and siblings. Damaged goods. They all loved her, but through the obligation of blood. If she was a stranger, she would just be another whelp on society's teat. Her family's gratitude wasn't meant for her.

Despite the chaos, she sank into her booth, fighting her own demons. Her tears found her cheeks as she began to loathe herself. Despite herself, she once again drifted off into slumber.

Her shallow, fitful sleep gave way to consciousness. Nearby, the family was feeding their now awake children. A glance at her phone revealed that she had been out for a while; it was now four in the afternoon. Glancing out her large window revealed no change. Still dark. Still snowing. She stood and gathered herself, purse slung across her chest. Straightening her skirt, she abandoned her booth.

At the bar, Manager, City Worker, and Businesswoman were halfway through a bottle of whiskey and laughing at jokes they were passing back and forth. Businesswoman, mid-laugh, pushed the side of her hips into City Worker. Jeanette wanted to punch her, but that would have to wait. Manager was the first to notice Jeanette, but he had just enough booze in him that his professional side was clocked out. Even his tie was loosened. He waved for her to join them as he placed a glass on the bar near the empty stool next to City Worker. The other two turned to watch as she approached. City Worker flashed a pretty smile; a faint dimple appeared on his right cheek. Businesswoman went from a comfortable slouch to a rigid posture; her smile shifting to annoyance. Jeanette assumed she liked being the center of attention, even with the day accumulating a death toll. But that was fine by her. Businesswoman could have all the attention she wanted. Jeanette just wanted Scotch.

She took the stool next to City Worker and offered a polite smile. Manager waved to get her attention—she really hated when people did that—and with a whiskey bottle in hand, offered her a drink. She shook her head. Manager looked confused, almost hurt. She pointed behind him at the rack of glass bottles. He followed the gesture and laid eyes on the object of her desire, Johnnie Walker Blue

Label. Manager turned, wide eyed, and smiled. She watched as he mouthed, "Yes ma'am." She scribbled a few letters on her pad of paper and turned it to him as he set the bottle in front of her. S&S. Manager smiled again and tapped his nose. It was then she realized City Worker had been watching her. Despite the sleep she'd caught, she was still sluggish and dazed. Certainly off her game. Manager sat a highball glass full of ice in front of her, filled about halfway with club soda. He then nudged the bottle of Blue Label towards her. She didn't hesitate. She poured a healthy amount into her glass and took a deep sip. It felt like burning heaven. Closing her eyes, she allowed the liquor to do its magic.

The lack of movement brought her back to painful reality. It's true what they say; when you lose one sense, your others grow sharper. But what they don't mention is that there are more than five senses. Many more. One of them is the sense of movement. Even when a person thinks they are still, they usually aren't. Subtle things like shifting in your seat or clearing your throat or getting that one itch. But right now, the people next to her were not moving. She glanced at the others at the bar and saw they were staring out the window near the front door. She followed their gaze. It was a firetruck.

Everyone ran.

Jeanette and many others pressed against the window. Deep in the world of snow outside were the unmistakable red and white strobing lights. The dense snow caused the lights to refract and expand, creating colorful clouds, contrasting hard with the gray of the day. Jeanette could make out the colors before she could see the large vehicle. It was moving fast. Jeanette sensed unease from the others nearby. They were muttering and pointing. People speculating and conversing. But Jeanette watched. The fire engine was moving too fast, and judging by the headlights, it was cutting across the parking lot, heading towards the restaurant nearby. That's when the rescue vehicle struck a parked car. It would have been difficult to see, but the truck hit the small car so hard that an eruption of sparks shattered in the snow. Everyone stilled again. The impact didn't hinder the truck, it kept barreling forward. A second later, another collision brightened the sheets of snow, another car being pushed out of the way. Jeanette held her breath as the truck hopped the sidewalk next to the neighboring building and slammed into it. The window in front of her rattled.

Shapes. So many shapes. Some big, some small. Some with odd proportions, all converging on the new chaos the fire engine brought. It was difficult to register what was happening because *so much* was happening. Fire was already blossoming from the impact. Figures that looked like people, survivors in that restaurant, were fleeing. The snow creatures hunting them. Carnage played out at a distance. It felt surreal from the vantage point of mild safety. Like watching something forbidden and secret. Jeanette watched as people died. The fire created a chaotic backdrop to the theatrics. As people fled the blazing building, things in the snow picked them off. Jeanette struggled to focus on the carnage, looking for a clue as to what was taking so many lives. That's when she saw a child running. She stifled a gasp as she locked on to a small figure zigzagging. She could make out a small pink parka with a matching beanie. The kid was trying her best to flee. Between the fresh snow, her restrictive winter gear, and just being so young, meant she wasn't moving fast, but she was moving towards Jeanette's restaurant. Others were screaming at things as the girl ran, and Jeanette watched as they shouted for help only to be ripped to pieces seconds later—but still the little girl ran. She was close enough now that Jeanette could see the terror on her face. Her little eyes were wide, and red. Jeanette grabbed for the front door. City Worker stopped her with a firm and gentle hand. They locked eyes as Jeanette realized she was crying. She pushed him away and went back to the window as the little girl came to a stop. Jeanette clutched at the glass, tears flowing. The little girl looked around before locking eyes with Jeanette. Her little face was red from the cold and crying.

She screamed for help, and that's all it took for her presence to be known. Two things grabbed her. One by her head and one by her arm. Both pulled.

Jeanette wept.

———

The restaurant was quiet. Jeanette sat at her spot at the bar. The cap to the Scotch was off. The fire at the nearby restaurant didn't last long. It wasn't big to begin with, and surely the snow helped to put it out. The lights on the firetruck were still flashing, but nothing moved. Here and there were the remains of so many innocents. The red and white lights showcasing the frozen menagerie of chaos.

It was almost beautiful after the right amount of Scotch. Jeanette thought of the little girl. Another pointless victim. She thought of her cat, Lazy. Were her parents up north experiencing the same fate? The same snow shrouded creatures lurking and waiting? Or was this isolated? There were too many questions and not enough booze. Why did they wait before attacking the child? She thought of the other poor souls that were freshly dead. The ones screaming as they ran only to be forced apart in moments. She thought of the little girl finally crying out. Maybe they were drawn to sound? That would explain the gap between Fat Man's exit from the building to the point he started yelling near his car. It wasn't until he started screaming that his life suddenly ended. Maybe these things had sharpened senses too, just like her.

City Worker sat next to her. She snapped out of her daze and straightened her posture. He smiled, that right dimple doing its damndest to win an award. She noticed others were gathering around the horseshoe-shaped bar. There were far more people on the other side of the restaurant than she had realized. Mostly adults near her age. There were a few kids too. Manager entered the back of the bar and gestured for everyone to gather closer. Jeanette suddenly found herself surrounded. She spotted Businesswoman trying to squeeze in closer to City Worker. She tried to hide her smirk, but the Scotch in her didn't care.

Manager turned and seemed to yell towards the kitchen. A moment later, three cooks came out, all looking out of place and awkward. The cooks gathered at the back of the bar, dressed in chef coats and aprons, listening as Manager began to talk. Jeanette watched as he addressed everyone in the restaurant. Once again, she relied on her other senses, and she was able to follow along.

He finally took his blue and green pinstripe tie off. Even his sleeves got rolled up. Jeanette watched him as he worked the crowd. Going on about how everything was going to be okay, they just needed to stay inside. As she watched the speech unfold, she caught a glimpse of City Worker giving her glances. Little looks, watching her and seeing how she was reacting to Manager's rousing speech. It was hard to focus on Manager when she wanted to focus elsewhere, but she tried to play it cool; the Scotch helped to tamp down the fire growing in her spine. Only if this man knew what he was doing to her . . . or maybe he did.

Suddenly people were applauding, Jeanette snapped back to the present and saw him mouthing the words, "On the house." Jeanette gave a bewildered look to City Worker. She added way too much enthusiasm, but it made the man laugh, so a win was a win as far as Jeanette was concerned. The servers started taking orders, and for the moment everyone was happy. Drinks were flowing and strangers were becoming friends. All around the bar, there were nothing but laughs and smiles, and in this small world, it felt okay. They still had power and a relative sense of safety. Manager did what Jeanette assumed he set out to do; give these people some hope.

Jeanette ordered the grilled chicken melt. The same damn sandwich that made her stop here to begin with. Bacon, sauteed onions, American cheese on grilled toast. A meal she's had for the better part of a decade. City Worker ordered Buffalo chicken tenders with three sides of blue cheese and gravy fries. Jeanette thought it was funny. Out of everything on the menu, this guy eats some fried food that a kid would order. Hell, this could be their last meal, and he picked an appetizer. Regardless, the food was amazing. They shared and drank and talked. Over the years Jeanette had become a pro at speed writing and shorthand to keep conversations going. Turns out, City Worker's name was Thomas. He did indeed work for the city and was a site supervisor for the nearby on-ramp being built. He asked a lot of questions and seemed intrigued by her answers. He watched as she described herself with ink and paper. He was patient and attentive. Despite the world going to shit with literal monsters outside, he just focused on Jeanette. It felt good.

As they laughed, Jeanette saw Businesswoman approach. The woman gave a forced smile and tried to butt into the conversation. Thomas was polite and smiled back as Businesswoman sought small talk. Jeanette knew what she was doing, but she didn't care. If this woman wanted to fight over this man as people were dying, she sure as hell wasn't going to participate.

Manager sat a big piece of chocolate cake in front of her and Thomas. Thomas quickly turned away from Businesswoman, wide eyed and excited. He had a childlike streak of enthusiasm, and Jeanette loved it. Thomas handed her a fork as he armed himself with a spoon. He waited for her to take the first bite, which she did with a smile. Businesswoman backed away, pretending she wasn't just blatantly ignored for a dessert. Jeanette watched as she retreated, glancing side to side to make sure no one witnessed the social faux pas. Jeanette wanted to laugh, but she was more won over by the moment. She was sharing a dessert with a cute boy she had just met, and it certainly seemed as if the world was ending too. The potential for something new with the threat of the loss of everything just on the other side of the glass. But damn, the cake was good.

The night meandered on. Over the hours, strangers became friends, and employees became patrons. There was talk about everything but the outside world. Mentions of movies and conversations of concerts. People telling jokes and employees playing Fuck, Marry, Kill. All the while, Thomas never left Jeanette's side. Even after all the food was finished, he sat next to her. They talked about their families and where they were from. Turns out Thomas was a college dropout. English major turned rogue. Leaving the world of academia behind in pursuit of something more lucrative. Thomas asked questions and patiently waited for Jeanette to write out her answers, never once seeming bored or impatient. Soaking up each answer and seeking more. It was a refreshing change. A much-needed reprieve. She even thought that maybe her parents and siblings would approve of this guy. But her family certainly didn't matter. Because she approved.

Businesswoman was the first to be cut off by Manager. Granted, no one was driving tonight. Was it night? But when she fell and broke her glass, she was officially tapped out. One of the servers, a young brunette, helped her to a booth at the far side of the restaurant where she covered Businesswoman with some black linen tablecloths. If Thomas noticed, Jeanette couldn't tell. Soon, others were calling it a night too. One by one, people found booths to sleep in, using coats and tablecloths to make the situation a little bit more comfortable. Soon it was just Jeanette and Thomas at the bar. His leg was touching hers as she wrote down her dream vacation destination, Tulum. She returned the question, and as he thought about it, he put his hand on her thigh. His other hand stroking the stubble on his strong chin, deep in thought. Jeanette held her breath. She didn't care what his answer was, she wanted to be there with him right now. Snow creatures or not, they were buying tickets and going there immediately.

Thomas slowly spoke his answer, France. Her heart skipped a beat. She loved French wine and French cuisine. She put her hand on his as she grabbed her pen with her other and wrote, *I've always wanted to go. It's a date.*

This made him smile. That pretty smile making his laugh lines show was almost too much. He locked eyes with her and said: "It's a date."

Jeanette felt her spine melt. The heat from his hand was as strong as the liquor. She tried her best to keep her composure. Stopping to sip some water, she picked up her pen and wrote, *if you could be anywhere right now where would you be?*

He leaned in and read the question. She caught the scent of his cologne—sandalwood and tobacco—making her lean in too. The question made him smile, his blue eyes sparkling.

"Where?" he asked, leaning in.

Jeanette nodded and leaned in more.

His hand glided up her thigh as he whispered, "Here."

They kissed.

Her back was stiff when she woke. There were tablecloths everywhere, and at first, she didn't know where she was. The vinyl on the bench was sticking to her as she forced herself up. Her mouth dry and head throbbing, her hangover in full swing. Steadying herself, she looked around, waiting for her blurry eyes to adjust. The smell hit her first. Blood. Everything came crashing back. The snow, the creatures, the deaths . . . Thomas.

Jeanette glanced at the other side of the booth. The table between had been moved; she couldn't remember when. The opposite booth was covered with makeshift blankets as well. Foggy memories tried to line up for inspection in her head, but they were stumbling over each other. Finally, she reached out and felt the other cocoon. Still warm. Where was he? Did they? But what about . . .

The blur of movement caught her attention. It appears they chose to sequester themselves to the far corner of the dining room last night. The booth furthest away from the bar or other tables. From here she could see the whole restaurant. And from here she could see what was left. Pieces and parts of bodies were strewn everywhere. The smell of fresh blood and bile crunched her hungover brain and twisted her guts. Wrapping her hands over her mouth, she fought the impulse to eject her stomach, lest she gain the attention of the thing moving near the bar. It was hard to see what it was. Some of the lights were out now, and there was no way of discerning what time of day it was. Glancing out the nearby window, she saw the same. Just sheets of snow, opaque and silent, blotting out any chance of light. The sight twisted her stomach. Such a hopeless visage, purgatory in the flesh. All the components of a nightmare laid out before her. Then something else moved. She turned back to the bar. On the other side of the horseshoe bar, something knocked over a barstool. That's when other things took notice. The sudden clap of sound summoned several creatures, and Jeanette watched as they all sought to investigate the noise. There was no reasoning to what she was witnessing. There was no logic to the things rummaging around the restaurant. Each one unique to itself, not sharing traits with any of the others outside of size; all about the size of large dogs. Some with limbs in the right places, most a mix of things resembling creatures. An odd one had what looked like a crab pincer, the biggest one Jeanette had ever seen. They all creeped and crawled their way to the far side of the bar. Sound. They were attracted to sound. She was right. Her gut instinct was right. She thought of Fat Guy crying out in victory when he made it to his car. The little girl screaming for help. Both torn to pieces in seconds.

Something happened while she was asleep. She glanced at the front door. Destroyed; shattered glass on the floor mixing with the snowdrift accumulating across the threshold. Something bad happened. Now, this safe haven was just like the restaurant across the parking lot. Carefully, she rose to her feet. All her clothes were still on. So, nothing too debaucherous happened with Thomas. She donned her parka, made sure her boots were laced, and slung her purse across her chest. She paused. The little alcove of her booth felt safe despite the numerous threats of death scampering around, and stepping forward was like a step into the unknown. Once she left the safe little booth, she would be in their domain. She stepped out into the aisle and paused. More creatures came forth from the lengthy shadows to investigate the sound. So many of them. So many that it was only a matter of time till one or more locked on to her. It was time to go. Keeping an eye on the congregated terrors, she walked forward and kicked a ketchup bottle. It rolled across the floor and met a metal table leg. She froze. She knew she hit it hard, and even more so, she knew it certainly gave off an affirming clank when it hit the metal table leg. It certainly wasn't quiet because she sensed the tone change. Her breath caught in her throat; she couldn't blink. She wanted to smack her forehead for making such a foolish move. Hangover or not, that was the dumbest thing she could have done.

Two creatures came towards her. Jeanette backed into her booth as she watched the shambling things draw near. Both caked with gore and viscera. One of the things seemed to have two mouths, both sets of lips rummaging around in its blindness, seeking more to eat. Jeanette climbed up onto her booth as the two predators found the ketchup bottle. Maybe they could smell her on it. They both shuffled closer to the booth. Jeanette, holding her breath, slowly raised her leg and stepped over into the adjoining booth. As she did, the one with two mouths clambered onto her makeshift bed. Any sense of security was now gone. She had no choice but to flee. With patience, she made her way from booth to booth. Climbing up and over, slowly making her way to the front doors. The process was slow, and her thighs were already burning from the slow and constant exertion. Dehydrated, hungover, and just being out of shape was making Jeanette make all sorts of promises to whatever god happened to be listening. If they just let her escape, she would never drink again. If they let her escape, she would lose twenty pounds and pick up yoga. If they let her escape, she would volunteer at the animal shelter she adopted Lazy from. Hell, she would strike a deal with the Devil just to get the hell out of this place. She crossed over into another booth. This one was slick with blood. Beginning to fall, Jeanette grabbed a cow skull mounted on the wall. It was just enough to steady her balance. Her lungs ached as she fought to control her breathing. The shock of almost falling put her into panic mode, and not breathing hard was just about impossible. She paused and gathered herself. Only four more booths and she would be near the front door.

Jeanette glanced around, still holding onto the wall decoration for balance. Everywhere she looked, she saw reminiscences of people she was surrounded by only a few hours ago. Near the lobby there was the lower torso of Manager. His entrails were beginning to freeze as the snowdrift drew closer to him. On top of the bar was the open chest cavity of one of the cooks. His chef's coat open but still intact somehow. It was too much to endure, nausea swelled up from her guts and her head spun as she struggled to maintain. Breathing deep, she stopped to compose herself. She couldn't hurry the process no matter how terrified she was; the urge to flee fighting for control. As Jeanette took another slow breath, feeling her face flush hot from the adrenaline, a motion caught her eye. It was a flash of something little under a nearby table. With her free hand she wiped at her dry and crusty eyes.

That's when she saw him. The little boy who had been near her original booth. There was Mom and Dad and their two little kids. She locked eyes with him. He was sandwiched under a table, but from Jeanette's vantage point they were able to see each other clearly. Jeanette immediately brought her finger to her lips and vehemently gestured for him to shut the fuck up. His open mouth closed and he nodded. Maybe there was a god or two still paying attention. Jeanette mimed zipping her mouth shut just to drive home the message when the two critters she had summoned drew closer to. She watched as the situation registered on the boy's face, his eyes grew big, tears flowing. She didn't have long. Just a few seconds before they would bumble their way under the table and directly into the boy. Holding onto the cow skull, Jeanette stooped down and grabbed the saltshaker from the table and whipped it across the restaurant. It crashed into the wall and shattered. The two creatures near the boy took the bait as they spun and made their way to the other side of the restaurant. She grabbed the pepper shaker and hurled it too. It shattered as well, summoning the rest of the bloated and festering creatures. Slowly, they all migrated towards the back. Jeanette, still trying to be quiet, hobbled to the floor and ran to the boy. She pulled him out from under the table and hoisted him up. He immediately wrapped his arms around her and wept silently. Jeanette didn't realize it at first, but she was sobbing too. She wrapped her arms around the boy and held tight. Glancing to the side, she saw what was left of the boy's family. Somehow, he was alive, though.

Another bottle smashed near the back; A steak sauce bottle that painted the wall. This extra chaos made all the remaining creatures stampede, leaving most of the building free of danger. Jeanette turned to see Thomas. He was smiling, and this made her cry more. He had a bag filled with food on his back and was picking up another wine bottle to throw. He lobbed it across the dining room where it hit one of the bigger creatures. It yelped in confusion and lashed out, striking another monster. The bottles and noise served their purpose. Thomas ran to Jeanette and wrapped his arms around her, the little boy sandwiched in the middle. Maybe the gods were listening indeed. The three survivors walked to the lobby. Jeanette clung to the little boy. Despite her handicap, Jeanette could talk. But being born def meant she didn't know how to say most words. But she still had perfectly functioning vocal cords. As the three of them stood in the lobby and stared out into the snowy oblivion, they could sense the creatures behind them growing restless. It was time to go. And with great care, Jeanette leaned in and whispered, "Paris?" into Thomas's ear. The man was exhausted and terrified, but somehow the smile Jeanette invoked washed away all the pain. He locked eyes with her and nodded. Slowly, Thomas mouthed, "Let's see your cat first." Jeanette read his lips and smiled. More tears flowed.

"I like cats," the little boy whispered.

Together, they carefully left the building and entered the snow.

Hexan Haus in Hammer Hill

At dawn, the Supreme Holiness will arrive with his envoy of gilded war machines, and I will be burned at the stake. For now, I sit in my stone cell waiting. A small barred window lets me look out at the humble settlement of Hammer Hill. I am alone and the last survivor of the Battle of the Heathens. Such a glorified name for a slaughter. I look out at my pyre, standing tall in the center of this village. A big stone circle filled with firewood around a twenty-foot tall, striped pine. I was supposed to be burned this morning, but word came that His Immortal Holiness was on his way. He wanted to personally see to my execution—to celebrate my death, which would mark the end of the rebellion. The end of the non-believers. The Battle of the Heathens, the last settlement not controlled by the church, was an extermination and nothing more. Just like Hammer Hill. I remember when this was a barter town. Just a village for hunters and trappers—earnest people trying to survive—but just like everywhere else, the church rolled in and converted.

The sun was setting as I watched the villagers head home for the night. What little vantage point I had showed me some brick row homes, a general store, and of course the lingering visage of my death pyre. For something that will light the dawn like a sunburst very soon, it sat so dark and quiet now, staring back at me as dusk cloaked it. A mother rushed her child past the shadowed pyre, averting her eyes. So much has changed in such a short time. When absolution is used as a weapon, there's no time for gradual shifts. People and places that were set upon by the church either converted or were tried for heresy. The witch's hammer, slamming against the anvil of righteousness.

My prison was nothing more than a small stone building with no more than a few rooms. No water and no bathrooms. The people put here didn't stay long. A stone construct built dead center of the village, adjacent to the newly built gallows and pyre pit. A lingering warning to any potential heretics. Outside, the building was covered with holy crests and symbols and wards; its craftsmen took no chances against the possible horrors kept inside. Strangely, it wasn't considered witchcraft when the church used ritual magic.

There were no other prisoners here. Just me. Other degenerates were kept in a different building. One with lights and water. Mine was reserved for heretics and witches, and the souls God has forsaken. In the cramped space was nothing more than a feather stuffed cot; stained and moldy. My last food was back at the settlement—mushrooms and leeks in a salty broth. That was two days ago. I was so starved that I stopped feeling hunger pangs. Not that it mattered.

As night came, the small prison became pitch black save for a few stray moon-beams when the clouds above cleared. The village was falling asleep, but I knew rest wouldn't find me. I paced and thought about those left back at the settlement. We had only been there for nine months, and now it was another mass grave left in the church's wake. I paced more, leaving footprints on the dusty floor when I heard something. Footsteps. More of a shuffling really. Irregular, shambled steps. I couldn't imagine a guard bringing me a last meal. Some simpleton with a bowl of slop. They say witches don't eat, but my stomach didn't agree. The shuffling grew louder as I tried to press against the bars to better see down the stone hallway. The few rays from the moon revealed nothing, but there was certainly someone there.

I could feel the air shifting as they approached. The scent of salt and juniper. The hair on my arms stood. I backed away from the bars, no longer curious.

"'Tis a full moon tonight," a dry voice muttered.

I heard him, felt him, before I could see him. Just outside my line of sight, he continued.

"But you needn't worry about the moon."

I backed against the wall of my cell. I was supposed to be painfully alone.

"Then what should I worry about this full moon night?" I asked.

From the shadows, a thin man stepped forward. The light from my cell window revealed his frail figure. He was stark naked and made no attempt at modesty.

"Yourself. You needn't fear me or the things you'll see on this longest night."

He stood there facing me. His face was worldly and wise. Was he an escaped prisoner? A roaming madman?

"And why should I fear myself?"

"You were tried as a witch, were you not? And found guilty?"

"I would scarcely call what I endured a trial. Seeing how I was gagged with leather and bound to dogwood and draped with silver chains. I couldn't even talk to defend myself."

The man stepped forward.

"Tell me. What would you have proclaimed given the chance? What would you say to your innocence? What would you have uttered to admonish yourself?"

The man gripped the cell bars and leaned closer. I stepped forward as well.

"Where did you come from? Is there an empty cell somewhere with a pile of clothes on the floor?"

He was old; there was no question of that. But he was clean and well groomed. His snow-white hair was brushed and beautiful.

"My shackles would have rusted to dust long ago if I were a prisoner. What of you? What shackles bind you?"

I crossed my arms. "If you don't mind, I'm preparing to die and would enjoy some proper solitude."

"Seek rest, but none ye shall find midst the longest night," he said.

He pushed from the cell, backing away, but keeping my eye.

"The longest night will be a many great and terrible thing, but restful it will not be."

The man turned and shuffled towards the shadows whence he had come.

I stepped forward. "Stranger, state your peace. Why have you come to me this night?"

He kept moving, the shadows swallowing him.

"Witches three ye shall meet. To them, ye shall bare ye soul. To them will you find your worth, and to them will ye find a fair trial. A trial unlike any you've seen."

The man disappeared. Once again, his soft shuffle filled the hallway. Moments later, he was gone.

Try as I might, I couldn't find a comfortable spot on the half-stuffed mattress. Fear mixed with the surreal knowledge that I had mere hours to live made me redefine exhaustion. My mind floated from one memory in motion to another. Roaming through thoughts and feelings. I recalled our first week in the valley. We were starving and wind burned and befriending death almost daily. Samuel went out to hunt. I stayed behind and tended to our people. Their combined woes and strife were too severe for my meager knowledge of healing. Doing what I could, I dressed wounds, gave out tonics and advice, but the newfound blessing of the valley and its untouched buildings gave us all hope. We could rest and regain our strength, our grit, and our purpose. Our small band fit comfortably in an old but solid building that bore the sign, Court House. Samuel brought down a big elk and carried it all the way back to us. That night we ate. We had fire and shelter, and we feasted and laughed. Our people were smiling, huddling in blankets around the fire. Our bellies full, we went to sleep. I cried that night. As I cry this night.

Sleep settled in as my eyelids grew heavy. The silence was bliss, and soon I drifted off.

"You're missing a beautiful moon."

The small voice startled me. Jolting up, I tried to peer into the dark. Once again it seemed that I was alone till I heard tiny, padded steps, almost too soft to notice. As I stood, I shivered. A crisp cold had come with the night.

"You're the second person to mention the moon tonight in a building that's supposed to be mine alone," I said to the dark, wrapping my arms around my torso, waiting for a response.

"I think you will hear about it a few times before the longest night is over."

I sensed movement close to the ground. A beautiful white cat sauntered up to my cell door. Fluffy, pristine, and so white she almost glowed silver in the moonlight. The creature was stunning, angelic even. Her eyes were an icy platinum that gave off an unnatural radiance as they regarded me. She didn't stop, simply looking back at me as she kept walking. A loud clank rang out as my cell door creaked open.

"Let's go. It stinks in here," she said.

Somehow, I knew the cat was a *she*. I could feel it. Rising to my feet, I checked the cell door. It was indeed unlocked. I would like to think that under a less dire situation I would stop to question this; first visited by an old man and now a talking cat. But between hunger and the shock of all that I've been through, I felt oddly at peace with this, safe even. I stepped out of my cell in time to see the cat's fluffy white tail turn a corner. She was headed to the front door of the prison. I followed along the brick hallway, turning towards the big iron door entrance as it glided open, allowing the celestial cat out. Barefoot, hungry, and crippled with exhaustion, I followed.

I had to shield my eyes as I stepped out. The moon was beyond bright and so massive and bold in the sky it was shocking. In all my years in this world, of all the wondrous and frightening things I've beheld, I've never seen anything the likes of this. Stifling a scream, I stumbled back towards the prison. Above, streaks of clouds raced by at storm speed, but there was no wind. The shifting striations above made the luminous moon dance all around, shifting and moving as if nature itself was running away from something.

"Hey, hey, hey! You're ok!" The cat finally stopped and turned to see me struggling. "Things are different here. But you're ok. If there were any real danger, I wouldn't be here." She turned and made her way down the short stoop to the cobblestone road.

I stumbled to my feet and tried to center myself. Outside, the sky was still a raging river, but it was whisper quiet. Settled. Almost peaceful. I followed.

The cat was two buildings down, waiting for me in front of a brick structure. The wooden sign above the door read 16 Ton.

"Join me. Will you?" she said, a pleasant smile on her face and in her eyes.

The door opened on its own, and she went in.

The taproom was empty but warm and welcoming. Lantern light and a proper fire in the hearth made me realize how cold I had been back in my cell. We sat near the fire at a small table. Atop was a bowl of cottage cheese in a fine crystal bowl, and across was a steaming bowl of lamb curry. My mouth ached as it watered.

"Cheers, love," the cat said as she hopped onto the table.

I sat and, with no hesitation, ate. It was pure divinity. Velvety curry with chunks of potato and carrot, tender lamb that filled my mouth with hot juices.

"Slow down, love, there's more if you're so inclined." The cat had finished her cottage cheese and was watching me eat. She was big. Larger than most cats I've seen. Her eyes full of spark and vibrance.

As my belly filled, my wits came back as well as a deep sense of apprehension. 16 Ton was empty. Not even a barkeep to offer more curry that the cat promised. And to that end, I remembered I had been talking to a cat.

"So, you're a cat. A talking cat. Does this talking cat have a name? You bought me dinner after all, and I would like to thank you," I said, wiping my mouth and leaning back in my chair.

"I do have a name, and you needn't thank me for the food."

I leaned in, elbows on the table, and whispered, "Am I dead? Is this how I am able to so freely leave my cell and talk so freely to animals? Is this the afterlife?"

"You're thinking much too narrowly. There are so many things between life and death and so many avenues and paths to explore," the cat said.

"So, I'm alive. Perhaps I'm dreaming? A sleep so deep and a dreamscape so powerful I'm in control of my facilities?"

"You're to be burned tomorrow. Shortly after dawn," the cat stated.

I leaned back as the hair on my nape stood. "Are you here to remind me of this? You needn't bother. I assure you I haven't forgotten."

The cat, still sitting on the table and presented as beautifuly as a painting, continued, "And why weren't you put to the stake today? This morning?"

The food in my stomach churned, and a wave of sour nausea rose from my gut. The delicious food was not settling well with such morose dinner conversation.

"You seem to be in control of this evening. You're the one to free me from my cell, feed me as you see fit, and keep me company on this night. I suspect you are very much aware of my unique situation." I was getting angry.

The cat could sense my apprehension but didn't seem to care as she regarded me as a tired mother might glimpse regret while dealing with an unruly child. The cat drew a long breath and slowly blinked at me. "You need to say it," she finally said.

My stomach twisted as I fought back the need to vomit. "Fine. As you wish. I am to be put to death tomorrow morning by the hands of His Immortal Holiness Pope Axtrath the First and Only. He will light my execution pyre himself. Standing next to me on a raised platform as I am tied to the top of a very long pole. He will spout rhetoric and preach the gospel as the crowd roars and cheers." I stood, my blood running hot. "And he will ask me to repent for my sins. He will tell me forgiveness is his to dole out as he sees fit and all I need to do is ask." I began to pace. "He will stand there in his robes and finery forged by the submission of countless innocent and wait for my recant."

"And what will you say?" the cat interrupted.

The question stopped me in my tracks. My chest heaving, vision blurring with rage.

"Why does everyone keep asking me that!" I screamed.

The front door creaked, drawing my attention. I froze. The oaken door swung in. Beyond the threshold was nothing but void. I should have been looking out at the sleeping village of Hammer Hill, but there was nothing. A wall of black. The absence of everything. Such a terrifying sight. I had to be dead, and this was my very own Hell. If not the afterlife or some other divine creation, then my own mind has betrayed me, my soul has relinquished my sanity.

A figure stepped in, appearing from the void with ease. It was a man wearing overalls and a dirty long-sleeved shirt. The left side of his face was caved in. Fresh, steaming blood soaked his chest and arm. Without a pause, he bellied up to the bar, hopping onto a wooden stool in front of a mug of dark beer. Had that always been there? As I struggled with the scene in front of me, another figure emerged from the black threshold. Another burly man draped in dirty work clothes; his chest littered with sucking bullet holes. He joined his friend at the bar, picking up a mug. I clutched my mouth. Another figure entered. This time a woman. She wore green corduroy britches and a thick woolen sweater. The front of which was a sopping wet mess of blood and gore. She didn't seem to notice as she sat at a small table near ours, where a big plate of fish and chips sat. I glanced at the cat, who was also watching the spectacle unfold.

I don't know how I didn't scream and flee for my life as I watched the next person walk in. I don't know how my brain didn't recoil and explode as I watched my Samuel walk in. I knew him instantly. Tall, broad shoulders, and a long auburn beard. Tears poured as memories of his fuzzy face brushing against my cheeks as he kissed me flooded my head. Samuel walked to the bar and joined the others as more people came in from the dead space outside. I backed against the hearth, the heat from the small fire biting me. If this was a dream, the fire felt real as well. All I could do was watch as the taphouse filled with people. *My* people. The people who were massacred. I began to recognize each one. Jeffery at the bar, his chest caved in by an explosive. Matty, chatting with others as if most of her torso wasn't missing. Carl, burned to a crisp, who I didn't recognize till I heard his laugh. And then there was my Samuel, sitting alone at the bar. Not conversing or drinking or eating. Just staring off.

"Cat. Ghost. Witch. Devil! Whatever you are! Why have you brought me here?!"

The cat had since laid out across the table, in between our plates, verging on sleep. She blinked at me. "Actions hold weight."

I sat down. The massive cat pulled herself up and sat on the table watching me.

"Must everything be so vague! Or can my own mind not justify the horror it's creating?"

The cat's face softened. "Creating? My dear, this *is* real. You did this."

"What is she talking about?" A deep voice came so close I shook with fear. Samual stood next to me, and before I knew it, I was standing. With his blood-soaked chest at eye level, I looked up. His big, sad eyes looked through me as if he had just awoken. "What is that woman talking about?" I looked down at the cat.

"What are you talking about? Woman? You mean the cat?" I asked. I grew dizzy from the familiar musk of Samuel mixed with fresh blood.

"To you I'm this creature. To him, I'm something else. Actions hold weight. And there are ways to help lift that weight. There are things you can do to ease the burdens. Our actions do not need to become our chains," the cat said.

"Please. What is she talking about?" Samuel pressed.

Fresh, hot tears fell from my cheeks. I wanted to hug him. Kiss him. I glanced down at the cat. "This isn't fair. How dare you!" I said.

Like a knowing flock of deer, all the patrons stood and faced me as one.

"Our time here is done. This might be your last chance to tell them. Lest that weight crush you. There is still hope. It will require sacrifice beyond anything you've known, but there is hope."

"No. No! It wasn't my fault! I had no choice!" I backed away from Samuel, smacking into the hearth. All my people gathered closer. Staring, waiting.

"I didn't do anything wrong!" I screamed.

"Do you think they believe you?" the cat asked, watching the encroaching group.

"Why can't I feel my face?" Samuel asked, staring into the fire.

"You could have warned us," Carl said, his white teeth the only part of him left not blackened.

"You could have been a good person, you selfish bitch," Matty said. She stood from her table and approached.

Everyone pressed closer. *How could you? We trusted you! You should be rotting with us!* It was all too much to take.

"It was the right thing to do! Any of you would have done the same! I did it for the children!" I screamed, but no one heard me.

I ran. I ran as hard as I could, pushing past my dear friends and family. Screaming, I flung myself towards the door. The threshold of the abyss. A few hands reached for me as I moved, stifling my screams. I pushed harder. Then I leaped.

Darkness. I was too stunned to scream. Too startled to cry out. Surrounded by abject gloom, I stood there flailing my arms, feeling for anything to grasp onto. Something to show me I was still capable of holding onto reality. The air was cold and clingy—thick with dew. Terrified to move forward lest I find the edge of a pit or something worse, I dropped to my knees and felt the ground. Cold, damp stone. Roughhewn but cobbled together. I was in some place manmade. My heart pounded so hard my body shuddered with every beat. Frigid, crisp air burned my lungs with each quick gasp. Fear was bubbling up in my chest; a panic attack was coming. I had to find control. I had to get a grip. Hands on the cold floor, I bit the inside of my cheek, the pain bright and sharp. My nails grated against the stone floor. Were those really my people? My own sweet Samuel? It felt like him. I couldn't dwell. Not now. I bit harder, focusing on the pain—pointed and pure, no room for interpretation. I inhaled. Held it. Slow exhale. Again. Again.

Still on my hands and knees, I sat straight up, resting on my bare feet. I wiped my face and did my best to smooth my hair. Another slow breath. I thought about the wide-open plains of my childhood. Remembering the warm breeze wrapping around my face, rushing down my neck. My mother carrying me on her hip, staring out across the rolling fields of amber wheat together. Nature is stirred by the wind, rippling like the sea. The blue and bright sky was host to gargantuan clouds rolling by. My mother hoisted me closer and nuzzled my nose. Her hair wisped around my face, and I felt her warm breath as she kissed my cheek. She smelled like flowers and linen. I wanted to melt into her. It was safe there. In that moment. That moment from so long ago. I took another deep breath. My mother was gone. Killed years ago, when the church invaded our ranch. Everyone I loved was gone. I took another deep breath and stood. But I'm still alive.

"This way," a hushed voice echoed from somewhere close.

"Stranger. Are you here to help or hinder?" I asked.

"Come. We must hurry."

A small and soft blue light lit up. Hazy, but enough that I could make out the figure holding it. It was something tall and gaunt. Its torso stretched and wrong. Frail limbs wrapped in paper thin skin made me step back.

"Who are you?" I debated running, but I still couldn't make out anything in this cavernous room.

"This chamber will be filled with fluids in a few minutes. I won't be here when that happens."

The thing turned and shambled away, leaving me once again in pitch black. I bit the inside of my cheek again and followed.

I kept a distance from the creature. It shifted from one unsure step to the next, looking as if it could fall at any moment. Its awkward height made it all the more unstable. Whatever magic it used to guide the way wasn't strong enough to reveal any discerning details, so I simply followed. Soon we reached a wall. The light shone across the rusted metal surface, and before us was a solid and angry looking door; its hinges and facade looked old, rusted and bitter. The short trek gave my panic time to mold into curiosity, which I was thankful for.

The creature used its pockmarked hand to operate the huge locking mechanism. Somewhere inside the massive door, gears resisted but finally gave in, creaking and moaning. The door swung open. I shielded my eyes from the blaring light.

I can remember seeing grand buildings and massive structures that used to house hundreds of families at once. Before the fist of the church came down, many structures serving various purposes. I had heard stories of some hosting elaborate events and performances. But even in my fevered dreams, I couldn't have imagined anything like this. Suddenly the big creature that was my escort didn't matter. I was in the belly of a titan. A massive steel and iron hall so big the ceiling was beyond my sight. To my left, a sky-high wall yawned into the distance. To my right was the same. I felt small and pointless in the presence of this monstrosity. It was beyond my knowledge, and all I could do was stare. Then I realized something was staring back. My guide had turned and was looking down at me. At least it seemed as such. His skull was stretched beyond natural proportions, and his chin came to a sharp point some half a foot below his head. His eye sockets empty; hollow and dry holes directed at me. His limp eyelids still squeezed together despite the absence of the organs they were meant to protect. He was a walking nightmare but made no move to threaten me.

"I think I preferred the cat," I finally muttered.

"This way."

It was hard to keep pace with the tall phantom as his long legs sped along the rusty corridors. My bare feet found every sharp edge of the metal floor in their haste. I dared not speak of my discomfort or fear lest my companion, the very vestige of discomfort and fear, should decide to leave me in his wake. I kept my mouth shut and my eyes open. The place was a colossal maze of hallways the width of hundreds of paces. So massive it defied any logic I dared to reason with.

Despite the magnitude, it all looked the same. Rusted walls riveted together. Cyclone fencing acting as walls and barriers. No ornamentation to speak of just endless walls and corridors.

"We are close," my guide said.

I didn't reply. There was no need; he didn't seem like the type to answer questions. Instead, I stayed in his shadow.

We neared a stairwell going up; even these were of gigantic proportions, easily two hundred feet wide. My eyes followed their ascent for what seemed at least half a mile, but near the top there was the hard brightness of red light. My guide began the climb, easily taking two steps at a time, his frailty seeming to vanish. Without turning to me, he spoke. "Rest not, witch; this is not a time for you. You are the vessel of change. A vessel of the light. You'll shed your sins, what you did to those people, and you will set things in motion. Now move."

I did as instructed. I was too close to the edge of shock to reply or put up a fight. As I climbed the stairs, I thought of his words. Somehow, he knew. He knew of my actions back at the settlement. I thought about my interaction with the cat. She knew too. But how? I wanted to cry, to object, to fight against this judgement, but who would listen? The cat didn't ask for my stance on the Battle of the Heathens. This forsaken guide surely doesn't care what I have to say about my actions. They don't know what it was like.

My legs burned, but all I could think about was the day before the attack. That terrible day. I was out foraging deep in the outskirts of the valley. Beyond the dilapidated buildings and overgrown roads we were calling home. I was picking berries and herbs, and the recent rains had made mushrooms plentiful. As much as I was falling in love with our small settlement, I still enjoyed foraging by myself. It was a relief to be alone with my thoughts and not have to tend to anyone for a bit. I was out farther than I had gone before, but the weather was on my side, and I felt at peace. I was deep in a berry bush—ripe blueberries and so many of them—thinking of all the ways we could prepare them when I heard him.

"Don't move," he whispered from behind me.

I froze. Berries in both hands.

"Turn around."

I did as he said. He was armed and well disguised. A scout. I had seen them before. The church had deployments everywhere. Large roaming armies converting one town after the next. Often, they would send out scouts to survey unknown areas, looking for smaller groups that were hiding in hard-to-reach places. Groups like mine.

"Go ahead. Shoot. It's just me out here." It was the first thing I could think of to say.

He was in full green camouflage. His face was painted as well. Lowering his gun, he said, "Noble. But a lie. I've been watching your refugees for two days. How many of you are there?"

This was not good. If he was here, then there was a fleet nearby.

"You tell me."

He rubbed his temples and muttered something under his breath and then stared at me. He seemed world wary and exhausted. A stark contrast to his high-end and seemingly new equipment. "Where are you from?" he asked.

I wasn't expecting such a casual question. I lowered my arms, tossing the blueberries into an old plastic bucket. "You mean where was I born?"

"Sure."

"Canada. Old Winnipeg. What about you?"

"Old Winnipeg?" he asked.

My hands went to my hips. He watched me, his body language neutral. "Yes. I was born before . . ." What was this man's angle? What was he trying to sniff out?

"Before the church turned it into a nuclear wasteland?" he finished for me.

"Yes. It seems that the Pope wasn't happy about people not conforming. But I'm sure you know more about that than I do," I said.

"Is it that obvious?" he asked.

"Comes down to the numbers. The crusade has been going on for what? Almost thirty years? All the rebel holdouts have long since been turned to ash. Everyone else converted. And judging by your equipment, I doubt you're one of the few godless traitors left."

"Maybe I took out a member of the Silent Congregation and stole his gear."

"Nope. A true heretic would have just said Scout," I muttered, looking at the ground. It was broad daylight; there was no way I could outrun him. Besides my buck knife, I was unarmed, but he was most certainly wearing lightweight armor under his ghille suit. I was stuck.

"You're smart. I guess that's why you're way the hell out here."

"Are you allowed to say that word? Hell?"

"Are you gonna rat me out?"

"Not if you let me go."

"Deal."

The scout pulled the shoulder strap of his rifle up his arm. Apparently, I was not at all a threat.

"Deal? What do you mean?"

He eyed me, scratching at his chin. "I'll let you go, but you gotta make a choice..."

I snapped back to the moment when I heard chanting. We climbed the large stairs for at least twenty minutes. My leg muscles were burning, shaking with each step. My guide seemed to have quickened his pace, or I had slowed mine. The gap between increasing.

I huffed and tried to concentrate. Somewhere far away was a deep chant. A bassy low tone that sounded like it was coming from a choir of giants. A profound pitch from the belly instead of the throat. The malignant chorus made my teeth hurt as my eyes strained to stay focused. I chewed the inside of my cheek and quickened my pace. In a few minutes, I was neck and neck with my guide. He didn't bother to observe or even acknowledge me. It didn't matter; we were both going to the same place. Ahead. The lights grew brighter and the chanting stronger. There must be an absurd amount of people to make such an overwhelming sound.

I sped up, my legs numb, on the verge of collapse. I had to make it. I didn't know what would happen if I collapsed or gave up. Neither were an option. I pushed my pace harder.

My knees buckled as I crested the summit. The last few steps were slick with dew, and I fell to my hands and knees. The hard concrete steps made my joints sing out in sharp pain as I collided with the floor. I pushed. I screamed. Only a few steps away. With what grit I had left, I scuttled up the rest of the way on my hands and knees and tossed myself onto the landing. Rolling onto my back, I fought to catch my breath as my body revolted and spasmed. I made it. Despite myself, I made it. Since I was still near the stairs, I saw my guide joining me on the landing. He didn't seem winded or even perturbed, nor did he glance down at me; he simply walked past. That's when I rolled over and looked towards the room I now found myself in.

I thought I had no more tears left to give on this strange journey—this sojourn I found myself in. This voyage into the darkness of my own soul. But fresh tears flowed as I gazed out towards the biggest room I've ever seen. We were high up, overlooking an arena. Tens of thousands of people filled the almost endless rows of seats. The steep rows surrounded and cascaded down to a show floor where a giant golden crucifix, ornate and beautiful, was etched. People in robes surrounded the podium at the center. The chanting continued. The combined drone of so many people made the floor vibrate. My heels throbbed as the feeling surged up my legs. I could do nothing more than witness. Nothing more than bare the glory of what man had created in honor and service of God. The energy in this massive hall could move mountains and make armies tremble. I had never been a believer, but in this moment, beholden to this poignant display of passion and power, I understood it.

The lights dimmed. The strong red floodlights softened and almost extinguished. The masses hushed and whispered with excitement.

"Tell me, witch, what am I witnessing?" I demanded.

"A clergyman is being sainted. His valor and conviction are being rewarded and celebrated."

"Sainted? I thought you had to be dead first."

"His Holiness, the mouthpiece of God, has changed the rules," my guide said.

A spotlight shot down onto the arena floor, illuminating a podium. Then, the crowd lost control. A shocking bellow of cheers and applause erupted, making me jump. Then I saw him. The Immortal Pope had entered. He sauntered up to the podium, his arms raised, his head back and smiling. He took to the pulpit as the crowd roared, waving and smiling, soaking up the adoration. I had never seen the man in person. Only in paintings and other depictions; murals, stained glass, and drawings. It was surreal being in the same room, breathing the same air, as this man.

Finally, the applause subsided and the red lights came back on, once again showing the thousands of zealots.

"Why are we still alive? So deep in this building of worship, why have these people not spotted us?" I asked.

"We are merely spectators of the past. They cannot see us, for we were not there."

"The past? When did this happen?"

"This morning."

The Pope beckoned for the clergy's attention and silence, of which he received both almost instantly. And then he spoke.

". . . Praise be to God."

The crowd thundered.

"And praise be to the Righteous. For they will inherit the Kingdom of God."

The crowd erupted again with palpable energy.

"And there are none more righteous than those that serve as the right hand of God himself. My Chosen. My Children. My Saints."

"His name is Joseph," my guide said, his eyeless skull never moving from the spectacle.

"Who?" I asked.

"The clergy you made the deal with."

I watched as a tall, blonde man walked up to the podium. And then it hit me as a jolt of pain shot through my brain. It was the scout.

He wore a cape and what seemed to be a golden laurel atop his head. He kneeled before the Pope.

"This morning will be recorded in the New Testament as the day the rebellion ended. The day the heathens were halted and their wickedness banished."

Once again, the crowd cheered, so intensely they seemed on the edge of rioting.

"And we have a special soul amidst our flock. A pious and worthy soul who spent weeks tracking the last remaining band of Pagans. He thought not of his own safety. He thought not of his own comfort. He thought only of his duty to God."

The crowd was brimming with edging chaos.

"And today we honor this person. Because without his servitude, without his conviction, there would still be unbelievers treading this earth. And I will not stand for that!"

The arena pulsed with adrenaline as the cheers continued.

"I present to this humble and righteous congregation, Joseph."

He waved his hand towards the still kneeling man, his head bowed.

"Joseph. Rise."

The man did as he was told, his head still bowed.

"Joseph. I have heard of your bravery. Your selflessness. Your unwavering dedication to the church. And despite such loyalty, I have been told you brought a gift unto me."

Once again, the crowd cheered.

"Tell me, Joseph, tell your fellow brethren, what do you offer?"

Joseph turned from the podium, and the Pope, and faced the audience.

"To the clergy. To the Church. To His Immortal Holiness, I offer the last of the Pagans from the Battle of the Heathens. To all mighty God do I offer the last of the sinners to you."

The robed figures near the podium parted as a cluster of small and bound children were ushered forth, front and center. I fell to my knees. The scout kept his promise. He didn't kill the children. I trembled as I kept watching.

"My dear Joseph. Are these the sinners I heard whispers of? The illegitimate, unbaptized spawn of the godless you helped to vanquish?"

"Yes, my lord, and I offer them to you. A tithe in flesh. A gift of blood. I have come before you as a soldier of God. And by His will I live and die. Please take these children."

The crowd hushed in awe. I wanted to scream, but I held it in and watched and listened.

"You honor me, Joseph. And in turn, I seek to honor you. Please come forth, my child. Come to me."

The Pope descended the podium as Joseph held his hands up to the cheering crowd. I couldn't take my eyes off that wretched old man. He didn't stand as tall and bold as all the depictions of him had shown me. He was smaller, more narrow and certainly more frail. He did not live up to his reputation. The old man paused. I studied him as he turned away in a coughing fit. He covered his face with both hands, coughing hard into a dirty handkerchief. His napkin was dark . . . with blood. He shook his head and tucked away the handkerchief and proceeded to the front of the podium, joining Joseph.

"Please, Joseph, kneel before me," the Pope said.

The scout did as he asked.

"Let the day be written that Joseph Rodgers of Baltimore, honored clergy of The Immortal Pope Axtrath, first and only of his name, has been divinely chosen as one of God's few. Rise and be witness here. I give you Saint Joseph of Axtrath!"

The scout rose, tears ladened his face as he openly wept. The masses let loose as lights flashed in a vibrant coronation. Trumpets sounded, and streamers fell from high above. A mockery of pageantry. A warped play of sacredness. I watched as the children were ushered away. The hooded figures swarmed Saint Joseph, patting him on the back and shaking his hand.

"What of the children?" I asked. I didn't realize the words had left my lips.

"Their skins are on display in the Holy Reliquary. Their remains were used as feed for livestock," the guide replied.

I stood, fists clinched, I hit my guide in his dried husk of a body. My fist pushed through it like the dried carapace of an insect. I pulled my hand out and hit him again, as hard as I could. I wanted blood. I wanted anger, rage, anything I could get in strong doses.

"Fight back, you coward!" I screamed.

My guide's large head looked down at me. He did nothing to stop my onslaught. He merely watched my feeble attempt at chaos. "I care not what you make of this. I have been lost and dead for eons. I am cursed to walk the planes forever. Lost in time. Lost in space. You are right. I was a coward. Thousands of years ago, far away. I did an unspeakable deed. As you have. We tell ourselves it was the right thing. The only choice. But we both know better. You can still save yourself. You can make things right. The blood on your hands may be dark and deep, but you can still redeem yourself. Think of what you have seen here."

"You speak as if you were there!" I backed away, my hands covered in flaky dead skin. "You speak as if you know my plight! My sacrifice! I had no choice! I didn't know these monsters would kill the children!" I backed away from my guide as he moved closer to me, reaching out with a thin, clawed hand. I could feel my heels at the edge of our observation deck.

"Words mean nothing. Nor do they correct the past. Go forth. Find a way to save yourself. Find your truth. Go."

With that, the gaunt visage of a haunted past pushed me.

I awoke in a field of grass, golden stalks rising all around me. The sky was clear and bright. My head ached. With a dry mouth, I tried to rise, pushing myself up. The last time I felt this bad was the morning after my birthday at the settlement in the valley. Some of the guys had set up a still and made a strong batch of mash. Samuel was always smart, always paid attention and remembered my birthday. So that night we drank. Such a warm memory for such a strange journey. I rubbed my eyes and tried to control my hair into some sort of ponytail. I stood and stretched and looked out at the wide and beautiful land. It was familiar and felt like a memory. That's when I turned and looked up the hill. A ways up in a small clearing, sitting upon an ancient log, was my mother.

The flood of emotions surely would have driven anyone else over the edge. Seeing their long dead mother perched atop an old fell tree, watching and waiting. But this—this longest night—was different. *I* was different. I brushed myself off and made my way up the hill.

"Beautiful, isn't it?" Her white and blue linen poncho flowed in the wind. She wore matching britches and simple sandals. Her hood pulled up, half covering her head. Soft auburn locks waving in the breeze. She watched the soft hills, spotted with clusters of trees.

I couldn't look away. Somehow, I was staring at my mother, the single most important person in my world. This long night was growing, changing into something beyond me—bigger than my narrow world of survival.

"Are you real?" I finally asked.

"As real as you are."

I followed her gaze, taking in the scenery.

"After this longest night, I don't know what I am."

"You'll be exactly what you need to be. And you'll always be my daughter."

A lump grew in my throat. I didn't know where to start. How would I? I blurted out, "How have you been?" Seemed as good as any place to start. Somewhere far away, a bird cawed.

"I'm doing what I can. Just like you. Just like everyone," she said.

"What's it like on the other side?"

She wrapped her poncho around herself. "It's not bad. It's like recalling a memory while dreaming; hard to hold on to and ever shifting. Not unlike what you're going through tonight. The longest night? That's one way to put it."

I joined her on the old oak trunk and stared out at the rolling beauty of nature.

"I need your help. I messed up," I finally muttered.

She looked at me, staring into my eyes. She was just as beautiful as I remembered. Soft blue eyes that instantly put me at ease. For all the death and destruction I was witnessing, this was a welcomed reprieve. I would take it because I knew it wouldn't last long.

"I heard."

"Wow. Word gets around fast." I tried my best to be normal. I wanted to just be a normal person with my mom. Why did we have to meet under such dire circumstances?

"The longer you've been dead, the quicker you hear things. And I've been gone awhile."

"You have. I miss you," I said, choking back tears. "It's been so hard. All we do is run and hide and run and hide. That's all I've known."

I couldn't hold it back any longer. I wept. I wept for my mom, for my friends and family, and for my sweet Samuel. I wept for the children.

"Hey, bugbear, get it out. Get it all out," she said, moving closer and placing an arm around me.

I haven't heard that nickname since she passed. She was the only person who called me bugbear. I cried harder, burrowing into her embrace. Warm and safe. We sat looking out over our old farmstead. I was home again. It's all I ever wanted. A quiet place to call my own. Away from the chaos. Away from those who claim they have all the answers. Those who want control and power. I burrowed into her and sobbed. She held me, showing nothing but love and patience. This was really her. This wasn't a dream. This was real.

I finally pulled away and tried to compose myself. I didn't notice the picnic basket next to us until she reached to open it. Pulling out a piece of bread and a dried fig, she handed them to me and told me to eat. I did. The bread was her own rosemary loaf. So simple and well made. I ate slowly. I didn't want this to end.

"No matter what, I am proud of you. You are putting up a good fight," she said, her voice low and soft.

"People died because of me." I thought of the damned scout. "That clergy said he would spare myself and the children if I left the door open that night. So they could convert us. It was that, or they would have put all of us in a shallow grave. I did what I thought was right. I couldn't take a chance and tell them. Everyone would flee, and then the church would kill us all," I said.

"You don't need to explain yourself. You were manipulated. Taken advantage of. You think I would have done anything different if I were in your shoes? You would be shocked at how many mistakes I made in life," my mother said, looking away.

"But none of it matters now. I'll be dead in a few hours," I muttered.

"Your chapter doesn't have to be over."

"Chapter?" I asked.

"We are short stories, just chapters, in the longest story ever told. All that matters is that the story doesn't end. Our chapters will close, but the story can't die. You made a hard call. People died. But we are at war. Your whole life has been a battlefield. But your chapter isn't over. You still have time," she said.

She smiled at me; a smile that felt like home. She wrapped her hand around the picnic basket handle and stood. I remained seated as she took a few steps down the soft decline.

"Will I see you? After they..." I couldn't finish.

"You don't have long. Your longest night is at an end."

I stood and watched her walk away.

"I love you," I said.

"I love you more."

———

I awoke to the ground shaking. My cell shuttered as I tried to make it to my feet, but my knees buckled as I wretched. Thin, bitter bile splashed onto the floor. Steam poured off my body as I realized how hot I was. It felt as if my skin was on fire, my limbs bright pink. I gulped the cold air and shambled to my window. The edge of night blanketed Hammer Hill, but the dawn's rays were crowning the horizon, making the day's first shadow fall across my cell. My own eclipse cast from the edge of town.

The dreadnought was here.

A colossal city on wheels, the roving herald of the church. Even from my cell, the morbid opulence showed. Gilded statues of saints and crosses midst gun turrets; its immense weight making the whole town jostle. At a glacial pace, the mobile city crawled to a stop. Massive flags unfurled, and trumpets sounded. I had to cover my ears as birds across the sleeping town took to the skies. From all over the vast manmade behemoth, large doors opened as walkways extended to the dirt below. They were here for me. It was my time. I looked down at my dormant pyre. It was still there, haunting me. Plenty of wood for a huge fire. Movement caught my eye. Along the waist-high stone wall wrapping around the pyre, a large white cat sat, licking its paw. It glanced up at me, staring. A moment later, it jumped down and away from my line of sight.

———

A group of elite clergy came to gather me. Wearing armor and capes and golden laurels like that given to the newly sainted Joseph. They shackled my hands and feet in pure silver cuffs with just enough silver chain to allow me to hobble onward. A reed of dogwood wrapped in leather gagged me, lest I use my words to incantate any spells, and at this juncture, this close to the end, I would have. I would have uttered every spell, hex, and curse I could muster. That is, if I were actually a witch. One capable of wielding such power. But my strength lies elsewhere. My strength has yet to be exhibited. I am something akin to a witch. After this longest night, I know now that I am more than the sum of my grief and pain.

Outside, the townsfolk were gathered. Mostly modest folk; farmers, hunters, craftsmen, and plenty of wives and children. A few well-dressed politicians were gathered on a nearby balcony. I guess this was as good an occasion as any to break out the finery and dress up. The Pope was in town after all. I was escorted to one of two mechanical platforms, and the clergy boarded with me. All the village of Hammer Hill watched as we ascended to the very top of the center pine, some thirty feet high. The stripped trunk was huge. The original tree must have been massive. Without a word, the clergy attached my wrist shackles to the very top. I would be left to dangle as the fire consumed me. It made for a better show if I was free to thrash about as I died. The hand of God wanted a spectacle after all. My hands were already beginning to go numb as the clergy ensured the cuffs were firmly attached. Without a word, they made their way down the ladder attached to the platform. Leaving me alone high above Hammer Hill. From here I could see the whole village; to the west were many small homes, most with smoking chimneys. I guess not everyone was in the audience today. To the north was the town square proper, shops, the taproom 16 Ton, and the town hall. South was a blacksmith and a few stables. Such a pretty little town. A humble place. A place I would live. These people didn't ask for the church to roll in and convert them. More casualties of religion.

Trumpets split the morning murmurs below me. Everyone jumped, myself included. I tried to rotate myself to look out towards the dreadnought. Below, people shifted and whispered. Some pointed, others crossed themselves or prayed while clasping rosary. The symphony was beyond loud and even rattled the pine I was now a part of. The crowd grew restless as they watched the procession below me. I couldn't see what was going on, but I could assume. Soon the cheering started. I could see some people smiling and clapping. Some were stoic and merely observing. But the spirit of the crowd grew as I heard the other lift being used. A mobile platform just like mine. I watched as it rose next to me. Then there he was.

"Good morning, my child."

He stepped onto my platform. Behind him, the two well-armed clergy watched over him, like parents watching their newborn walk for the first time. He ignored both of his devotees and came closer to fully stand on my platform. Both henchmen stayed back but kept a wary eye on the old man.

"Good morning," I muttered from behind my gag.

There he was. Flesh and blood. My suspension meant I had to look down at him as he looked up at me with big blue eyes. With a simple smile, he stepped forward.

"It pains me greatly to meet you in such circumstances," he said. Reaching up he pulled my gag from my mouth.

"Unchain me and we can have a coffee and catch up proper."

He laughed and looked at the crowd below. Giving a gentle wave, they cheered.

"The chance for pleasantries is beyond us," he went on. "We are now in the realm of punishment and precedence."

He was close now. Close enough I could smell him. The stale scent of old sweat wafted from his robes. His breath was sweet with rot.

"And what if I ask for forgiveness?" My cuffs dug into my wrists.

"Your trial was held. You were found guilty of witchcraft. I have looked at the documents. And despite your namesake, you have strayed from the path. You and your small band of Pagans strayed too far from the light of God. Like so many before you. I am so sorry it had to come to this."

"God seems to have a lot more rules as of late. There was a time when all people could be forgiven. A time when religion tried to make the world better by helping others, by accepting people of every race and age."

The Pope continued to look below at his followers and wave, his soft smile ever warming. "What would you know of our church's complex history? The age-old tapestry of faith and devotion?"

"I know, despite any history or legacy, nothing gives you the right to kill."

He lowered his hand. His pleasant, crowd-pleasing grin seeped away as he turned back to me. His clear blue eyes locked onto mine.

"That's where you're wrong." He stepped closer. "He speaks through me. I carry His will and judgment. Through Him, I have a divine right over this earthly domain. I have lived countless lives."

I thought of my sweet Samuel. How I sacrificed him.

"Throughout the ages I have seen to His holy purpose," he continued.

I thought of the children. The ones I thought my terrible bargain spared.

"And I will continue to bring the heathens to heel. And usher forth the will of God."

I thought of my mom. Cut down too early merely for not kneeling.

"For I am his immortal vessel!"

I thought of the blood-stained handkerchief the Pope coughed into.

"I don't think you're immortal," I said.

I lifted both legs, bringing my knees to my chest, and kicked. Those bright eyes widened as he fell. Flailing, his hat flew to the side. Screams erupted as he hit the fire's wide stone embankment, neck first. His body draped in a foul shape as blood rushed from his cracked head. Both guards rushed me, drawing their swords, pulling my legs back up. I jabbed at them with my feet, knocking one off the platform. He screamed as he fell atop the dead holy man. The other raised his sword; I closed my eyes and waited for the blow. Yelping as a loud bang rang out, opening my eyes in time to see the guard collapse onto the platform, a deep hole in his forehead. I glanced around frantically. Screams and more gunfire erupted from below me. All chaos occurring all at once. I spun around facing my pole; it seemed that my chain was held by a steep hook. Twisting, I wrapped my legs around the big pine and did my best to shimmy up, pulling myself upward. All around was an eruption of confusion and far more gunfire than I would have imagined. Towards the top of the pine, I raised my joined hands and slid my chains off the hook. I fell onto the bloodied platform, the dead guard softening my landing. My shackles had enough length to allow me to defend myself. First, I took the guard's sidearm; a high caliber hand cannon more for looks than efficiency, but it would do.

"Mary!"

My name. Someone was yelling my name. It had been so long since I'd heard it that my head almost didn't recognize it.

"Mary!"

Across the town circle, on a third floor, a man was waving his arms. We locked eyes as he smiled.

"Run!" he screamed, shouldering his rifle and shooting another clergy below my platform. This man saved me. That beautiful white hair—it was the old man that visited me in the middle of the night. I pressed the down button on the lift's control panel.

Amid the chaos and confusion, no one seemed to notice the witch on trial escaping. So many townsfolk had taken up arms. All around me were dead or dying guards. Nearby the Pope lay, head split open, eyes looking in different directions. Guess I was right.

"Mary!" Across the wide town square was my hero. The lone man who saved me. I ran to him. He smiled wide as I approached, glancing side to side with his rifle still in tow.

"Mary! You must flee. The town will be ransacked as soon as the word spreads."

"You saved my life." That was all I could say.

"Aye. Now go pay it forward. There are groups of rebels in almost every town and village. We have been sleeping, waiting for the church to think they had won. Now's the time, Mary, now is when we attack." He raised his rifle and shot a guard coming at us. I muffled my ears.

"How do you know my name? How did you know to come to me last night?" I asked.

The man shouldered his rifle by the strap and reached for my shackles. Pulling pliers from his hip pocket, he made quick work of the lynchpins.

"You wouldn't believe me if I told you. Regardless, we've been planning this attack for days. Since we heard of your execution. I was meant to shoot him." He glanced at the corpse of the holy figure. "But you beat me to it. I can't believe it. Mary the Redeemer." He beamed with pride at the moniker.

"The church did not make my name public, lest I be made a martyr." I stepped closer; his eyes widened. "How do you know my name?"

"Last night. A spirit came to me. In my sleep." He looked away but continued, "She asked me to help you. Said Mary was to be put to the stake, and if I could be of any use, I should see to it. See? I told you it was daft."

I was speechless, stunned. Despite how lucid last night was, it was already growing hazy and distant. The morning taking away the night's edge. "This spirit. What did she look like?"

The man looked around, still watching as more guards were rushing to the scene. Other villagers were armed and fighting.

"A cat. A bloody big one. Pure white. Now listen, Mary the Redeemer, head south. You'll find an old deer path. Follow it to the coast. You'll find a stronghold there. A safe place. Maybe the last one. Follow it. Please. Run."

Before I could argue, the man shouldered his rifle and fired. The fray was upon us. More Clergy than villagers. The act I committed was so sudden, so spontaneous, people were still deciding how to respond. I ran.

I found the southern deer path and ran till I collapsed and passed out. At some point I awoke and ran more. It took me two days to reach the coastline. By which point, I was close to death. On the beach, I finally went down. This time, no spirits nor phantasms came to me. But someone else did. I awoke in a soft, clean bed, my bare feet washed and bandaged.

I went to the edge of the world looking for salvation only to have it find me. There weren't many here. A small band of survivors, but it was enough. Word of my actions had already reached this settlement and many others affected by the church. They knew my name and my deeds. The village of Hammer Hill was now scorched earth. The Pope's dreadnought laid waste to the entire area. I don't know if that man made it out, the one who saved me. I don't know if anyone made it out. But I do know the church is in ruins. Soon after the word spread that the immortal Pope was dead there was massive turmoil amongst their ranks. Within weeks, the empire was crumbling, and throughout the cities and farms and villages, they talked of the one who brought it down. The one who lit the fuse of revolt.

I have seen and made many sacrifices in my life, but my chapter is not over. I will spend what time I have left fighting against those who would do us harm. I am more than the weight of my sins. I am someone my mother would be proud of. Mary the Redeemer.

RETURN TO SENDER

"**I**'ll take it," Ryan said.

The realtor gazed at him with half-lidded eyes. As if she didn't understand what he said. She took a long moment, staring through him.

"Really?" she asked after a bit of computing.

Ryan took a deep, satisfying breath and re-declared his statement.

"Alright, I'll get the paperwork ready." Her subdued demeanor unchanging, she turned and consulted the pile of documents resting on the kitchen island.

Ryan gazed around his new place, a beautiful ranch home; simple and understated like his writing. Cassie wouldn't have liked this house, but that didn't matter, he liked it. Tucked away in the rural periphery of Philadelphia, it suited him quite properly. He was already imagining the layout. He would rest his sleepy head in the master bedroom with an ensuite. He would convert one of the two additional bedrooms into his library and writing room, the one facing the backyard with windows looking out towards the small creek cutting through the bordering property. He imagined summer night having parties on the back patio with his friends and brand-new agent.

This time last year, Ryan felt that his novel was polished enough to land him an agent, and after several well-written query letters, someone took the bait. In Los Angeles, Sidney Miller with the Blackwood Literary Agency was the first to respond. She was green, with just a few clients, but she got Ryan's book and knew she could make things happen; a few phone conversations later, Ryan was another one of her clients. A few months after that, she landed a huge publishing deal. It was a Cinderella story. Ryan had come from nothing, a poor child from a poor family. After several pointless jobs, he began playing around with writing. He honed his skills, and after years of practicing his craft, he was now standing in his new home that he would pay for in full. His mother would have been proud.

"Okay, just need a few signatures and we will be good to go," the realtor stated.

"I can't wait. Thank you for everything."

The realtor feigned her best smile.

A week later.

"So, what do you think?" asked Sidney from the speakerphone.

"I love it. This is just what I wanted." Ryan bustled about the kitchen, unpacking boxes and loading the dishwasher with freshly unpacked dishes.

"Well, I'm glad. You've earned it. But down to business. How's the second coming?"

Sidney was referring to Ryan's second novel. His throat constricted at the question.

". . . Good. I should have the first draft to you soon," he lied.

"I can live with that. You made the bestseller list, so we need to keep the momentum going. You're hot and I don't want to lose that, nor should you."

Ryan nodded in agreement. He thought about the second act of his new novel; he was stuck.

"I agree. It's going well. I just want to get my office up and running, and I'll be right as rain soon enough," Ryan stated with authority.

"That's what I like to hear."

She bought it.

"Can you at least give me a hint? Just a clue. Will it be a sequel to Far Beyond the Fall? Or something new? I'm okay with either, but I'd love to give a nugget to the designers at the publishing house."

His first book was about two lone souls who managed to find each other in the vast wastes of a ruined Earth. Cassie didn't like sci-fi. She always said it was juvenile and a waste of paper. Ryan ground his teeth and spoke up, "This one is called The Lonesome Road. It's about redemption and how far a person is willing to go when pushed to the edge."

There was a long pause. Ryan glanced at the phone, making sure it was still on. "Chills. That gave me chills, Ryan," Sidney finally said.

"I'm glad. I'm going deep on this one. Getting real personal."

"Fantastic."

Hours later he had begun to unwind, a stiff gin and tonic helped. He stored away countless books on his study's bookshelves, tomes that he revered and studied, and works of fiction that he read and re-read all the while critiquing the intricate plays of description and dialog. Analyzing the way different writers dealt with conflict and suspense. The dog-eared books that he scoured through while Cassie looked at him with those eyes. Those eyes that said, *grow up*. Those heavy eyes held such judgment and contempt.

The sun was beginning its inevitable descent when Ryan found his way to the backyard. He meandered this way and that, surveying the sturdy trees that he now owned. He made his way to the creek about fifty yards back that separated his property from the adjacent land. Clear, swift water that ran left to right, just like his words on paper. The gin and tonic he had been nursing perhaps piqued his adventurous side, and he followed the flow downstream along the rocky bank. With confident feet, he made his way into the forest that surrounded the development where his house resided. Despite the sinking sun, it was exciting tempting fate; he knew that he would have to navigate the way back with no light, save the glow of the cell phone in his robe pocket, but he didn't care. Writers explore; they adventure and take chances. How else do they convince a reader that a character is taking a chance but to know its effects firsthand?

After a bit, Ryan came to a small pool where the stream ended. A rock-rimmed pond with a gaping maw at the far end into which the water dumped. It looked like a half-submerged cave opening leading into a perfect pitch-black. He watched as the spring water spilled into the void, going somewhere he didn't want to see. With an empty drink in hand, he was suddenly on edge. He was nervous and didn't like it. After a few motionless moments, he became aware beyond the spilling brook; he heard a growl.

His body tensed, and with wide eyes, he surveyed his surroundings, trying to pinpoint the possible predator. The cavernous waterfall played tricks with his ears, tossing the low growl from his left to right. Slowly he reached into his robe pocket and gripped his keys into a fist with a key pointing out between each finger. If he was going to die, he meant to at least make the beast regret it. A moment later, he caught the eyes of his audience. In a thick bush across the pond, he spotted a large dark figure squatting low to the ground, wide yellow eyes unblinking.

If he bolted, he may gain a few yards before the creature navigated its way across the open pond, but he wasn't the athletic type; he was a writer. A high-pitched whistle ripped the tension. Both beast and human snapped out of their embrace and looked up the nearby hill where the noise came from. The hulking beast in the bushes turned from feral animal to domestic pet as it trotted upwards to a figure making its way towards the pond.

"Get yur ass ova hea," said the figure.

A gangly, elderly man in dirty overalls sauntered towards the now docile dog and kneeled to pet him. Ryan took in a deep sigh of relief and felt the tension leave his bones.

"You had me for a moment," he blurted out, startling the old man who stood and pulled up a shotgun that Ryan hadn't noticed.

Ryan threw up his arms, trying to display a sense of surrender. The old man read the writer and knew there was no threat. Lowering the shotgun, he offered a dirty tooth grin and laughed.

"Sorry thea friendo, usually when Kevin gets down inta tha thicket, he's got tha scent of a bear."

The writer looked on shell-shocked and stumbled for words. "I'm so sorry. I just moved in, and I was just checking out the stream."

The old man offered a laugh and made his way down the rise towards Ryan, ending up on the opposite side of the pond, shotgun in hand and beast by his side.

"Na worries friendo, nuttin but neighbors over hea," the old man offered.

"Look, I wasn't trying to trespass. I don't want any trouble," Ryan proclaimed.

"Na harm, na foul. Glad to meet ya, names Wilfred but most folk call me Fred."

The writer relaxed, letting his shoulders loosen. He regained his natural calm composure and wished he was able to shake the old man's hand. With no effort, he let his thoughts slip.

"So, you been here long?" A stupid question he realized instantly, but it was enough to break the ice.

"All ma life," the old man replied without hesitation.

Biting his lip, Ryan effortlessly slipped into writer mode: he envisioned the old man as a character in one of his stories. As a writer, he understood the subtle back-and-forth play of dialog between two characters. He understood that no written line was in vain: like a movie, every frame counted.

"This creek crosses behind my property. I followed it here, and it seems to lead into the ground."

"Indeed!" The old man found a toothless smile and was happy to share his thoughts. "Kinda funny you shoul' mention. Truth be told, no one is sure where the creek drains off ta." The old man settled on a nearby flat rock with his giant dog panting next to him.

"Nary ten years go some folk from the city came by surveying an such; they wanted to know if the creek fed into an underground cave and came knocking on my door. I didn't know an I told 'em such."

Ryan followed suit and found an old log opposite the man and hunkered down.

"So no one knows where this leads? It just disappears?" he asked.

The old man cleared his throat and eyed up the gaping mouth that ate up the fresh flowing water.

"Well, those folks threw Ping-Pong balls with their info drawn onto them into tha creek. Like addresses and phone numbers and such, and then they waited."

The old man paused and withdrew an old wooden pipe from his overalls, struck a match, and began puffing. After a few moments, the pipe found life and began to emit a steady cloud of thick white smoke. After a few steady puffs, the old man continued.

"'Nutin," he said with absolution. "After a long bit a wait, nutin came bout." The old man took a long, faithful draw on his pipe and let out a confident stream of smoke circles. His dog looked on, glancing at Ryan.

After a moment, Ryan found his voice. "So, the Ping-Pong balls . . . no one found them?"

"Nope. And I reckon no one has since no one has come here to lay claim to them."

"Makes sense." Ryan paused and glanced over to the gaping dark mouth that opened into the very black of the earth itself.

He felt as if he were in one of his own short horror stories. One of those quick reads that give you goosebumps; a quick "Boo" and moves on. He already saw his next line of dialog on the stark white page in his head. As the words passed his lips, he felt the click of the keys on the back of his teeth.

"Well, I guess I should be making my way home; the sun is going down," he continued.

"I suppose I already knew that." Fred began to find his feet and pulled himself up.

Ryan cocked his head at the strange comment. The notion left his head as quickly as it came to him. "The name's Ryan, by the way. I suppose you might be seeing me around. I just bought the house right over there." He pointed his thumb behind him, towards his new home.

"Ah! Yo tha writer everyone has been gabbing about," Fred returned. His back to Ryan as he made his way up the steep incline, one slow step at a time.

This also caught Ryan off guard. "Oh? I'm flattered. That's nice of you to say." He wasn't sure how to take the old man's words. There was a hint of irreverence in his voice mixed with a twinge of actual politeness.

"What's it about? Ya book that is," Fred asked, grabbing a low-hanging tree branch to steady his ascent.

Ryan thought about the pitch he had given his agent. It had taken him weeks to formulate the perfect query letter. But it had done its job. He glanced at the black opening of the stream's pit. The water disappearing into the nothingness below. He thought of his ex. She didn't care for his book. At first, she didn't even want to read it—a sign Ryan should have picked up on. When she broke down and took in the pages, she tossed them back at him. She said his prose was too dramatic and his dialog was as fake as it comes. Her words hurt him. The night of her feedback, he almost quit writing altogether. She had been drunk and in rare form. She had ripped into him about how he needed to get his shit together and get a real job. Her words still rang in his ears.

He looked up and saw that Ol' Man Fred was waiting for a response.

"It's about escaping," he said.

That night he unpacked. He wasn't in a hurry and had no particular direction or purpose. He had an old horror movie playing on the T.V. in the living room and his iPod pumping out punk music in the kitchen. Every light in his new house was on.

By good grace and fortune, one of the first boxes he opened after stumbling through the dark back to his house had a few bottles of high-end gin in them. He amused himself with the notion that they wanted to be consumed, and, by God, he wanted to help them with their goal. The new fancy fridge had two things in it: prosciutto stuffed peppers and artisanal tonic. His earlier trip to the grocer down the street proved to be ineffective; he was never good at buying groceries and just grabbed his usual and departed.

A glass of ice later, he was making another stiff gin and tonic as the Ramones blared from the kitchen island. He was alone. But he wasn't lonely. He felt the dusk of depression creeping in; the wounds Cassie had left were still fresh and wet, but he was too happy to give in. A few months ago, he would have let the darkness take over—he would have welcomed the self-slandering into his head about how he wasn't good enough to get published or keep a job or take care of Cassie. Months ago, he would have let the demon in his head berate and belittle him, but tonight, in his new house and with his new life, the demon lay silent.

The gin was good and cold. The music loud. His phone was lighting up nonstop with the endless notifications of people wanting to be his friend. If this was what fame felt like, he could get used to it. The drinks flowed, the music roared, and the fans adored.

Eventually, Ryan stumbled into the living room. He was drunk. The whole room was host to boxes upon boxes; his life quantified by possessions, all stored away in cardboard tombs. He entered the room with purpose. He sought to find some books he had been thinking about. Tomorrow he would have to get down to the business of writing, and knew if he pulled these out tonight, his sober self might be inspired. He opened a few boxes marked *BOOKS* and perused them as he might in a bookstore. The first box didn't contain what he was looking for. He opened a second and a third until he found it.

He pulled out an old book. It was a collection of short horror stories. It was one of the first he ever read as a young man, initiating his writing career. He smiled as he opened the book and fondly flourished the pages. That musky smell of old parchment filled his face. This would indeed help him tomorrow; his drunk self knew it implicitly.

He grinned as he closed the book and shuffled towards the couch where he would sleep for the night. As he made his way across the living room floor, walking around stacks of boxes, the old book he was carrying caught the corner of a box tower and fell to the ground. He stumbled to pick it up, pinching the spine with his thumb and forefinger. As he brought it back to his grasp, something fluttered out from behind the hardback cover. He fumbled for it, trying to catch it. Stumbling, he fell to one knee, and as he tried to steady himself, he paused.

Staring back at him was Cassie. It was an older photo, back from when they first met. It must have been their fourth date, maybe. It was one of those awkward pictures that get forced on you at the entrance of an amusement park. It had been a pushy young man who spoke little English and had practically begged them for a picture. Begrudgingly they agreed. He could still recall how nervous he was to put his arm around her waist. It ended up being a good picture despite everything. And now, here it lay.

He stared down at the happy couple. A lifetime ago they had discussed kids' names. They dreamed about retiring to Colorado after those kids had grown up and left the nest. A lifetime ago, he had the love of his life. But now he sat slumped on the floor. A drunk heap. He had made it; he was published. He was the new writer on the scene, and people were adoring him. But in this moment, he had never felt more alone. He sobbed.

After a few minutes of weeping, the overwhelming wave of remorse had passed, for now at least. He tried to clear his head and shake off the icy, dull grasp of loneliness. He shuffled to his feet, leaning against a towering stack of boxes. The tower slumped over under his weight. He tried to grab the top box, but it slid off and toppled onto the sandy-colored carpet below. The tussle was enough for the box lid to come off, spilling its contents out; more things and artifacts from a life lost to the angel of regret. He rubbed his face as a hard sigh let loose from deep in his lungs. He gazed down at the spilled contents. The box had been the lucky recipient of the belongings from the junk drawer. Bobby pins, bottle caps, paper clips, and an assortment of little things with no real purpose. He began scooting the loose items back into the box with a socked foot. He was too drunk and full of grief to care. A wave of tears was coming on again when he stopped in his tracks. He stared into the box. A hot bolt of clarity shot through his head. Without thinking, he dropped to his knees and pulled six Ping-Pong balls out of the box.

If Ryan were to be interviewed about this night sometime in the future, he would refer to this moment as "the turn". The moment in a story where the readers start to piece together the clues the writer was leaving behind and the point where the reader and writer alike take a turn towards the unknown. But Ryan would never be interviewed about this night. For better or worse.

In a flash, he was out in his new backyard. Robe pockets filled. Full drink in his left hand and a flashlight in his right. It was a starless, black night. The sky was an oppressive dark, like the thick curtains of an ancient playhouse. The air was thick, too. Each breath was a struggle.

Despite the obnoxious amount of booze racing through his blood, his feet were deft and swift. He followed the black creek that he had so casually walked earlier when the sun was still out. But now he had a purpose. Earlier, he was just a happy writer exploring the countryside. Now he was something else; something dark, something alone and forgotten. Before he knew it, his drink was once again empty, his house slippers and the bottom of his bathrobe were laced with loose dirt and leaves. His flashlight lit his path with a faint, alien white light. There wasn't a star to speak of above. He picked up the pace, head swimming, heart thumping in his throat. Where was the mouth? He had been walking too long. Had he gone the wrong way? A thick branch snapped somewhere in the dark distance. He pretended not to notice, hoping that it was his stupidly overactive imagination. He trudged on, his mouth hanging open.

For a moment he thought about turning back. The sudden and powerful notion he had back in his new living room was beginning to lose its glamor. But then he heard it. That distinct gurgle; the sound of helpless water going to some other place. He trudged forward. In the dark of night, the open mouth of the underground seemed predatory. As if it were looking back, unblinking and unremorseful. Ryan stood at the shore of the small pond, its contents pouring into the black rock opening. He thought about why he was back out here, back at the mouth of the abyss. He fumbled in his pocket as he dropped the empty rocks glass to the mud below. He pulled a permanent marker out of his right bathrobe pocket and a matte white Ping-Pong ball out of his left. He took a deep breath and wrote on the plastic ball. Once he finished, he gently blew on the ink. A lump formed in his throat as he re-read the simple words.

He looked up at the gaping jaws of the cave entrance. It taunted him; its bitter, jagged stone teeth wanted to tear him to pieces. He considered not tossing the ball in, not wanting the little lone messenger to embark on a journey it would never return from. In a way, the words were a part of him, and he was afraid. His light flashed, its battery was low. He snapped out of the strange kinship he was experiencing with the simple Ping-Pong ball. He tossed it. Slowly it bobbed its way to the dark, stoney entrance. With no epic gesture, it disappeared.

The curtains were open, letting in the early rays, and Ryan's position on the couch gave him a direct audience. He stirred and moaned, covering his eyes, fighting against a wave of gin-induced nausea. Somewhere in the kitchen his phone was erupting with texts, emails, and alerts of new fans following him on various social media outlets. Normally, such adoration would be a great way to start any day, but this morning would be a rough one. Slowly Ryan rose, swore off booze, and began his day.

Despite the throbbing in his front brain, some coffee and a croissant sat him proper and before he knew it, he was blaring music and singing along. Every window and door was open, and his laptop was taking in a windfall of words that were pouring from the writer's soul. The Ramones were once again singing to him, and in the early morning charm, he found a piece of serenity.

He was working on a heady piece; a short story that wasn't tinged with the normal horror and dark lurking things. This piece was more of a thinker, and he was happy to have a short reprieve from the norm. He knew he should be working on his next book, but this felt right. He emptied two carafes of black coffee and four Ramones albums before lunchtime. He was beginning to feel as if he had his stride back. Thus, he decided that after lunch he would open the manuscript of his second novel and attack it with teeth.

Ditching the bathrobe, he opted for jeans and shirt, and decided to venture out for an Italian sub. There was a local place down the street that he was sure he would frequent. Keys in hand, he opened the front door and stepped out. That's when he saw it. He stopped in his tracks, mind reeling. Stumbling back, his foot caught the lip of the threshold, and he fell. Never taking his eyes off it, he crawled back like it was a poisonous thing; something that could do him harm. Maybe it would. Stunted and stunned, he stared unblinking. Upon the welcome mat of his new home rested a single Ping-Pong ball.

It took Ryan a few shaky moments to reach his feet. The door stood open as he stared out onto the porch and the small white sphere. His hands and feet trembled as he forced himself out onto the porch. Birds sang, absent-minded to the sheer panic being presented before them. He glanced around; the street was empty. Standing above the small object, he pondered the night before. It was gray in the back of his mind, too much booze. He stooped down and gently plucked the ball off the mat. Rolling it around in his hand, his breath lodged in his throat as he read the single word written upon it 'yes'.

Who did this? he pondered as he choked back sudden tears. Hands trembled as the bold-faced letters stared back at him. Such a simple word in all respects, technically of course, but as a writer the word could, and did, hold so much more. And in this moment, it held everything. Alone and confused, he stood in the early summer breeze. Staring at the single, three-letter word. Shock and cold and fear iced his joints and throat. He needed a drink.

In the kitchen, the ball sat on the counter as his trembling hands poured liquor. No ice, just booze. He thought through the scenarios that could have led to this. He replayed the previous night over in his head, recalling it the best he could. He poured burning warm liquor down his throat. It wasn't long till he felt it working. The ball sat unmoving, glaring and white, and out of place; it didn't fit in his house. Suddenly Ryan was mad. Furious even. The only way this made sense was if someone had seen him and decided to play a prank on him. But he was alone last night. He picked up the ball and studied it. The lettering was bland; a simple *yes*. He rolled it in his hands. Enraged, he threw it across the kitchen. It landed with a hollow, mocking thud in the dining room. He took a pull from the bottle and winced as the remanence of his hangover reacted. Bottle in hand, he stormed into the living room and yanked open the box holding more white spheres. Soon after, he was stomping along the shallow stream, headed to the mouth.

A quarter of the bottle was gone by the time he stood in front of the maw. Despite the sunny day, it was shadowed and black with wetness. Ryan stared into it. *Yes.* The word haunted him. If this answer was true, he had to know *how.* The writer in him summoned up the age-old storyline of the artist descending into madness. *This must be a short story,* he mused to himself. Because in a proper narrative, the descent was much slower, and methodical. Perhaps this was a parable, a short cautionary tale. The booze was hitting him hard as his mind drifted; he swayed as he stood on the flat rock across from the open mouth.

He sat down with a thump and stuck his legs into the icy water. The bottle tucked between his thighs. He trembled as he etched another question on the Ping-Pong ball in permanent marker. With quivering lips, he blew the ink dry. He stared into the black opening. It looked back, cold and uncaring. He tossed the ball in. Alone, he watched it drift across the pond. Alone, he watched it drop into the cavernous underground. Alone, he drank and wept.

Ryan awoke. He had fallen asleep next to the pond. The mouth was still there, watching him from the other side. His head was throbbing, and he turned onto all fours and vomited. Painfully he made his way back to his house in the dusk of the setting sun. Muddy and covered in his own filth, he entered the back patio's sliding glass door; the phone was ringing.

"Hello."

"Jesus Christ! Where have you been?" It was Sidney. And a side of her he had never seen.

"I'm right here," he muttered as he poured a glass of water.

"I've been calling you for days. I even came by! Your car was there, but you weren't, I even walked into your house!" she screamed from the other end of the line.

He drank deeply and sat the glass aside. "What are you talking about?" None of this made sense.

"I left a note on your door! I was about to call the police!" She was calming down, but the tinge of concern was still there.

Ryan walked to the front door and opened it. "I seriously don't know what you're talking . . ." Before he could finish, he stared out onto his porch. He dropped the phone from his grasp as he stared down at hundreds of glaring white Ping-Pong balls. The phone cracked and malfunctioned as it bounced off the hardwood floor. Despite his head being dulled by yet another hangover, he reeled back from the scene. Then he screamed.

<hr>

"So, the call just dropped?" the police officer asked Sidney.

"Yes. He was saying something and then . . ." She trailed off as she lost herself in the stacks of boxes in Ryan's living room. She had decided to call the police after Ryan abruptly disconnected. She had been calling Ryan for days to no avail, and when he finally did answer, it wasn't him that was talking, it was something else. Now she stood in his empty house with several officers searching the premises.

"Okay, thank you for the info. We will take a look around. There are a lot of empty liquor bottles around, maybe he's sleeping one off somewhere," the cop said, jotting notes on a small pad.

Sidney didn't respond, she was lost in her own thoughts. Something was off, and she couldn't help but feel like she should run fast and hard away from this place. Something was in the air, and it was almost more than she could handle; if she had been alone, she surely would have left.

"Sir, we found something." Another cop stated from the back patio door. Sidney looked up at the cop she had been talking to, waiting to see his reaction. He didn't say a word and exited the back. Sidney followed.

They followed a dried-up creek bed. Three officers and Sidney; the dried and cracked stream lit by their flashlights. "Up here. There's a cave," the officer in the front of the line said.

Sidney was the last to walk onto the scene. She stifled back a scream as she stumbled back. A dried pond filled with Ping-Pong balls. In the center lay Ryan, dead. Across the dead pond was an open cave into the earth. A cop picked up a Ping-Pong ball. "Hey, there's something written on these," the first cop said, tossing the ball to the second cop.

The second cop read it aloud, "Does she still love me?"

"They all say it," the first cop stated, staring out in awe at the strange sight.

"It's like a scene from a horror novel," Sidney whispered.

PENNSYLVANIA PYRAMIDS

She was the kind of girl that gave you wet dreams.

She stood there in front of him, talking, smiling, and laughing. He did the same back at her as nicely as he could. She was oblivious, as she should be, since he gave no sign or hint of what he was thinking. If she could have peered into his mind at that very moment, she would have either blushed, screamed, or slapped the shit out of him.

Jeffrey had only been working at the bar for a couple of weeks now as a new manager. She, on the other hand, was the head bartender and, in every way, the kind of woman that Jeffrey sought to find, fuck, and worship. The clincher was the establishment's strict anti-fraternization policy, so Jeffrey kept all his thoughts to himself.

The girl, Kristen, had taken to him well enough, and within the weeks, they had become work friends. Jeffrey took every opportunity to talk to Kristen: liquor inventory counting, stocking, and scheduling the other staff kept him by her side enough for him to become even more infatuated. And now as she stood before him, telling a funny story about something or other, he nodded and smiled as he sipped a glass of ice water. He even liked her voice. It was soft and expressive. He smiled as he listened. The nearby barflies paid no mind.

". . . so, then she says, 'no, that's my monster in-law'," she said as she snickered at her own joke. Jeffrey watched her and laughed along. He took quick glances at her massive tits, the buttons of her blouse struggling to keep them caged in.

She was short. With dark hair and even darker eyes, curvy and thick in all the right ways. The kind of girl you might find swinging swords and robbing ancient tombs in an issue of *Conan the Barbarian*. His jeans were getting tight; he had to snap out of it.

There was a lull in the conversation, and he took it as an opportunity to focus on the task at hand. "Did the liquor store fax over the invoice for our order?" he asked, looking over the liquor rack, avoiding the girl.

"Yup. I was going to send Steve to pick it up. Is that cool with you?" she asked, studying a clipboard.

He liked that she was in the habit of asking him for permission. He never thought of himself as the alpha type, but just her presence was stirring something in his soul and deep at the base of his spine.

"Yeah. That's fine. He should only break a couple of bottles," he said. She snickered at the jab. He knew it wasn't funny, but she laughed regardless.

The receipt printer started printing a drink order from a server, and Kristen set down the clipboard. She glanced at the ticket and began making the drink. "I heard a little secret about you," she said with a sheepish smile, in that soft tone that meant she wasn't being professional at that moment.

"Oh, yeah?" he asked nervously, thinking about anything and everything he may have done that could be interpreted as bad or questionable. But short of constantly eye-fucking the girl in front of him, he couldn't think of anything.

"Yes, sir. One of the bartenders has a bit of a crush on you." Her words were syrupy and smooth.

"That's not allowed," he blurted out as if this were a test he was damn sure going to pass.

She fought back her laughter as she strained the mixed liquors into a glass of ice. "Jeez, relax, I didn't take you for a rules Nazi," she said, placing the finished drink on the bar. A Fuzzy Navel, the glass already sweating.

Caught off guard, Jeffrey suddenly felt awkward and uncool. "Nah, just that one rule is pretty black and white," he muttered, still feeling like it was a trap.

"Well, it's probably best I don't tell you, anyway. Wouldn't want to tempt you to the dark side," she said, picking up her clipboard once again.

"I have many admirers, but I'm married to my work," Jeffrey responded, trying to put the issue to rest. He preferred his private fantasy world where he could fuck Kristen on the bar top. Besides, all the other bartenders were barely above the south side of hideous in his book.

"Got any plans tonight?" she asked, studying the numbers and counts on her paperwork.

"Just a movie and bed. I have to be up early to open this place," Jeffery replied in his best casual voice.

"Nice. What movie?"

"Nightlife. Some mockumentary about vampires."

"I've seen that one! Def worth the watch," she replied, not looking up from her clipboard.

"Normally I only watch horror flicks, but tonight I'm changing it up."

This made her drop her clipboard and smile from cheeky dimple to cheeky dimple. "I love horror movies! I see them all in theater, even the shitty ones."

The receipt machine whirled and clanked as it spat out another drink ticket. She grabbed it and started making the order as if it were second nature, and Jeffrey assumed it probably was for her.

"You should see my Blu-ray collection. Over two hundred titles. I even have rare foreign VHSs. Stuff that's never been released on DVD," she continued with a twinge of excitement in her voice.

"Well, I have a pretty healthy collection myself. We will have to set up an exchange program."

"I don't lend out to just anyone," she stated as she built another drink. "But Thursday night is new movie night at my apartment. Just saying," she offered in an almost hushed and playful voice.

Blood rushed to Jeffrey's cheeks as he turned a light shade of pink. He wasn't expecting an open invite. And from a girl he would punch a baby to dry hump for thirty seconds. He tried to block out the sudden flash of her bent over and naked on all fours as he was fucking her, all the while some slasher flick roaring on the flat screen.

He had to say something quick; something, anything that wasn't stupid. "Don't threaten me with a good time," he retorted with a casual and very forced snicker. He could have punched himself in the dick for saying such a stupid line. But it was too late. It had escaped his mouth before he could even analyze it.

"Oh, it's not a threat . . ." she said in the same hushed and playful tone. She turned to him and handed over the clipboard.

"Inventory is done, sir," she said in a mockingly official tone.

"At ease, soldier," he returned in his own mocking tone. She laughed easily and turned to head towards the bar's kitchen. He watched her walk away, her curvy hips framing a full and tight ass that was showcased by perfect jeans. It looked as if she were dipped into liquid denim from the waist down. As she disappeared around the corner, Jeffrey was now alone behind the bar, holding the clipboard. The receipt machine spat out a drink order.

The next day, Jeffrey sat in a cramped and cluttered office, hunched over a dirty keyboard staring at a monitor. Last night, his sleep was shallow and unsatisfactory. Tossing and turning, he must have changed positions a hundred times; his pillows and blankets were the victims of his fitful night. He stared, blurry-eyed, at a spreadsheet of endless and rather dull numbers. All the lines and digits made a useless roadmap to nowhere.

"Hey there." Her normally soothing voice made him jump. He quickly straightened and sucked in his gut like a soldier caught off guard by a drill sergeant. He tried to pull off that cool, casual vibe but failed instantly. Believe it or not, he was capable of such a thing, but not when surprised like this. He tried to prop his elbow on the little desk, but it was taken up almost entirely by the decades-old clunky keyboard.

"What's crackin', gangsta?" He immediately regretted the words as soon as they left his dumb mouth.

She snickered and smiled, and suddenly, his uneasiness melted away as quickly as his own iciness brought it on.

"Sleep well, cowboy?" she asked with that sweet smile. She turned her hips towards the little desk he was half working and half sleeping at, and rested her firm ass against it. This act put her within Jeffrey's personal bubble. Normally, he would have backed his rolling chair away a few inches, but her essence and perfume kept him steadfast in his spot. Her scent was a subtle floral spirit, and a spicy sweetness of tobacco swirled together with her own chemistry. It was intoxicating. His jeans began to tighten again.

"Like a stone. How 'bout you?" He couldn't distract himself by pretending to work because her ass was perched on the table in front of the keyboard. There was no out short of standing up and walking the fuck out of the office. *What is she doing?!* His brains were screaming.

Ignoring the question, she brought her small backpack up to her chest, paused, and then asked, "Can you keep a secret?"

There was a flash of perversion in his head. For a moment, her knees are over his shoulders, and he is thrusting hard. "Yes," he said with no comedic touch; just a straight, honest, and flat *yes*.

She grinned and pulled out her smartphone, tucking in closer to Jeffrey. She was so close he could feel her soft body heat. He didn't realize it at first, but he was holding his breath.

"I know how much you love horror movies, so I gotta show you what I did last night." Holding up her phone, she plugged in her passcode in front of Jeffrey. *6663*. He smirked.

Once in, she tapped on a video and swung it around to grant him the best seat in the house. He was thankful for the momentary distraction; her presence so close to him was almost too much to take. He watched intently.

Blackness. A subtle rustling. Tree branches brush by as the cloudy sky lets through a whisper of illumination. Slowly, the thick brambles and trees pass by—no path ahead, nothing to follow. Moments pass, and so do the trees. Blackness eats everything as soon as the moonlight finds it. Confusion and a sense of lost sets in.

Then a noise gives pause, stopping, waiting for the noise again. In the distance, a subtle hum comes. With just enough spirit behind it that it's known not to be an accident. Cutting through more trees, the darkness begins to give way to a warm glow. Ahead is a clearing and the source of the warmth and light. A bonfire. The hum is alive as more trees slowly pass. Ahead, the fire flickers in the clearing, viewed safely from a distance as shadows start to move around it. The fire burns brighter showing a surrounding circle of hooded figures. The hum of a chant from human throats swells. A deep brassy melody.

The whole spectacle is hypnotic. The robed figures continue their melody as the fire grows; wild flames reaching heaven bound. The chanting increases, matching the flames. Suddenly all the cloaked figures stop and spring their arms upward while letting out an eerie note. The flames higher yet give light for the first time to the behemoth on the far side of the clearing—a pyramid. It was small, maybe fifteen feet high and marble white. All at once, the engorged flames withdrawal into themselves and the massive stone structure returns to the shadows. Slowly turning from the grand scene and back to the darkness of the woods, trees pass by and the rustling from below returns.

Jeffrey blinked hard as he stared at the phone slack jawed "Um . . ."

Kristen stood, clenching her phone to her chest and hopping from foot to foot with a wide grin. "Well?! What did you think?!" she asked, barely containing herself.

". . . I'm speechless. Was that real?" he wondered with a genuine sense of dread creeping up his neck.

"Yes! I had heard about this weird cult that meets in the woods near my house, and last night I snuck out there, and sure enough, they were there!"

Any sexual frustration that Jeffrey had been feeling was suddenly lost. All he could think about was the fire framed image of the stone pyramid he had just witnessed. "Yeah, I'm gonna call bullshit on this. That was *not* real. No way. You found that on online or something."

"No! I swear to all the gods above and below, this really happened," she exclaimed.

"You are so full of shit!" he claimed as he laughed out loud. "This is modern day U S of fucking A. That doesn't happen around here. Maybe four hundred years ago, but not today."

"I thought you liked spooky shit?" she asked, putting her hands on her cocked hips.

"I do! But I don't believe that's real for a second. But don't worry, your secret is safe with me," he said, repositioning himself in front of the computer.

"I'll prove it to you." Her voice dropped back into that sweet, calm, and raspy tone that made Jeffrey's spine melt.

"And how do you plan on that?" he asked, genuinely curious.

"Tonight. We are going back. Come with us," she stated.

"Us?" He knew what she was going to say before she could say it. Girls like this weren't ever single, at least not for very long.

"My boyfriend," she said, aggravated. "I know we aren't allowed to hang out, but I think this is grounds enough to break the rules. We are going to go there tonight to see what's in that big ass pyramid."

The image of the pyramid held fast in his mind's eye. Dark and complex. Steadfast and stone hard. It seemed to look back at him in his own head.

"Have fun. I'm not getting arrested for trespassing on private property and then losing my job for hanging out with you." Jeffrey was getting annoyed. He didn't know why, but the whole situation was rubbing him the wrong way. Maybe it was the fact that there was someone other than him plowing Kristen, or maybe it was something deeper. Whatever it was, it was starting to piss him off. He started working on one of the spreadsheets glowing on the monitor.

"Suit yourself. Just thought it would be fun. A little Scooby-Doo style snooping around . . ." she said, trying to convince him. "At least think about it, okay?"

"Yeah . . . I'll think about it," he replied, not looking up from the monitor.

She grabbed her bag and left the small office. He took a deep breath, trying to relax his frazzled nerves. She had a talent for putting him on edge in more than a few ways; he didn't like any of it. He hadn't felt these types of base emotions since high school when he first dared to talk to a girl about anything other than schoolwork. He cracked his back and put her and that stupid pyramid out of his head. There was work to be done.

Later in the day, after getting most of the bar's administrative duties done, Jeffrey's stomach rumbled, and realized he had missed lunch. He went to the bar's small kitchen and made a tuna hoagie with extra peppers and onions then sat at the far end of the bar where the service well was. He ate in silence as he skimmed a newspaper that had been left behind by one of the regulars. The headline read *Comet Closer Than Expected!* He glanced across the columns of print that were speculating on the effects of Beasley's Comet and what it could possibly do as it passed by on its cosmic field trip.

"Motherfucker." Kristen was mumbling under her breath as she approached him on the other side of the bar, typing away on her cellphone.

"You kiss your mother with that mouth?" he asked playfully. Maybe it was his full belly, but his annoyed mood had passed.

"Yes, and your mother too," she returned. It seemed as if his foul mood had passed to her.

He glanced down at the newspaper. One of the scientists had guesstimated that Beasley's Comet could just smack into Earth and kill the whole damn planet. This scenario made Jeffrey laugh; maybe, just maybe, the world would be ending in a few weeks. It was a sobering thought, but a strangely uplifting one all the same. He glanced at Kristen, who was resting on her elbows on the back display bar where all the bottles were racked. She was texting furiously with her firm and perky ass stuck out towards him. *So, what if she has a boyfriend?* he thought to himself as he studied the curves of the hips and ass cheeks. *The world could be dead in a few weeks.*

Before he could run the notion through all the responsible adult filters in his brain, he simply blurted, "So, what time we leaving tonight?"

Kristen stopped her angry typing and turned on her heels, smiling wide. "For reals? You're in? You wanna go?"

He glanced at the black-and-white photo of Beasley's Comet. "Might as well. Only live once, right?"

"You are fucking awesome!" she squealed while trying to contain herself.

This made him smile. She bounced happily, which made him even happier.

"I will meet you here tonight. We can drive together. I know where to park so that it's easy to get there," she stated as she picked up her phone and began typing quickly. "I'm so glad you're into this. My stupid fucking boyfriend just backed out."

This made Jeffrey crack a smirk that he tried in vain to hide. "Oh no, that's too bad." His words dripped with so much sarcasm he was surprised she didn't pick up on it.

"He is an idiot. I'm kinda over it," she said as she finished a text and slammed her phone on the counter in front of him. "Yeah, I'm sure you're devastated."

Her tone and her grin made him blush instantly. She was flirting with him. And it was the best feeling in the world.

It was a starless night. Low-hanging clouds formed a shallow ceiling, and the sudden drop in temperature once the sun went down made a heavy fog form off the still hot ground. It was almost too perfect an environment, Jeffrey thought as he sat in his car outside the bar, sipping from a metal flask.

The final lights from inside the bar turned off; she was done and heading his way any second. He sniffed his shirt; his cologne was just right. Glancing around his car, he made sure it was clean and free of clutter. If he was going to go down this road, he was going to do it right. He wanted her, and once she got into his car, it would be the point of no return. At that juncture, he could lose his job; it would be his word against hers if she decided to throw him under the bus . . .

If . . .

She opened the front door, closed it behind her, and locked it. Crossing the road quickly, she got into his car like she had done it a thousand times before.

"So, are you Shaggy or Fred tonight?" she asked as she adjusted herself in the seat.

"Always thought of myself as a Hardy Boy, to be honest," he said with a smile. The three nips from his hip flask were enough to take away his anxiety.

"Fuck that. The Hardys were a couple of fags. Get on Route 76 and head south," she stated, then pulled a bottle of whiskey from her bag and took a strong sip. He gladly did as he was told.

"Up here, take a right," she went on as she pulled a draw off the whiskey bottle. She handed it to him, and Jeffrey followed suit.

"So, this place is real, or at least you claim, so what if those people are there right now?" Jeffrey inquired.

"That's a real chance, Frank Hardy. A chance you'll have to take." Kristen had made herself comfortable. Her window rolled down the second she got in, as she'd been chain-smoking the entire ride thus far.

"But how did you manage not to be seen? And what about that . . . that pyramid thing?"

"What about it?"

"What is it?"

"The better question is *why* is it," she said while lighting another smoke.

"Okay, I'll bite. *Why* is it there?" he asked.

"Good question. I wish I knew," she returned with an almost annoyed look.

"I assume it's a good old-fashioned spot for human sacrifice, if horror movies have taught me anything," he joked, trying to block out the blurry image of the towering and bitter pyramid that loomed in his mind's eye despite the whiskey burning in his gut.

She seemed to not hear, or maybe she didn't care. She rummaged through her backpack as she continued her cryptic musings. "I've heard some say it's a portal to another world. Where old gods shamble across a burning landscape. Infinite in their madness and hunger."

"Jesus." His raging hormones, now fueled by cheap booze, didn't know how to compute the sudden change in climate.

"Calm down," she said with that smile. "The truth is kinda boring. Some Masons built it for ceremonies a few hundred years ago. Does that make you feel better?"

"Well, that's kind of boring by comparison," he returned, holding out his hand for the bottle.

"I guess you'll get everything you want tonight." She pulled out the shirt she was looking for, unbuttoned her work shirt, and stripped it off. Maybe it was the liquor, or the fact he had gone further than he could have imagined with this girl already, but he stared at her chest. He didn't sneak a quick peek; he didn't pretend it wasn't happening to spare her or himself any dignity; Jeffrey turned his head and stared at her big tits. They were resting in a black push-up, and they were perfect. Smooth porcelain skin and lots of it. They looked heavy and delicious. He took in the show and spectacle as an unashamed participant.

She readied her shirt, a small black tank top, and gave a little smirk at her number one fan. "You enjoying the show?"

Jeffrey took a savage swig from the bottle and wiped his wet mouth with the back of his hand. "Fuck yes," he uttered breathlessly.

She slowly pulled the shirt over her head, embellishing the struggle of slipping the tight material over her full breasts. "Good. Cause they will probably be in your face later." She took the bottle back and drank.

They drove on, cutting a path through the thick fog.

"So how did you hear about this place?" Any uneasiness Jeffrey had melted away with the warmth of whiskey in his gut.

"My dad showed it to me years ago. I've been hooked ever since."

"But those people? How did they not see you?"

"You saw the video. They were pretty out of it. Trance like even."

"I suppose. Just weird is all."

"Don't get cold feet on me now. We are almost there. Your next right, take it." Her voice dropped to a softer tone, as if she had just walked into a library.

Fifty yards further up the misty farm road sat a narrow dirt path cutting its way through a dense wood. He eased his sedan to a stop at the would-be road, staring out the passenger side window down the black path to nowhere good. Jeffrey didn't like the way this felt. His confidence was short-lived as a sobering moment of hesitancy thrummed up his throat and spine in steady pulses.

". . . well?" Kristen poked, almost annoyed.

"Don't worry. We are doing this." With a feigned confident grin, he tried to change the subject. "So, does this place have a 'Meet the Cult' night when comets are this close?" For whatever reason, his mind went to the science article he had been reading earlier. Beasley's Comet. He assumed they were named after whoever happened to discover them. Maybe he would be so lucky. He glanced at Kristen. Perhaps he had a comet right next to him. She was, by all means, a heavenly body.

"Funny you should mention it. That comet is thought to be important to several religious groups around the world," she said matter-of-factly.

He hadn't been expecting any response other than a joke or two. "Oh. I didn't know that. I mean, aren't comets pretty frequent?"

"Yes. But this one is different." She stared out her window up towards the sky.

"How so?"

"They say it's the eye of God—the judgment of the world, of mankind. It's meant to pass our planet and make a collision course with the sun. From here it will take three years to reach it. Once it does, it will crash into it and destroy it. Leaving the world in darkness for eternity. The righteous will rise to the heavens and rest for eternity in the light of God. But we must wait three years, unfortunately," she said, never looking away from the dark skies overhead.

"We?" he asked.

"I'm speaking figuratively, you fucker. Right here, make a right."

The *road* was nothing more than a hole in a cattle fence. Some lightly worn tire tracks showed that someone had been here not too long ago. Jeffrey sighed and turned the car down the pitch-black path. The car's headlights were the only light for miles. His head was just on the verge of swimming. He knew he had better lay off if he wanted to be any use to himself or anyone else later this evening.

"Good boy . . ." she said smoothly as he cautiously traversed the grassy field.

He was too busy concentrating on the phantom road ahead to respond. Slowly, they rolled up to a thick wall of trees. He thought about the video Kristen had shown him. This seemed as if it could be the exact spot.

"Okay. Kill the car. We walk from here," she said.

"How far is the walk?" he asked as he killed the engine and opened the door. The dull dome light shone down on the dewy grass. The landscape was slick and warm; the remaining spirit of a hot summer's day.

She disembarked as well and sauntered around to his side of the car. "By the way, I never told you who has a crush on you." She leaned against him, pinning him to the side of the car, her tits against him. She looked up into his eyes. The eerie, faint moonlight gave her dark eyes the feel of bottomless pools. He couldn't help but be caught off guard by her beauty. Words escaped his head. Every fiber of conscious thought was focused on feeling her pressed against him. He stared down into her face, just inches from his. Her full lips pursed and slightly parted. Her smooth cheeks porcelain and perfect. Slowly, her hands traced up his arms, feeling his tense biceps. He was beyond comprehension. His soul was frozen in the moment, and she was in charge of the universe.

"I'll give you one guess . . ." she whispered as she pulled Jeffrey's face down towards hers. He grabbed her hips firmly as they kissed hard. The night's heat, the whiskey, and the sheer and blatant defiance of all the rules proved too volatile a mixture. They kissed each other like the world was truly going to end. Mouths danced, and hands grouped with the hottest fever any star-crossed lovers ever felt.

Jeffrey's was someone else, in a place he had only dreamed of. Her lips and mouth were making him more drunk than any liquor could dare to do. He squeezed her firm ass with one hand and rubbed her tits with the other. They felt better than his vivid imagination could have alluded to. He could feel her hard nipples through the padding of her bra. She held the back of his head steady as she continued to kiss his mouth. Her other hand reached down below his belt, and she instantly found what she was looking for. She whimpered as she squeezed his ready manhood.

Suddenly and abruptly, she pulled away from him. She took a few steps back and took a deep breath. Jeffrey did the same. He composed himself as he centered his brain and caught his own breath. They both stood by the car, calming the heat between them.

"Holy shit, you're a great kisser," she said breathlessly. "I hate to break this off, but we got a job to do."

Stepping up to Jeffrey, she kissed him once more. "We will finish this later," she said as she grabbed his hand and led him to the forest edge.

Jeffrey felt like a stranger in his own head. He padded along behind his voluptuous field guide, numbly trying to regroup. If he had been a betting man, he would never have fathomed such a scenario. Kristen had always been the woman he wanted but never had, but here in the middle of nowhere, in the shadow of a comet from the heavens, he found himself in her presence, in her essence. He could still feel her tongue on his as he dumbly glided along behind her.

"Game on, Boy Scout. We are almost there. You may have to save me from scary cult members if the going gets tough." She snickered as she pulled him into the thick of the forest.

Kristen's video played out in his head as his eyes watched it play out in front of him. The close-cropped trees gently wiped wisps of leaves against his burning cheeks. The warm dew does little to squelch his tempered fever that had his heart still in his throat and his manhood throbbing.

"Where's the whiskey?" His voice was deep and bassy; it was an odd side effect from drinking that he had always dealt with.

"It's in the car. Shut up and keep walking," she snapped in a hushed whisper, yanking his hand.

With his free hand he reached to his hip pocket and pulled out his flask. He fumbled to open and finally poured the hot liquor down his throat. He was only getting drunker, and was still high from Kirsten's mouth and body. His eyes blinked heavily and blurry. Trudging along, his feet dragging against the forest floor as he ambled along on autopilot, one foot in front of the other and so on. So drunk from the booze, the heat, and the lust that he didn't notice she had stopped until he bumped into her from behind.

"We are here," she whispered.

It took Jeffrey a moment to understand what she'd meant. He wiped droplets of sweat and dew from his eyes and strained to focus. He looked left and right, searching for something to anchor to, and he found it; dead ahead stood the grim pyramid. The firm hand of fear slapped a lightning strike of sobriety through his skull. He stared straight across a small clearing and up at the towering stone structure that was staring back. Jeffrey lumped forward as Kristen stepped out into the small field; she still had a firm grip and wasn't letting go.

With a wide stride, she led him from the shelter of the forest canopy into the openness of a neatly trimmed yard. "Right here. Hurry."

At first, he couldn't make it out, but within a few feet, he saw what she was referring to. A thick and heavy raised rock slab positioned under the soulless gaze of the pyramid. Without further words, Kristen turned on her heel and grabbed him with both arms. Slowly, she guided him to the raised slab and laid him on it.

"Wait. What are you doing?" Jeffrey muttered dumbly.

"Just shut up," she said softly.

He watched sideways from the cold slab as she undressed. A moment later, she was completely naked.

"Seriously. What is going on here?" he asked. He was too drunk to ask more.

He watched as she climbed up on top of the rock table. She paused to pull her long, dark, and curly hair back into a ponytail. Her pale, naked body glistened with a sheen of dew and sweat in the moonlight. She was breathtaking.

"Well, I see I'm not gonna have to do much work," she said.

She grabbed his ready crotch and made quick work of his belt buckle and zipper. She pulled his cock out of his jeans. Her hands were soft; she clearly knew what she was doing. Jeffrey gave himself over to the night and to Kristen. A soft moan slipped from his lips as she pulled him to attention.

"Woah there, cowboy. Not yet," she commanded softly.

She let go of him as she positioned herself. She threw one leg over his hips, straddling his pelvis. "See? I said my tits would be in your face tonight," she said, lowering her massive chest.

He reveled in the moment, rubbing his face back and forth drunkenly. They were heavy, slick, and hot. His sweltering tongue lapped at one of her nipples.

"You are so fucking sexy," he mumbled.

"Way outta your league, that's for sure," she replied.

"The fuck does that mean?" he asked. Despite the wild amount of booze in his veins, the jab landed squarely in the side of his heart.

"Shut up. Let's do this," she snapped.

Quickly and without grace, she lowered her hips onto his. In the exact moment they both hold their breath.

Jeffrey had always considered himself a simple man. Throughout his life, he had taken his mediocrity in stride and, to some point, considered it a blessing in disguise. He never wanted much and was usually happy with whatever life ended up serving him. But in this very instance, no matter how small a sliver it was, he was a king. Her heat enveloped his hard length. She was ready for him. Her wetness let him easily in, and she was melting all over him.

"Alright. Tie him up," she said.

"Huh? What are you talking about?" he asked, still entangled in the throes of the moment.

From nowhere, strong hands grabbed his arms and pulled them upward toward the head of the slab. Without warning, he felt the sharp bite of rope, so tight that he could already feel his hands going numb. While still inside Kristen, he looked around in vain, trying to make sense of his sudden captive nature. From all sides, sudden firelight gave life to the dark clearing. Shadowed figures shambled all around him as he struggled against his bonds. Despite all the confusion, Kristen rode him as if her life depended on it.

Terror mixed with pleasure. The robbed figures began to chant a deep, throaty hum that only heightened Jeffrey's dawning sobriety. He quickly realized that fighting against the roughhewn ropes was pointless. He looked up to see the naked and glistening Kristen riding him, despite the act of intimacy, she seemed a million miles away. Some of the cloaked figures were close now, up next to the slab. She began talking to them in some scratchy, bitter tongue. They seemed to understand her commands as they bound his feet just like his hands. A moment later he understood why the precaution was taken.

At the head of the stone, as Jeffrey saw from his upside-down point of view, appeared a red cloaked figure. The others, donning black, seemed less imposing compared to the one in red. And to make his stature even more affirming, Jeffrey noticed he wore a crown of antlers that stemmed from his head.

But still Kristen writhed. She dipped her chest onto his face once more, giving his manhood a needed boost of vigor.

"Stay with me. This is important," she whispered while near his face.

As the chants grew louder, Kristen rode harder . . . faster.

He looked toward the sky. Above, he saw a full and pale moon looking back. There was also the faint aftermath of Beasley's comet; its eerie green twinkle sparkling in the sky. It was beginning to make sense, and all too late.

Kristen spat out another command. This one was projected from deep in her diaphragm. He was the only one there that night who would know that little fact, and all thanks to his VIP seat six inches deep in the grand wizard of a star gazing cult.

The horned and red cloaked figure extended a gloved hand. In its grasp laid nestled a bejeweled blade. She grabbed it with an uncaring abandoned not quite suited for such a beautiful piece. The chanting grew to an almost yell. Each in sync with the other.

He looked up at Kristen. His face must have exposed his worry and confusion, as she instantly tried to console him. One hand rested on his face, the other wrapped around the pummel of the jeweled blade.

"I think you will end up being my favorite. Such a shame," she breathed into his ear.

His body let out its own telling pulse at that moment. One that Kristen felt. He was about to climax as his manhood grew even harder. Despite the place and the situation, he couldn't picture anywhere else he would rather die. Old and alone on a hospital bed didn't seem right. Suddenly in a car crash didn't seem right either. But here, on the verge of erupting in the angel of death seemed most satisfying.

She brought the jeweled dagger down hard and fast. She planted it squarely in his heart as he released himself deep inside her. Every possible muscle spasmed in ecstasy and terror. His biceps burned as they strained against the ropes. Kristin's angelic face started to blur, and he looked over to his side only to see the pyramid staring back.

Red Red Ruin

"I quit," Amelia lied.

It wasn't a mean lie. Or a lie meant to hurt someone. It was meant to postpone reality. To put off the unwanted repercussions. Even if just for a few hours. The harsh truth was that she got fired.

"Good for you! That job sucked anyway!" Bethany said from the other end of the phone.

Amelia walked towards Deerborn Street Bridge, people passing. She wondered how many of them were living a lie at this very moment and what kind of lie it was. But the idea of solidarity didn't make the burden lighter.

"You're right, so I'm done. I'm out." She hoped the lie would start to feel more real.

The night was hot, and she was hoping to cool off once she was over the Chicago River. Her tote bag was full, all her personal crap from her desk. Well, it wasn't her desk anymore. Some other sap would come along and fill her place. Just like she filled it. And so, the wheel turns.

"Okay, I'm formulating a plan," Bethany said.

"I'm not coming over."

"Bullshit. Stop by Woody's. I'll order us a couple Italian hoagies, come over and we will drink that case of prosecco my mother got me for Christmas."

"Let me guess, is Rob working tonight?" Amelia asked, adjusting her tote.

"Who the Hell knows? I'm just hungry. Hurry up! I have a surprise for you. Fuck your job, fuck your boss. Stop by Woody's and get over here!" Bethany demanded.

"Surprise? I don't know if I'm up for any shenanigans tonight," Amelia muttered.

"Please. Shut up. If it sounds like I'm hanging up, it's because I'm hanging up. Woody's. Now."

Amelia's handheld went black. So much for going home and wallowing in self-pity. In an apartment she could now not pay for. But Woody's was only four blocks away, near her subway stop. She took a deep breath and stared out at the Chicago River. This sucked. No savings. No nest egg. Her parents wouldn't help. But this would all still be here—and still suck—tomorrow. No matter what she did tonight, she wasn't changing any bit of this. So, this will be a problem for tomorrow. Tomorrow, when the sun was up. Right now, it was late, and the promise of food and booze and the natural dysfunction of Bethany sounded more and more like a grand alternative to stewing in her own misery. Amelia took a deep breath. "Fuck it".

As usual, Woody's was packed. When they built the claustrophobic building some hundred years ago, they clearly didn't understand how popular this place would be. The line to sit inside was out the door. Thankfully, she could sneak her way into the to-go counter, but even that was proving difficult. Despite the late hour, damn near all of Chicago was there.

"'Melia!" A dark-haired man in a chef's coat shouted from a nearby counter. Amelia waded through the crowd, dispensing a continual muttering of apologies for existing and being in the way. Mean looks be damned, she managed to squeeze herself between the counter and an angry couple waiting for a table.

"'Melia! Is goot to see you!" He reached across the high counter, grabbed her hand, and squeezed. Amelia understood what Bethany saw in this guy. Handsome, tall, and a fierce smile. Far from Amelia's type, but she could appreciate the menu even if she wasn't hungry.

"Good to see you too. I'll be quick, I know you're busy. Did Bethany call? How much do I owe you?" Before she could finish, Rob already had a large paper bag on the counter.

"For you, my queen? Nuttin'. A friend of Bethany's is a friend of mine."

"I can't do that." Her pride wanted to be fair, but her bank account was more than happy for the handout.

"You can, and you will. What are you two doing tonight?"

There it was. His motive. Rob really liked Bethany, but the feelings were unfairly one sided. Bethany enjoyed his late-night company and the benefits it brought, but Rob wanted more, and he was not shy about being persistent. It was charming, but Amelia hoped Rob wouldn't get hurt.

"We are hanging out at her place." She didn't feel like getting into the grim details of the purpose of the night with so many people around. And maybe, just maybe, if she ignored her plight hard enough, she would wake up, and it would have all been a dream.

Rob smiled. "Maybe I come by later."

"That's between you and Bethany, but I get the guest room."

His smile widened, and he nodded. That's all he needed. Rob was nothing if not determined. He turned to the customer he had been ignoring since spotting Amelia and went back to his job. Large bag in hand, she squeezed back out of the restaurant.

The street was thankfully quiet. Soon she was on the subway; the car was air-conditioned, and it felt like heaven. Readjusting in her seat, she heard a faint clicking from the bag Rob had given her. Curious, she looked inside. There were two giant sandwiches, the smell and oil and vinegar mixed with oregano made her mouth water. There were two bags of chips. Salt and vinegar. A box of three cannoli's; Rob really put some thought into this and about a dozen little glass bottles of liquor. She smiled and reached inside, grabbing a small bottle of Sambuca. *Might as well get the night started,* she thought as she cracked open the nip. The sweet anise liquor felt velvety on her palette as that familiar warmth took over her cheeks and chest. Maybe things would be okay. Maybe she could go back and beg for her job. Promise to never fuck up again. Maybe she would move back home, start over. Listening to all the "I told you so's" her folks could muster. Maybe she would find another job. The liquor lit a glimmer of hope in her belly, and her brain was suddenly okay with being unemployed. "Thank you, Roberto." She finished the little bottle.

Leaning back, she rested her head against the window. The rhythmic pulse of the subway car pulled the tension out of her shoulders. Maybe things were going to be okay. Rubbing her eyes, Amelia glanced around the empty car when her vision settled on some graffiti. Across from her in red marker was RRR. The wall was bare, except for the three matching letters.

A couple stops past hers was Bethany's. Amelia accidentally drank another mini bottle and was almost skipping out of the subway station. Even the humid and stale summer air did not deter her newfound mood. She was in the nice part of town now. Bethany lived in a high rise on Kinzie Street by herself, which meant Amelia often stayed over, especially after long nights of drinking. And tonight was shaping up to be another one.

It was late enough that the door clerk was gone for the night; thankfully though, Amelia had a key. The door opened and a wall of cool air ate Amelia as she entered.

"Boo!" Bethany screamed. She was hidden behind one of the large, gray couches in the lobby.

"Jesus!" Amelia jumped. After hours, the massive lobby of the high rise was dimly lit. As if to put the building to sleep for the night. And more than once Bethany has used it to her advantage in scaring the crap out of Amelia.

"That never gets old." Bethany stood and approached. She was clad in pastel sleepwear, a fuzzy robe, and well-worn slippers, carrying two bottles of prosecco, one open and half empty. "I may have started the party without you." She drank from her bottle and pushed the other towards Amelia.

"Woman. Calm down. My hands are full." Amelia dropped her bags on the large coffee table in front of Bethany's hiding spot and took the bottle. It was well chilled, so she pressed it against the back of her neck, under her ponytail. With a sigh, she closed her eyes. If it felt this good on the outside, it will be even better in her stomach. She twisted the top off and took a swig. Soft and sweet and sudsy. "Holy shit, your mom has good taste."

"No, but her sommelier does," Bethany said. "You got the goods?"

"Yes, your boyfriend hooked us up. I may have started the party early too, so your social faux pas can be admonished."

Bethany snooped in the bag and pulled out the empty mini bottles. "You whore. And he's very much *not* my boyfriend."

"Does he know that?" Amelia asked, gathering the bags.

"Look. He knows his place. It's not my fault he can't get enough." Bethany took a swig and led the way to the elevators.

Amelia followed, lugging the goods. "That's gross. Can we please change the channel?"

Bethany stopped, pressing the UP button in the bay of six lifts. They waited.

"Funny you should say so . . ." An elevator chimed, and Bethany spun on her heels and dramatically fanned her arms, gesturing for Amelia to enter the empty lift. She did as she was beckoned and sat upon the cushioned bench along the back of the elevator. It was large, with lots of wood and brass. Waist high mirror covered all three walls. She took a small swig of the cold booze and sighed. "Yes?" she asked.

Bethany entered and pulled the left side of her robe up like a vampire hiding behind its cloak. Amelia rolled her eyes. "Tonight is a very special night," Bethany began, trying her best with a European accent, but the booze had other plans. Instead, she fumbled over her words like she had a mouth full of marbles. Amelia fought back a smile.

"Tonight, we are in the midst of a very special event," Bethany continued.

"Great. What movie are we watching?"

"No! Tonight, there will be no bullsheet moooovie!" Bethany moaned.

Amelia leaned forward to press the eighth-floor button, but Bethany slapped her hand away and continued her performance. "Tonight, we embark on the most dangerous journey of our lives!" With a grand sweeping gesture, she turned and tapped the button for the thirteenth floor.

"Is this the surprise? B, I'm so not in the mood for a house party. Can we just go to your place?" Amelia was getting annoyed.

Bethany stood straight and dropped the dramatic act. "It's not a party. Just chill. We are trying something." The elevator doors slowly drew together. Amelia stared out into the world beyond the lobby. The hot and oppressive dark night. She was leaving her world of regret behind.

Bethany sat next to Amelia and pulled out her phone. Amelia watched as she scrolled through her pictures and a series of screen grabs. Bethany pulled the device closer, studying the small print. "Okay. There are a lot of steps and it's pretty convoluted, so I might need your help."

The lift passed the floor Amelia was accustomed to getting off at.

"Okay. Once we get to the thirteenth floor, the doors will open. We wait until they close and then press the button for the basement," Bethany instructed.

"B. What are you doing?"

"Red Red Ruin."

The elevator slowed to a smooth stop, and the doors opened. Amelia stared out into the long, straight corridor. The hallway looked identical to Bethany's floor. Off-white walls, finished wooden floors, brass light sconces giving off a dim light. The apartment doors, all red, matched as the hallway faded into the distance. The doors slid closed. Bethany stood and pressed the button for the basement level. With mechanical ease, the sealed box lowered itself.

"That doesn't answer my question."

Bethany sat next to her friend, pulling her robe closed. "This is the super-secret I was talking about. We are playing a little game I found online."

"And this is supposed to distract me from losing my job?"

"If you wanted it, why did you quit?" Bethany asked.

Amelia wasn't good at lying, and now it was showing. Did she know? Did Bethany know Amelia was lying? B was her best friend, so maybe she had more insight into her head than most. If she did know she didn't seem to care.

"I know. I'm just processing. Is this one of those Creepy Pasta games?" Amelia asked.

Bethany took a swig of her sparkling wine. Seeing this, Amelia remembered she had one as well and took a sip.

"I guess, but this is supposed to be the real deal," Bethany muttered, not looking up from her phone.

Amelia leaned back against the cushioned backrest. No use fighting this. She loved Bethany and had followed her on many wild goose chases. And, after all, Amelia wanted distraction.

"They all claim to be the real deal." Amelia chuckled to herself.

"But this one came to me."

"What? Like in an email?"

"No. This morning it was open on my phone. Like I had searched for it," Bethany said.

"And I'm assuming you didn't? Weren't you drinking last night?" Amelia asked.

"Well, yes, thanks for calling me an alcoholic." Bethany took another swig.

"Oh, shut up. I mean did you actively look for this game on your phone?" Amelia asked.

"No! That's what I'm trying to say! It was just there. So, I took a bunch of screen captures just in case. Cause I wouldn't believe me either," Bethany said, perching on the edge of the bench.

Amelia took a sip and settled into the bench. "Fine. I'm in."

"Well duh. We already started."

The elevator passed the second floor.

"So, what do we win?" Amelia asked.

"I don't think it works like that. But I didn't finish reading everything. It keeps mentioning Carcosa, but I have no idea what that means."

The elevator car slid to a smooth stop, and the doors quietly slid open. A gust of cool air rushed in. Both girls stared out into the dark basement level. Amelia had never seen this floor of the building. It was a long, singular corridor like the floor they were just at, but this one was unfinished cement; dusty and grimy. Instead of solid walls creating rooms and homes, there were only chain link fencing creating divisions. Forming small places for storage and equipment. Lots of chains and padlocks keeping out the curious. It was quiet. Still. Breathless.

The door slid closed.

"Okay. Did we win a Toyota Corolla?" Amelia asked.

Bethany stood and pressed the top floor, the Penthouse suites. She grabbed Amelia's hand, beckoning for her to rise. Amelia did as summoned.

"Okay. We gotta hurry. Repeat after me: *Dominus pastorum.*"

Amelia, feeling past the edge of tipsy, grabbed Bethany's hand and repeated the words.

Bethany continued, "*Permitte nos intrare . . .*" She glanced at her phone. The elevator moved along its journey to the top. "*Ubi di vagantur.*"

Amelia repeated the verses.

"*Anima mea pretium,*" Bethany uttered, her eyes closed.

The elevator stopped, and the doors opened. Amelia let go of her friend's hand and took a step forward. She knew B lived in a nice building, but this floor was something else. This one had close cropped carpeting that looked brand new. Greens and grays. The hallway was long like the others but had a scarce few doors on either side. Small, delicate chandeliers hung every thirty feet or so giving off a haunting, soft white light. "This floor is amazing. Do you know anyone who lives here?" Amelia observed the hallway, waiting for a reply. She turned to see Bethany standing still, eyes closed. "Hey. You okay?"

The elevator doors slid closed with a hiss as Amelia turned to face her friend. Bethany stood still, eyes closed. Her right hand still gripping where Amelia had been. She watched her friend, waiting for the jump scare. But Bethany stood still. She backed away, pressing against the closed door behind her. Bethany wasn't breathing. This had to be a prank. Amelia reached for her friend's shoulder as Bethany unfroze and reached for the button terminal, pressing the button for floor three.

"Hey," Amelia said, wide eyed.

"Hey," Bethany replied, taking her seat and a long pull on her wine bottle.

Amelia remained standing, waiting for the gag to continue. "Are you okay?" she asked.

"Yeah. Why?"

She tried to read her longtime friend. They met in high school and hit it off right away. And even attended the same college until they both dropped out at the same time. Amelia knew Bethany well, but right now she didn't know her at all. She finally sat down, the elevator doing its thankless job.

"Just making sure," Amelia said.

Bethany busied herself with the rules of the game. Studying the screenshots.

"Floor three. Just let it be."

"So, it's rhyming now?" Amelia asked.

"Chill. You don't have to be mean about this," Bethany snapped.

Amelia didn't reply as her friend went back to studying her phone. Instead, she sat on her side of the bench and nursed her wine. This was odd. Maybe Bethany was drunk. Maybe she had more to drink than she realized. It's certainly a possibility.

"It says no matter what, we have to ignore what happens next, and we can't leave the elevator," Bethany said, not looking up from her phone.

Amelia didn't feel like pushing it. She would just let this unfold and hopefully it would be over soon. The lift slid to a stop, and the doors opened. It was a carbon copy of the thirteenth floor. Identical in every way, from the floor to the ceiling. They both stared down the dark corridor. Watching. Waiting. Bethany glanced at her phone, and Amelia watched her as she tried to discern more meaning from the text.

"Help!"

Both girls froze. Amelia felt her spine constrict; a chill shot up to her scalp.

"Hey! Help me!"

The voice called again. Amelia stood and strained to investigate the darkness at the far end of the hallway. Bethany grabbed her hand, keeping her from exiting.

"You heard that?" Amelia asked.

"Yeah," Bethany said.

They both stood near the door, staring.

"Please! I need help!"

The girls looked at each other, breathless.

Amelia slipped closer to Bethany and whispered, "Please tell me this is a prank."

"Hey! Do you hear me?!" The voice was distant and little. Sharp and thin. A girl's voice, or maybe a child. It was just soft enough and far away enough that it was hard to discern.

"N-no," Bethany whispered back.

Amelia lurched forward a fraction and shouted, "Where are you?!"

There was no answer. She strained to focus her eyes, to latch onto anything in the darkness. But there was nothing. The hallway lights were on, but the illumination they gave off was shallow and unhelpful.

"We have to wait for the door to close," Bethany whispered.

Amelia turned from the hallway. Bethany was studying her phone again, holding it with both hands, shaking.

"Fuck this." Amelia jabbed the button for B's floor.

"Hey!" Bethany yelped and slapped away her hand.

The button didn't light up. They both stared and waited, but nothing happened.

"Really?! Not gonna do anything?!" the voice yelled. "You two hear someone calling for help and you just ignore them?"

"Where are you?!" Amelia tried again.

The doors began to slide together.

"See you soon!" the voice called out as the doors came together.

The car remained stationary. The closed doors did give some sense of security.

"B. Please. I won't be mad. I just wanna know. Are you messing with me?"

Bethany placed her hands on her waist and cocked her hips to one side. "No, Amelia. I'm not messing with you."

"'Cause now's the time to tell me. This has been a great prank. If I had a scorecard, I would hold up a '10'. Please, just tell me." Amelia wanted this to be a prank. Needed it to be. Because if it wasn't . . .

Bethany pressed the button for the ninth floor. This time it lit up, a cloudy orange color. She took her seat and let out a heavy sigh. Amelia remained standing as the car lifted.

"B." Her voice quivered. "You're scaring me."

"It's just a game," Bethany muttered. Not caring about comforting her friend.

Amelia almost felt mad. A mixture of fear and anger. She knew she owed Bethany a lot. She had helped her out on more occasions than she could count, but she never felt like Bethany minded. She seemed like a genuine friend who enjoyed her company. Until now.

The car stopped, and the doors slid open.

Amelia turned to Bethany and said, "I'm getting off."

Bethany, wide eyed, slowly took to her feet, staring past Amelia, her jaw dropping.

"I don't know where you're gonna go . . ." Bethany uttered.

Amelia followed her stare and turned to look out the elevator. It was another hallway, identical to the others. Wooden floors, off-white walls, brass light fixtures. But no doors. There were no doors on either side of the hallway. No entry points for apartments. Amelia fought back a scream.

"What?" Amelia whispered.

"Don't get off. You'll be stuck here," Bethany whispered back.

Amelia stared down the dark and endless hallway. Nothing but smooth off-white walls and simple brass light fixtures. No openings to apartments or the outside world. Nothing. She strained to hear something, anything. The sound of air conditioners running, people walking, muffled conversations. Any normal city sounds, but there was only silence. The hair on Amelia's arms stood on end.

The door slid closed.

Bethany looked up from her phone and pressed another button.

"How . . . how are you not losing your shit right now?" Amelia asked.

She was shaking, breath stuttering, staring at Bethany.

"It's just a game." Bethany seemed mildly annoyed.

"A game? A fucking game? Are you high?" She glanced at the bottle in her hand. "Did you drug me? How are you not losing your goddamn mind?!" Amelia backed into the corner of the elevator, dropping her wine bottle on the cushioned couch. Shaking, she pressed against the mirrored wall.

Bethany stood still. Staring at the long panel of buttons. The elevator hummed as it ascended. Something was wrong. All of this was wrong.

"Bethany Sanders. Tell me right now. What is going on?" Amelia's voice trembled.

Bethany turned. Wine bottle in one hand and phone in the other. "*Novi lunae circulo.*"

Amelia whimpered, tears flowing down her cheeks. The elevator stopped. The doors slid open. It was another long hallway but there were plenty of doors this time.

Amelia eyed Bethany, who was now standing still again, staring straight through her. And then she eyed the hallway. This was all too much. She edged towards the exit, holding the door open but making sure not to reach past the threshold. She leaned towards the hallway; it looked normal. Sounded normal.

"Hello? Is anyone there?" Amelia asked.

A loud bang erupted, and she spotted movement at the furthest point, right where the hallway disappeared into darkness. It was a door, slamming open, crashing into the wall it was attached to. Amelia jumped, standing straight and grabbing her mouth. On the opposite side of the hallway, a matching door slammed open, just like its twin across from it. With a rush of chaos, one by one, the red doors slammed open. The wave of commotion coming towards the elevator at a deafening speed. Amelia withdrew her hand and began jabbing at the close door button. Each set of opening doors getting closer each time. The noise was painful; her ears popped, and the elevator car shook from the percussive impacts.

The doors slid closed.

Amelia stumbled back and crashed onto the couch, sobbing and shaking. Her hands and feet were numb, and she was feeling waves of hot and cold across her body. Wiping at her face, she heard a soft whimper. Amelia looked up to see Bethany looking down at her, eyes wide, her color drained from her normally rosy cheeks. She was the effigy of grief. A perfect saint of sheer terror. Trembling to the point of lunacy, she fell into Amelia's arms and wept.

The car didn't move. Time passed, and not once did the car move or its doors open. They held each other and cried.

"So, you don't remember what happened?" Amelia asked. It took some time, but they regained some composer, just enough to make an attempt at reason.

"No. I was reciting the words, and then everything went dark. But . . . those doors. Why?"

Amelia didn't have an answer, but she was glad to have her friend back. "I don't know. But we need to get out of here."

They tried pressing the button for Bethany's floor, but nothing happened. The button didn't light up, nor did the car move. It simply hung there.

Bethany tried to use the emergency button. Nothing happened.

"I don't get it. We've been stuck right here for at least twenty minutes," Bethany muttered, once again checking her phone for service. "How is there no service? This is the city. We are downtown. How is there no service?"

Amelia looked at her phone, too. Zero service, but her battery was still full. "Maybe there was some sort of attack?" The words felt dumb as soon as she said them.

"Attack? Like a terrorist attack?" Bethany asked.

"I guess so, or maybe a meteor hit. I don't know. Like that comet that is supposed to be flying by us tomorrow. I don't know I'm just taking shots here . . ." Amelia trailed off, feeling helpless.

"Speaking of shots . . ." Bethany reached into the paper bag between them and pulled out two little glass bottles, handing one to Amelia. She took the bottle and opened it.

"I'm just glad you're better. Or acting normal, I guess," Amelia said.

"That's the part that scares me. Something is off."

"What about the directions? For this game?" Amelia asked.

"Fuck. I forgot about that. My head is not doing good."

Amelia eyed her little bottle and sat it aside. Watching as Bethany studied her phone.

"What do you mean not good?" Amelia asked.

Bethany looked up, her eyes sharp and fierce, red from tears and fright. "Like my thoughts are getting jumbled. I'll think one thing and things out come but different." Realizing her mistake, Bethany pinched the bridge of her nose as she squinted away the faux pas.

"Oh, sweetie. It's okay. I don't know what happened. Maybe you had a little panic attack," Amelia tried to console, but her palms grew sweaty.

"Here." Bethany handed Amelia the phone. "I'm hard time having read right now."

Amelia took the phone and tried not to notice her jumbled words. Despite it, she understood what her friend said. She scanned the device. The battery was at sixty percent. No time shown nor any symbol signifying a connection. Strange. Instead, she focused on the pics. Scrolling through the screenshots. It was her first chance to investigate the very thing that now seemed to have them stuck. It looked like a PDF: black text on a white background. No bells and whistles, no pop-up ads or flashy banners. Just text.

Amelia swiped to the beginning, scanning the steps that they had already taken. Every so often there were bits that looked like symbols. As if the creator had switched to a type of Wingdings. She couldn't decipher them, but they didn't replace any of the other texts. The symbols were randomly inserted. Scrolling along, she found the passage Bethany had recited. Scrolling further, she caught up with their current objective; Go to the seventh . . . *strange symbol* . . . floor. Don't turn your back on it.

"It?" Amelia muttered.

Amelia looked up. Bethany was sitting on her side of the bench, wearing her old pink bathrobe, fuzzy slippers, and with messy hair. She looked small, like a child. Shoulders drooping, staring off into nowhere. A nearly empty nip of sambuca in her hand. She looked tired. She looked scared. So was Amelia.

"B. What do we do?"

Bethany looked up, eyes puffy, she stared at her age-old friend, as if hoping Amelia already had an answer. "I guess we keep going. I don't know what else we can do."

This made sense. Phones weren't working. The emergency button wasn't working. Bethany's words stuck in Amelia's head. The smell of sweat and sambuca making for an odd and unsettling palette. She stood, took two steps to the button panel, and pressed seven. It lit up.

Bethany rose to her feet as the car started to move. She grabbed Amelia's hand, who returned the sentiment. "No matter what happens, don't turn your back on it," Amelia whispered.

Bethany shook her head, not in disagreement but as if to dislodge something or to knock her balance right. Then she nodded. The car came to a stop, and with a soft whir, the doors slid open. Amelia and Bethany were staring at themselves. Opposite them was a mirror image. A whole other elevator with them inside. "Holy shit," Amelia uttered. The reflection did the same.

"Is that . . . us? Or a reflection of us?" Bethany asked.

"I don't know," Amelia said, raising her right hand and watching her copy do the same. "But don't look away. We just gotta wait for the doors to close."

The mirrors at the back of each elevator gave a smoky infinity effect, making it all the more distracting. Behind Amelia's reflection was an endless number of her, fading to a point of singularity. Both women watched, studying their reflections. Something was off. Amelia could feel and smell the atmosphere from the matching elevator car. She could feel the heat from and kinetic friction coming from their copies. There wasn't the cold indifference a mirror had. This felt real.

Bethany reached out, a single finger, dangerously close to the threshold. Her doppelganger doing the same.

"Stop," Amelia whispered, voice trembling.

Bethany did as such. Her other stopping as well. Amelia strained to keep her eyes on her reflection and keep her friend from doing something stupid at the same time.

"Don't. The door will shut soon," Amelia said.

Before Bethany could pull her hand away, her copy reached out and grabbed her. She screamed. Amelia broke away from the staring match with herself and reached for the tug of war raging beside her. The other Bethany had a death grip on her B and was yanking and screaming. Instinct took over and Amelia threw a hard right jab at the jaw of the other, sending it back and against the bench in the reflected elevator. That's when Amelia realized her copy was still standing, unmoving. Just staring at her. She pulled a sobbing Bethany away from the door. Forcing her to the back of their elevator. Turning back, she locked eyes with her other. Bethany's copy was still resting on the bench, watching. The door started to close when Amelia caught a glimpse of the mirror behind her, two arms somehow reaching out and grabbing her by the shoulders, dragging her into the mirror. She heard Bethany scream and knew she was scrambling to grab onto her, to fight off the strange abduction. Amelia managed to grab onto B's robe, but the arms were strong. Strong and cold. They pulled, and she followed, her head entering the looking glass. There was no shattering. No collision of fragile face upon sharp mirror. Instead, Amelia plunged in, like a sink full of water. She was now somewhere else. She tried to scream, but nothing came out. The arms that had dragged her to this place were gone. Now she was leaning into somewhere else. Some place she desperately didn't want to be. Far away there were titanic monoliths reaching high into a black and starless night. Two silver moons cast a bleak light over the towering masses. Harsh winds pulled her hair, the cold hurting her throat as she tried to inhale, wanting only to scream. But even the luxury of responding to fear was taken from her as she caught a glimpse of something massive on the horizon. Something bigger than she could believe. Something so immense it had its own pull, its sheer mass felt from what had to be hundreds of miles away. It lumbered behind the miles high and massive obelisks. Tears streamed down her cheeks, the dark winds grabbing them and whisking them away. That's when the thing stopped and began to turn towards her.

Amelia crashed to the floor of the elevator; she found her voice again as she let rip a hoarse cry of terror. Bethany collapsed onto the floor, gripping Amelia and squeezing her tight. The two friends clung together and sobbed.

"Holy shit, I thought you were gone. I don't know how I pulled you back." Bethany tried to wipe away tears, but her hands trembled too hard.

Amelia, gasping the air she was used to, brushed her messy and mousey auburn hair from her face. "Thank you thank you thank you thank you thank you," she said, once again hugging her best friend.

"What happened? I don't understand. How did you not destroy that mirror?" Bethany asked.

Amelia looked up at the elevator doors, making sure their other halves were still closed off.

"I don't know. But we need to get out of here. Right fucking now." Amelia's voice dropped to a whisper. She was beyond panic. Beyond the visceral reaction of fear. She sat, ghost white, trembling and silent.

"Yeah, I agree."

Both girls managed to find the other side of shock. They wanted out. They wanted to end this. Bethany grabbed her phone and looked at the next step of Red Red Ruin.

"Holy shit," Bethany gasped. Her eyes brightened as she wiped her face, trying to regain composure. "The next floor is my floor."

"What?" Amelia said. They both stood, trying to gather their wits. "What's it say? Is this the end? Are there any other instructions?"

Bethany jabbed at the button for her floor. It lit up and the lift obeyed.

Amelia, impatient, grabbed the phone. With shaky hands, she read the current step out loud.

"Remember. Don't get off. But someone can get on. But think twice." She turned the phone off and rubbed her face. "Shit. I was really hoping this was it."

"It doesn't matter. I'm getting off," Bethany said.

"I don't think that's how it works."

"I don't give a shit. If this voodoo crap won't let me off, I'll scream for one of my neighbors," Bethany said, staring at the button plate, watching the floors pass.

The elevator cart came to a halt and the door opened. Bethany started to leave, but Amelia grabbed her. "Look," she whispered.

The hallway was just as they both expected; one they were both warmly familiar with. And three doors down on the left, where Bethany's apartment sat, was Rob, knocking on the door. He turned at the noise of the lift opening. He smiled big, that beautiful face.

"Hey! I was just about to leave! I was banging on the door for ten minutes. Are you getting my texts?" Rob said, turning to face the girls.

Bethany's face lit up with her own perfect smile. She hopped in place, making the car shake. "Oh my god, I've never been so happy to see you!" Bethany shouted.

"You know I like the sound of that!" Rob said, walking towards the elevator. "What we doing? Partying on the lift tonight? I can get down wit dat!"

Amelia had her own easy smile. The sight of a familiar face was instantly reassuring. Even if Rob was Bethany's flavor of the month, she was beyond happy to see him. Further down the hall, a glimmer caught Amelia's attention. Rob must have heard whatever Amelia was seeing because at the same time he turned to look into the distant hallway.

"Oh, sheet!" Rob yelled, turned and ran.

"Rob! Run!" Amelia screamed.

Something was skittering down the dark hallway. Numerous legs making light tapping noises, fast and chaotic. Soft lights flashing and then dying, a quick cascade of void shooting down the hallway towards the elevator, keeping the crawling chaos barely covered. But it didn't matter what the thing looked like; Amelia didn't want to know.

The doors began to close.

"Run you fucker!" Bethany yelled.

Rob did just that. Long strides caused him to barrel toward the closing entrance. The avalanche of limbs and darkness closing in. He was sprinting at full speed.

Turning sideways, he launched himself into the car as the doors slid shut. Amelia tried to catch him, but he was going too fast and collided with the back of the elevator car. As the doors closed, Amelia caught a last glimpse. Something in the darkness was looking back at her as the doors sealed.

"Holy shit! Oh my god! Are you okay?" Bethany fell onto Rob, who was panting on the cushioned bench. They both embraced each other, kissing and touching. Amelia stepped back and wrapped her arms around herself, trying to give them a much-needed moment. She settled into the corner, sinking to the ground, wishing to be as little as possible.

"What . . . What was that? What's going on?" Rob huffed, catching his breath and brain.

Bethany and Amelia looked at each other. Such an honest question. Pure and earnest. But a question with no answer.

"Something is happening. Something happened to us." Amelia hugged her knees.

"Do you remember when I texted you this morning about that game I found on my phone?" Bethany asked Rob.

Rob, wide eyed, just stared back.

"Holy shit. Did you hit your head? This morning. I texted you about a dumb game I found on my phone," she tried to force the recollection.

"I'm sorry, I don't 'member," Rob said.

Amelia stood, back to the corner. "Something bad is happening. We started a game. A creepy pasta type thing. But it's real. And it almost killed you."

Rob stared at Amelia and then turned to Bethany. "Wow. You guys are really fucking with me! You had me! That was good! I was scared sheetless!"

Amelia shook her head and rubbed her temples.

"Robby. Baby. We aren't messing with you. This is for real. We are so fucked right now," Bethany said, her voice raspy.

Rob, looking even more confused, stood and turned to face both women. "Okay, I'll play along. You know I'm always down for good time." His grin only grew.

"I can't believe this. You're an idiot," Bethany said, already giving up.

"Rob, please listen. We are in danger. You are in danger. Your phone. Can we try to use it?" Amelia asked.

Rob reached into his jeans, paused, and then began to pat his pockets. "Oh no. I don't know where it is." He raised his hands in surrender.

"You would lose your dick if wasn't glued on," Bethany mumbled.

"When did you get here? How long were you banging on her apartment door? Which elevator did you use to come up?" Amelia rattled off.

"I don't know? Not long?" Rob replied.

Amelia eyed him. He looked like a lost puppy. Stupid and innocent when he should be panicked and afraid. She turned and looked at the elevator door, still closed. She touched it. It was cold and smooth shiny brass. Her hazy reflection stared back. Dark eyes watching her. The door was still. No vibrations or shifting pangs. Just still.

"B, what's the next step in the game?" Amelia asked.

Bethany and Rob were both sitting on the burgundy lined cushion seats. Rob was picking at one of the cannolis from the paper bag.

Her friend tried to smooth her hair into place as she picked up her phone. She read the softly lit screen and paused.

"Well?"

"Floor two. Don't give in no matter what they do," Bethany read.

"For fuck's sake," Amelia said as she pressed the button for the second floor.

The little car shifted, and Amelia felt it in her stomach. They were going down.

"Rob, did you hear the direction? We don't give in," Amelia said, pulling her hair into a ponytail.

"Give in to what?" Rob asked.

"He will get it soon," Bethany said.

Rob remained seated as both women stood facing the door.

"If we make it out of this, I'm moving to the first floor," Bethany mumbled.

"If we make out, I'm never getting on an elevator again," Amelia said.

The car slid to a stop. Bethany grabbed Amelia's hand as the doors slid open. The girls could hear them before they could see them. In the hallway on floor two, just on the other side of the door, was Amelia's parents.

"There you are!" her mother declared. A thin, well aging woman with silver streaks in her head full of auburn hair. She wore khakis and a fleece.

"We've been looking all over for you," her father chimed in. A bald man with thick glasses and an easy expression. He wore stripped button down with his sleeves rolled up.

"The fuck . . ." was all Amelia could get out.

"Language! Sweetie, I raised you better than that!" her mother said.

"Wait, is this real?" Bethany whispered.

"Of course we are real. And we are to take you home," her father said in a soft voice.

Amelia could feel Rob stand up behind her.

"Oh! I see you got company! And a handsome one at that! Who's your friend, dear?" Amelia's mother asked, looking Rob up and down.

"How did you two get here? This makes no sense." Amelia's breath quickened.

"Hi mister and misses Smith," Bethany said.

Amelia froze, realizing what B had just done. Bethany had never met her parents. They had been friends for a long time, but her folks lived in Kentucky and never visited. And more importantly, Amelia's last name wasn't Smith.

"Well, hello Bethany! It's so good to see you!" Amelia's mom said.

"Hey, we want to thank you for helping our daughter during this difficult time," her father said. His voice deep and serious.

"I'm afraid I don't know what you mean," Bethany said with a fake smile.

Both of her parents looked at each other, concern washing over them. Her bubbly mother suddenly became serious.

"About Amelia's job," Father said in a hushed tone.

"Oh yeah. Fuck that job. She's better off without it. I'm glad she quit," Bethany said.

Amelia watched as Bethany glanced at her phone, presumably to anticipate the next step.

Both parents exchanged another awkward look, Dad's big eyes made bigger by the thick glasses.

"Is . . . is that what she told you?" Mom asked.

"Look, it's been real. But we must get going," Bethany said. Reaching out and pressing the button for her home floor.

"She was fired," Dad said.

Amelia turned red. Her palms clammy.

"Yuppers. I'll take it from here. Y'all have a great night." Bethany smashed the floor button again.

"Her boss called us. She was fired today. She was stealing from her company," her mother said, wiping away tears.

"And I already slapped her bottom for it, now if you'll excuse us," B said.

Amelia was frozen. Was this really her parents? How did they know her ugly truth? It wasn't a lot of money. Less than a hundred. And it was a mistake. Something she could sweep under the rug. Or at least she thought until she was escorted out today.

"How did you know that?" Amelia finally spoke up.

"Let's go home sweetie. We will get this all sorted out," her father said, extending his hand.

She watched as he stopped right before the threshold. Looking up, she locked eyes with the old man. He looked like her dad. Those big eyes. Light hazel and full of patience. She reached out.

"No!" Bethany slapped her hand away as the doors began to close.

"You're still a disappointment. You always have been," her mother said.

The doors closed, and Amelia wept.

"Was that really your parents?" Rob asked.

Amelia huddled on the bench as the elevator car went up. Bethany held her.

"Okay, I know that was fucked up, but I need you. We need you. I don't know what to make of this next floor," B said.

Amelia wiped her red eyes and said, "What does it say? Are there any nips left?"

Bethany reached into her robe pocket and pulled out a little glass bottle, handing it over. Amelia took and tossed it back as Bethany recited from her phone.

"The wheel of fortune has many faces. Many choices. Many starts and many ends. Spin the wheel and take the fate. Pick your next floor."

Amelia stood, eyes wide, empty bottle falling to the floor. She stepped to the button panel and pressed the capital L button.

The elevator whirred to life and began to descend.

"Holy shit. You're smart," Bethany gasped.

"I'm starting to get scared," Rob said.

"Starting? You should have shat yourself when that thing on my floor was trying to finger fuck you to death," Bethany said, not even looking at the man.

"If this works, if the door opens, we make a run for it," Amelia said.

"But what if there are more things or shitty parents or fuck knows what else?" B said.

"I don't care if there is a slip n slide made of razor wire. We are making a run for it. This keeps getting worse. Something happened to you at the beginning, and Rob is acting weird. Like, not normal. Our phones aren't working, and we've been in here for at least an hour! And my parents?! What the hell is going on?!" Amelia began to cry.

Bethany hugged her friend and they both let loose loud sobs of anger and anxiety. It was all too much, but Amelia found a warm comfort in her friend. And as much as it might sound like a death sentence, she was glad Bethany was with her. She didn't want her here for the pure sake of protecting her friend, but she was glad to have her by her side.

Bethany let go and tried to dry her face. "Okay, we got this. Let's do this," she said.

Amelia tried to right herself as well. "Yeah, fuck this game. It can't beat us. We are gonna win this."

"Hey, why did your other mom say you got fired? I thought you quit?" Bethany asked.

The elevator stopped. All three of them looked at the smooth brass panel above the door. All the round floor lights were black except for the floor they were currently on, the ground floor.

"It's . . . it's not opening," Rob whispered from the bench behind the girls.

Neither turned to acknowledge him. Instead, they stood frozen. Amelia held her breath, waiting for the doors to glide open and witness some bizarre form of torture. Some creature or apparition that shouldn't be. But the doors stayed sealed.

"Okay . . ." Bethany muttered.

Amelia reached out with a hesitant hand and tapped on the door, then quickly pulled back.

"Did the directions mention anything else?" Amelia asked.

"No."

"Wait. Can you scroll ahead? Maybe there's more to this? Mentioned later in the rules?"

"About that . . ." Bethany said, crossing her arms.

Amelia took a sidestep away from her friend and eyed her up and down. "Yes?"

"Well. I tried that . . . scrolling ahead. Cause this morning I must have taken like thirty screenshots. There was a lot. Just page after page. I don't know, I just saved it all, but figured we would get bored after the first few moves and just go back to my place." Bethany was fidgeting.

"What are you not telling me?"

"My phone. The screenshots. They aren't there."

"Did you delete them?"

"No."

Amelia felt her skin prickle, the thin hairs on her arm raised. "Then what is on your phone? What rules are we following?"

Bethany pulled out her phone and pushed it towards Amelia like it was a cursed thing that she sought to get rid of. And in a way, it was.

"Here. Take it."

Amelia did, grasping the device. "Why didn't you say anything?"

"Because this shit is scary enough. And I feel terrible." She began to cry once more. "This is all my fault."

"What's your fault?" Rob asked.

Both girls turned to look at the forgotten third member of the game.

"Goddamnit, Roberto, I told you. The game I found on my phone this morning! Did that creature cast a dumbass spell on you?!"

"B, be cool, he's in shock," Amelia said, raising a hand to her friend.

"Sorry! I'm sorry! I don't know how to handle this. But there you go. The rules changed or went away, or whatever. I didn't want to alarm anyone, but the next direction won't appear until we figure this out. So not only is this real, it's wildly unfair!"

Breathless, Bethany plopped onto the bench next to Rob and grabbed his arm as she wept.

Amelia pocketed the phone. There was no point in double checking, she knew Bethany was right. She wiped away some fresh tears and tried to fix her frazzled ponytail. A pointless task, but the normalcy was comforting.

"I got fired," Amelia said.

Bethany wiped her face and perched on the edge of her seat. "What? You said you quit?"

"No. I was fired. I found a discrepancy in the company's records. It was ninety-eight bucks. So, I kept it." Amelia stood a little taller. The freedom that comes with the truth was palpable.

Shocked, Bethany grabbed two nips from her robe and stood. She handed one to Amelia and held her own up for a toast. "Fuck 'em." She waited for Amelia to join her. Amelia followed suit and tapped her little bottle to Bethany's. They both chugged the sweet liquor and grimaced in equal measure.

"And if you ever lie to me again, I'm gonna make you play Red Red Ruin by yourself," Bethany added.

"Deal. Now let's get this door open."

The open door button wasn't working, and there was no further text for this floor. After a bit of floundering, Bethany pressed all the buttons. Nothing worked. It was time for brute force.

"Rob, get on the right side. B, on the left. Both of you pull, and I'll pull in the middle," Amelia instructed.

They did as they were told. Using their fingertips to achieve what little leverage there was. Amelia did the same, forcing her thin fingers between the two doors.

"Ready. Pull," Amelia said.

All three pried, huffing and cussing. Just as quickly they gave up. The doors were not budging.

"C'mon. Let's do it again," Bethany huffed.

They all grabbed the lips of the doors and heaved. Something shifted inside the car, and the doors opened a fraction.

"They're moving! Pull!" screamed Amelia.

Her arms trembled as she pulled with all her might. On either side, her friends grunted and screamed, pulling hard. The doors parted slightly. Amelia pressed her face against the crack, fighting for more leverage. More grinding sounded from the inner workings of the door, signs of mechanical resistance. Amelia held her breath and pulled as hard as she could. The doors parted just enough for her to see out. She could see the lobby. The front door. And Rob on the other side trying to get in.

Amelia screamed and fell back. Her long nails scraped against the lips of the doors. Both Rob and Bethany let go and the doors closed.

"What's wrong? Are you hurt?" Bethany asked, rushing to her side.

Amelia glanced at Rob. He stood there, looking concerned. She tried not to seem obvious or scared or confused, which only intensified her already nuclear level of anxiety.

"No. Fine. I'm fine. I broke a nail." She stood, focusing on her hands, as if trying to assess the damage but keeping Rob in the corner of her vision. Bethany swooned over her like an overbearing mother with a drinking problem.

"It's not that bad. I have glue and band aids in my apartment," she said.

Amelia tried to concentrate. Did Rob have a key card to enter the front lobby like she did? Or did Bethany buzz him up when he visited? The act was so ubiquitous it was as if Rob just appeared whenever he visited. She was growing dizzy, and it was getting stale in the small elevator car.

"I'm ok. But that door isn't opening."

As if the thought had summoned it, Bethany's phone lit up. Amelia and Bethany froze. It was the next step of the game. Amelia backed into the far corner of the elevator, away from Rob, who was still standing near the door eating chips. The smell of the salt and vinegar chips mixed with their own fear induced musk made the warm car too much to take. Amelia eyed her bottle of wine, almost empty. She grabbed it and finished it off. Then she tucked it between her and the wall of the lift, just in case she had reason to swing it. Rob didn't notice. He was preoccupied with the chips. In fact, Amelia just realized that Rob had been eating their food since he got on the elevator.

"Hey, Rob, can you lay off the food? It's all we have, and who knows how long we will be stuck here," Amelia said.

Rob looked up from the now empty bag of chips. His eyes were wide. Amelia palmed the neck of the wine bottle next to her. He looked hurt by the comment and slowly shrugged, crumbling the empty bag in his hands. Bethany studied her phone. Her grip tight, eyes narrow.

"Shit," Bethany muttered. Rubbing her eyes with the back of her free hand.

Amelia, still gripping her bottle and watching Rob out of the corner of her eye, inched closer to B.

"What's up? What's next? Lingerie floor three? Abusive family members on floor five?" Amelia asked.

"It's . . . gibberish. It's nothing. It's not letters," Bethany whispered.

"What about the screenshots?"

"We stopped using those already."

"Let me see." Amelia grabbed the phone. Still holding the empty wine bottle. The screen showed a text from an unknown number. The text bubble was just fuzzy, mismatched symbols.

"Does this mean the game is over?" Amelia wondered, handing the phone back.

"It never was a game," Rob said.

Both girls looked up at Rob. He was standing there, shoulders sunk forward, staring at the floor. Amelia pulled her bottle forward and gripped the neck with both hands.

Bethany, sweet, nurturing Bethany, who under normal circumstances would console Rob and tell him it would be all right. But tonight was different. Or was it daytime yet? This was different, and B stood next to her friend. Amelia could feel her go rigid.

"Okay, Mr. Garbanzo, can you tell us what it is?" Amelia asked.

Bethany stopped breathing.

This Rob looked down at his hands. Studying them as if he had just got them back from the repair shop. Normally Rob would never shut up. It was a charming but slightly annoying trait of his. He was funny, a good talker, a great storyteller, but he was a bit much for Amelia. But now . . . here in the elevator . . . he was quiet.

"How did I get here?" Rob looked up, eyes watering.

Both friends backed up against the elevator wall.

"Let's just try every floor," Bethany said. Ignoring him.

She began stabbing each floor button one by one, but they were all dead.

"I think you're in shock, buddy. Why don't you sit down and have a drink?" Amelia said, taking a half step forward and gesturing towards the bench. "I know you love booze."

She reached into her pocket and pulled out a nip of Sambuca and handed it to him.

"What is this?" Rob asked.

This made Bethany stop and turn. She watched the bizarre interaction for a moment and then frantically started pressing all the buttons again.

"It's your favorite. We ordered it from this sandwich place. Really good food. It's called Woody's. Ever been there?" Amelia talked slowly and with measured words, and watched for any sudden movements.

Rob, eyes wide, shook his head.

"Okay, I get it. But we need to get out of here before . . ." Bethany trailed off.

Amelia was also thinking of all the possible scenarios that could erupt at any moment. But B was right. They were still in the game. Amelia turned to see why B suddenly went silent. She gasped as she witnessed the revelation. One by one, every button on the brass button plate was lighting up, starting with the lobby floor. The small buttons illuminated one after the other, going all the way to the floor thirty.

"Nononononono . . ." Bethany backed away from the panel and reached for Amelia.

"Holy shit. Do you know what this is? Do you have any idea what's happening?" Amelia asked, already knowing the answer.

"Fuck no. We've been off script for a while."

The lobby button went dark as a soft bell rang, the normal and non-terrifying sound the lift makes when they reach the requested floor. Only now that bell was a potential death sentence.

The doors opened. The light was blinding. Both girls stepped back, shielding their eyes. It was daytime. And Snowing. And Christmas. The lobby was filled with bustling families wrapped in festive winter gear. People coming and going. Outside, the day was bright and iridescent. No clouds, but snow was falling. Everyone was smiling.

A middle-aged woman in a bright red sweater bearing a knitted snowman on the front walked into view as if she were getting on the elevator.

"Oh! Hi there! Looks full! I'll just wait for the next one. Merry Yuletide! You guys are doing great! No one's gotten this far before."

The elevator door began to close.

The festive woman turned to walk away but continued to talk, "But there's only one winner! So good luck!"

The doors closed and the car shifted, beginning its ascent.

"I shouldn't be here," Rob muttered.

Both girls, tears flowing in stunned silence, turned to Rob.

"Yeah, none of us should be here," Bethany said.

Rob was still seated. Staring at the carpet of the elevator. "I shouldn't exist. I can't feel my soul." He sobbed.

The elevator glided to a stop on the first floor. Rob stood. Amelia and Bethany backed away.

"He wants me to attack. He wants me to hurt." Rob wrung his hands together, his nails cutting open his hands. Thin cuts opening and bleeding.

The door began to open.

"But I can't. I won't. I'm sorry that you two are here. Humans—those with souls—shouldn't be here." He looked Bethany in the eye. "Your soul is golden. He wants it."

Rob slapped himself hard across the face and ran.

"No!" Bethany reached for Rob; Amelia pulled her back.

"Someone has to win! Or it will never end!" Rob yelled as he sprinted down the darkened corridor.

He didn't make it far. He neared the first apartment on the left as the door ratcheted open, almost torn off its hinges. A hulking and large thing bombarded out of the apartment. Rob didn't try to defend himself. Maybe he could have ducked and weaved around the monstrosity, but he didn't. Instead, the thing grabbed him and, as if happy, the thing let out a squeal of excitement. Like a train making an emergency stop. High pitched and bassy at the same time.

Bethany and Amelia watched, too shocked to scream.

The fleshy and boney thing had Rob held in place by several arms, one of which reached for his head and twisted. Rob was now looking back at the girls. The thing didn't stop there. With unnatural ease, it pulled Rob's head off. Just as a child might pull the wings off a butterfly.

The doors began to close.

The thing squealed at its exploits, as if pleased with itself, and then whipped the detached head at the elevator. Both girls ducked as the head came screaming in, crashing into the mirror at the back, smashing it into pieces. The heavy cranium landed on the bench, blood still pouring out. Rob's blood shot eyes looking in the wrong directions.

Amelia and Bethany screamed.

The doors closed.

"I can't do this anymore." Bethany sobbed, tears and snot flowing freely.

Amelia reached for the paper bag, ripped it open, and tried her best to cover the head.

The elevator ascended once again.

They both gasped and huddled into each other. The car moved in smooth, gliding motions. There was nothing to say. Nothing to do. Nerves fried, emotions exhausted, adrenaline in overdrive. The car slid to a stop. And the doors opened.

The hallway was dark, humid, and hot. There were no lights, and any illumination revealing the confines came from the lights of the elevator. This floor was not like the others; it was a fleshy and veiny tunnel, not tall enough to walk but just enough to crawl. The swollen and irritated flesh puckering along the edge of the threshold, pulsing and bruised.

"No. You've got to be kidding me . . ." Bethany muttered.

"It kinda looks like a—" Amelia was cut off.

A soft cry came from the flesh tunnel. A muffled wail, painful and angry.

"Yeah . . . I think it is," Bethany said.

The claustrophobic passageway constricted and pulsed, and in the dim light something moved. Something hairy.

"Fuck no!" Bethany yelled. Rushing to the button panel and pressing everything.

Amelia backed away, remembering the disembodied head behind her, she jumped. The walls were closing in. Nowhere was safe.

Amelia turned back to the tunnel in time to see something looking back. So many eyes. So many things looking. Big eyes, some the size of her head. Some split pupils like an animal. Some vertical slits. Far too many eyes. Amelia's skin shivered with itches, an intense urge to rip apart her own hide shook her hands. Repulsed, she vomited.

"What the fuck is that?!" Bethany screamed, jumping away from the entry up onto the padded bench.

The thing was shimmying its way out of the fleshy confines. It managed to shove an arm forward and out, desperately close to the threshold. A mixture of a claw, hand, and a hoof scraped the raw walls restricting it, trying to free itself. It howled again, its mouth too big for its body.

The door began to close.

It howled again, freeing more arms and reaching out.

"Fuck off!" Bethany screamed, throwing her empty wine bottle.

The glass made contact, smacking into what should have been the thing's forehead. It clawed at the bottle, pulling it into its mouth. It bit with animal instinct and the glass shattered without hesitation.

The door closed.

They cried.

The elevator moved up.

The door opened.

This hallway looked normal, as if whoever was in charge of this was offering a temporary reprieve, a moment of solace.

"Should we run for it?" Bethany asked, as she tried to regain some semblance of composure.

"No. We know none of this is real. We know there is something out there."

The hallway felt warm and inviting. Soft lights and rich carpet. Amelia wanted to feel the rugs in her apartment at this moment. Maybe even the plush carpet at her parents' house. She wanted to be clean and free of this place. She would give up an organ for hand sanitizer.

The doors closed.

Amelia settled for drinking another nip. The booze hit easily. Her stomach was empty, so her head began to swim almost instantly. But it felt good. The only reprieve from this ever-evolving mountain of bullshit they were in. And the only food they had access to was here with them, so the longer they could do without, the better. She looked down at the head of the Rob creature; the thought of cannibalizing was out of the question at the moment. But was Rob even real?

The lift went up.

"Bethany. I love you."

Bethany wiped her face and looked at her longtime friend. Amelia sucked at expressing her feelings, but tonight felt like a good time to try.

"Oh, sweetie, I love you too."

She could tell her best friend was done. Cashed out. Expired. Down for the count. But so was she. They were just subjects of some terrible experiment.

"And we are only ever taking the stairs after this," Bethany said.

Amelia laughed from her belly. She couldn't help it. As silly as it was, it meant Bethany still had a little hope. And if she had hope, so could Amelia.

The elevator stopped.

It was another normal hallway. Both girls took a cautious step forward, looking and listening. There were the telltale hum of air conditioning and the soft pulse of life unrequited. It was the most normal hallway thus far.

"This feels . . . right," Bethany whispered.

Amelia felt it, too. The warmth. The ease. It was effortless.

"Don't. It's a trap," Rob whispered.

Amelia yelped despite herself. They both turned, hands drawn up, ready to defend. There was no one there. That's when Amelia noticed the paper bag covering Rob's head moving.

"I should have seen this coming," Bethany whispered.

"Please. Uncover. Me." The voice was small and hurt.

Amelia hesitated. If the booze wasn't in her, she may have just turned and bolted, but she stayed put. Against her better self, she reached down and uncovered Rob.

The head was alive.

Bethany started crying again. "Robby, I'm so sorry!"

"Please stop. I'm not Rob. I'm trying to help you."

Bethany kneeled and sobbed into her hands.

"Fine. I'll bite," Amelia said. "I'm listening. Help us."

Rob's odd set eyes turned independently, each looking for the right angle on their own accord. The visage was nauseating, but Amelia watched. Soon both eyes drifted into the right place and locked with Amelia.

"I can't save you, you're both doomed, but I can help you stay alive."

"That sounds worse somehow," Amelia said.

"I'm sorry you're wrapped up in this," Rob whispered.

"What is *this* exactly?" Amelia asked as she kneeled next to Bethany, hugging her.

"This is how it feeds," Rob's head said.

The elevator moved.

Amelia looked over her shoulder at the button plate. So many floors left. So many damnable floors. This was no longer a fun creepy pasta misadventure. It was no longer a game. This was torture.

"Fine. Talk. I'm listening," Amelia said.

"This ends when you both get off the elevator. The first one out loses. The second one out wins," Rob explained, blood bubbling from his mouth and ears.

Bethany and Amelia stare at Rob and then turn to each other.

The elevator stopped. Both girls stood, turning their backs to their new tour guide.

The doors opened.

It was another normal hallway. Same brass sconces and same red doors.

They both stared down the hallway, waiting, listening.

"And what if we never get off?" Amelia asked, not taking her eyes off the hallway.

"You will. You both will."

"I don't like you anymore, Robby," Bethany muttered.

The head ignored the jab and continued, "I'm expiring. I wasn't meant to be, and certainly not meant to still be. This is how it feeds. One of you spoke the words. One of you made the pact. It is only a matter of time now."

The head stopped, so did the flow of liquids leaving it. Bethany gasped and began to pace as the door closed.

"What? What's wrong?" Amelia asked.

"Me. It was me. I said the words. That bullshit gibberish on my phone. From the website!" Bethany was yelling now.

It took Amelia a moment to recall what her friend was saying. Between the booze and the floors of living nightmares, her brain was cooked. Then it hit her.

"Oh shit. You're right," Amelia said.

"Thanks, asshole, I know I'm right! What do I do?!" Bethany panicked.

The elevator slid to a stop at the next floor. The panic attack would have to wait. They both turned to see a new floor. Technically, it was like the last floor, but upside down.

"The fuck?!" Bethany yelled.

"Okay, that's pretty wild." Amelia was too engrossed to entertain Bethany's crisis.

Amelia took the final swig from her little plastic bottle and tossed it into the hallway. The bottle did what it should have until it passed the threshold of the elevator. It made a downward arch, but once it passed the doors, the bottle shot upwards towards the floor of the topsy turvy hallway. They both watched as it rolled across the hallway's floor. The part they would call the ceiling.

"Impressive, but this is kinda silly. I wouldn't call this scary," Amelia said.

"The fuck you want, you stupid bitch?! Reversing gravity isn't terrifying enough for you?!" Bethany screamed.

It then dawned on Amelia that her friend was losing it. And maybe in her own private way she was too. She shouldn't be taking all this in such a casual stride. Maybe she should be freaking out too.

"Sorry. You're right. I don't know what's wrong with me," Amelia said.

Bethany bit her lip. Amelia knew her friend wanted to lash out more; they both did, but at what? They were both at the mercy of this thing that the head was referring to.

"Look, I've been fucked up since I said those words."

"What do you mean?"

The door closed.

"I mean I thought it was the booze at first," Bethany said, trembling, wiping away tears. "I kept seeing things in the mirror." She gestured to the shattered mirror at the back of the lift.

They both turned. Amelia half expected to see something, but she was wrong.

"It was nothing at first, just shadows. But I keep seeing more and more things. And in the hallways too."

The elevator slid to a stop.

"Oh, sweetie, I had no idea. I wish you had told me sooner. What did you see?"

The door opened.

"Me. Dead."

Bethany, pale and exhausted, tears flowing freely, ran.

She ran hard. Frantic. Animal-like. A person driven beyond logic. Her pink fuzzy slippers kicked off mid sprint. Amelia, buzzed and shocked, reached for her friend, but it was too late. She made it about twenty feet before the floor opened below her. Too fast for her to avoid and too small to fall through instantly. Instead, a single leg plunged into the narrow hole. Her hips and free leg wedged enough to keep her from falling all the way in. Amelia watched in horror as the screams started. Something was pulling her friend deeper. Amelia joined the chorus of screams as she watched her best friend contort and bend in unnatural ways as some unseen force made Bethany fit through the narrow trap. It was over. Amelia stared at the small hatch as the elevator doors closed.

The elevator did not stop for hours. The constant low hum and the rhythmic mechanical workings were hypnotic and strangely calming. It reminded Amelia of the fan in her bedroom. She would always keep it on at night. The noise was soothing in a weird way. There she sat on the bench next to the head of the imposture Rob. She covered it at some point. More out of respect than fear. A modicum of normalcy in a place of madness. She was sober now and starving. It was finally time for one of Woody's famous sandwiches. Lots of meat and veggie goodness. The oregano and oil made her feel alive. A feeling she didn't want. She didn't feel like she deserved such pleasures after all that had conspired. Despite her mixed feelings, the food made her feel good. Amelia only ate a quarter of one sandwich and wrapped up the remaining.

There was no indication of which direction the elevator was going, nor did it really matter, but Amelia was growing stir crazy. She wanted to pace. She wanted to run, to see something besides these four goddamn walls. Hours passed. Maybe even days. But eventually, she got her wish.

She was asleep on the cushioned bench, bent at an odd angle, avoiding the mess of the severed head when the lift came to a stop. The shift in ambiance awoke her. No floor button was lit on the button panel, and above the door, no illuminated number revealed her location. She stood, holding her breath and an empty bottle.

The door opened for the last time.

A sight beholden by anyone not as primed as Amelia was would surely have set them to madness. But Amelia stared out the elevator, bearing witness to her prize. A place vast and endless. A dark ocean stretched out before her. A black sky filled with moons and onyx stars made her skin grow cold. Across the shimmering and hazy landscape, monoliths reached for the gray clouds above. More massive than any building in Chicago. Bigger than any structure should be. And somewhere on the horizon gargantuan creatures roamed, their huge lumbering effigies cast shadowed thousands of miles long. And Amelia watched in awe.

Days passed as she stayed put in the elevator. The head was beginning to smell, and she was out of food. She was beyond thirsty. As the days passed, she watched as this world existed in front of her. It didn't care for her. She was pointless. Eventually the lights flickered and died, and she took her first steps out of the elevator. It was cold, and over the several days of observation she never saw a sun. This was it. This was her world now.

She won Red Red Ruin. She won Carcosa.

———

Malady and Her Fevered Sisters

1

And In Came Death

A long time ago, there was a dark land ruled by a dark Queendom. In that dark Queendom was a dark palace, and in that dark palace lived the witch goddess Diana. Diana ruled this shadowed realm for a thousand years. Till one day she suddenly fell ill. Her four daughters rushed to her side. Malady, the youngest, raven-haired. Entropy, with auburn locks. Fallacy with golden curls and Heresy, the oldest with a fiery fringe.

As Diana lay upon her silken deathbed, she admired her four daughters. Diana told them that they would rule the Queendom together when Death arrived for her. This declaration upset Hersey, who thought the throne was her birth rite as the eldest.

"I am the eldest of Mother's blood! I should rule!" she screamed from behind clenched fangs.

"The land needs the four of you. You will rule together. My will is the law, dead or alive. So mote it be," Diana whispered.

This only served to enrage Hersey, who stormed out of the royal chambers. Malady, Entropy, and Fallacy watched as their eldest sister spat fire and left. Slowly, Fallacy turned back to Diana and took her mother's fragile hand in hers.

"You are wise, Mother dearest. But these lands have only known one ruler since their very creation. Perhaps you would be so kind as to continue such sacred traditions and elect but a single heir to the throne . . . mayhaps myself . . ." Fallacy said with warm dandelion curls framing her sharp cheeks.

"My will is the law. In life or death. You will rule as one, or each will perish by the hands of the other. As above, so below," she said, her eyes pale and milky.

Fallacy rose from her chair, her feet dangling a hint off the ground. She floated there beside the silken deathbed, and she gazed down upon her mother. "Your will is weak, and in death, you will find but the same fixtures that you held in life. A lone and Cold Throne that will see no future." Fallacy brushed her shining golden waves of hair aside and floated away, leaving the sacred chambers.

Malady and Entropy watched as their sister glided from view. Entropy gazed back at Malady, her auburn bangs showcasing her prismatic eyes.

"I am afraid this will be our demise. Mother wants the simplest of requests. Yet our own sisters defy her." Tears welled up and rolled down Entropy's cheeks. She stood, shoulders stooped and walked away. Leaving her mother and the sacred chamber.

Malady watched as Entropy padded away in soft black sandals. Then, Malady turned back to her mother, ebony streams of hair tucked behind her pointed ears. Diana was already gazing upon her youngest as a hint of a smile brightened her wistful and aged face. "Malady, my youngest, my last chance at keeping peace in this hallowed Queendom, I must task you with a burden most heavy."

Malady glanced back at the doors of the sacred chamber. They were alone. She leaned close to her mother as she took her frail hand. "I will do all I can, Mother, but perhaps one of your other daughters would be better suited. For I am young and weak."

Diana smiled at this and said, "You may be young, but you are far from weak." She took her youngest daughter's waif-like hand and pulled. Malady rose from her bedside chair and leaned into her dear mother. Diana whispered, and Malady listened. The words like a blue moon chill. As the youngest of Diana's daughters listened, the hair at her nape rose. The onyx doors to the sacred chamber clicked open. One hundred candles lining the marble walls flickered, and Malady turned to see that Death had entered. His black cloak was a dark mist following all around him. The gaunt visage had to stoop to enter the sacred chamber. Despite his size, his presence felt weightless. Malady stepped in front of the deathbed.

"Hear me, O'Death! Please, I beg of you. Return another night. You may have her, but not now," Malady commanded with quivering words.

Death slowly glanced down, observing Malady, then Death spoke, and the world trembled.

"The choice was made and not by me."

Malady gasped as new tears began to flow. She turned back to her dear mother.

"Tell me this isn't true!" she said, running to her mother's side.

"My lovely Malady. The decision is mine. Go, my child. Remember my words. I love you."

Before Malady could protest, her mother was gone, and Death had vanished.

***

2
Cherries and Funerary Candles

The moon was full and red for the funeral. Denizens from all dominions traveled to this dark Queendom called the Shadow Keep to pay their respects.

From the frozen halls of Tyr far in the north came Valkurl, the ancient frost giant, an old friend of Diana.

From the western coastal keep of Nohope came Nautilux, a once brave sea captain who took over as warden of the west at Diana's behest. All that was left of the man was a floating phantasm of greens and blues ever swirling.

From the stronghold Voplenheim came Barrenjur. The keeper of the East and protector from the horrors that haunt beyond the Badlands. His blood, the vestige of were-folk from time immemorial, clad in only a kilt, his onyx talons glistened in the moonlight.

And then came Throng from the peaks and chasms of the south. Smoldering and broad-shouldered, cloaked in his own massive and veiny wings. Appointed by Diana as a liaison between her world and what lies beneath the mountains far to the south, the city of Dis.

The only keep not represented was that of Hellheart, which was laid in ruins since the great war. Man, nor beast stir in that accursed place.

And so countless others joined and converged at the Shadow Keep. From villages and farms and ranches and temples, they came. The villagers and common folk gathered at the Fountain of Helen outside the palace. They sang and cried and talked of Diana. Many brought offerings, rare spices, exotic fruits, and many tithes of cherries, Diana's favorite. They burned black candles and white sage around the Keep. Wine flowed and people watched as the procession of family, friends, and comrades walked in silence.

The winding line of funeralgoers snaked through the streets and thorough-fares of the Shadow Keep. At the front, the Royal Guard led the way, followed thereafter by many of the Royal Family's staff. Then, the realm's nobility and finally, the late Diana's brood. Their four-door coach of gilded burgundy pulled by a team of six Nightmares. All four daughters rode in silence. Behind them was Diana's sarcophagus. The elegance of the whole affair stopped when it came to her final resting place. It was her desire that she be laid to rest in a simple pine box; the wood taken from the trees near the Emerald Plateau. The day after her passing, a rough-hewn box was built and now she rests there, soon to be interred in the labyrinth beneath the palace with so many others.

The procession meandered past one of the many statues and memorials that spread across the city; this one a statue of Helen, stood the tallest. Naked, she looks upward, her arms stretched above her with open palms reaching for the stars.

"That dreadful thing should be demolished," Heresy said, glancing out the carriage window.

"Three generations from now, it will collapse. A ground quake," Entropy muttered.

"You're always wrong," Heresy returned.

"She is always right. But things change, and then she's always wrong," Fallacy added.

Heresy rolled her eyes. "Same difference."

Malady stared out the coach window. The lacy black curtain was closed, but she could still see the citizens gathered on the streets. Countless faces watching, some lost in prayer, rolling prayer beads through their hands. Some whispered to others, pointing and gesturing.

"That should be Mother up there or one of us. Helen caused the Chaos Opus after all," Heresy said.

"She did no such thing. She alone stood against the hoards whilst all the other Keeps turned their backs," Fallacy whispered.

"All but Hellheart, and we all know how that turned out," Entropy added.

Heresy's fingers drummed on the silver dagger tucked into the folds of her cloak. "Look at them." She gestured out the coach window. "They came to watch us mourn and cry and lose ourselves. Vultures, all of them."

"If you love them, they will love you. That's how you rule a dominion," Fallacy replied.

"It doesn't matter. When I look out that window, all I see is a sea of tombstones," Entropy said.

"Hells bells, you're so dramatic. Could you spare me one day, this day, from your depressing dribble?" Heresy shouted.

Fallacy leaned forward. "And perhaps you could calm down and act like an actual high-born princess."

Heresy flashed her fangs as her hand gripped the hidden ceremonial dagger. "And perhaps we could leave one more body in the labyrinth tonight . . ."

Malady reached for the coach door and flung it open.

"Halt!" a coachman yelled from somewhere behind. The entire procession ground to a halt as Malady fought against the narrow opening and her mourning gown. Onlookers watched in confusion as the princess fumbled her way out of the cart and onto the muddy road. She stumbled, a guard reached for her hand, catching her before she fell.

"Thank you," she huffed as she slammed the coach door shut.

"Onward!" the unknown coachman called out.

Like a giant hulking beast, the procession lurched forward. Malady gathered her gown as best she could and ran towards the front of the coach and into the ranks of the Royal Guards, each soldier stepping aside, giving her a path to wherever she was going only to fall back into position once she passed. Malady made it to the front; breathing hard and slowly becoming mist drenched, she found who she was looking for. The soldier was large, easily three heads higher than the tall and lanky Malady. While all the soldiers around him were clad in heavy plate mail armor and dark red cloaks, this one was fitted in brushed silver chain mail and a forest green cape. Malady matched his pace and tried to blend in.

"Did you manage to miss the coach, my princess?" the large soldier asked without looking down.

"I know exactly where it is."

"We will be at the cathedral soon," he said.

"Matters will only get worse from there."

"Do you know what I loved about your mother?"

The question caught the young woman off guard. "What?" she asked.

"Her patience. When the four of you were just babies, you nearly tore the palace to the ground. Every day it was something new. Some new fight or dare or tantrum or disaster. Every day. The four of you would have driven me to death by wine if you were my brood. I would have strung up all of you by your toes and left you for the crows."

"Maybe you should have."

The big man ignored the comment and continued. "But not your mother. She had infinite patience."

"Even for Heresy."

"Even for Heresy, but you were a handful too, lest we forget. Remember when you and Fallacy decided to bake winterberry pies?"

"That's not fair. It was an accident."

"It took the carpenters a week to rebuild the oven. We didn't have bread for days. That alone would have made me leave all of you for the wolves."

"I would like to think most of our transgressions and ill manors did not survive into adulthood. But my sisters love to prove me wrong daily."

"Speaking of which. I need to ask you a question of a sensitive nature." His voice lowered, rough and morose.

Commander Nicodemus was a friend of Malady's and a loyal liege to the Shadow Keep, the Cold Throne, and all Diana stood for. Since she was a child, he has been a figure in her life. A figure of safety. A figure of authority. Almost like a father, but both were too shy to ever admit it. So when Nicodemus took this tone, it made the breath in Malady's throat catch.

"Go on."

The commander looked from side to side, observing the mourners. "One of my sentries came to me at dawn. He tells me he witnessed Heresy entering the coffers. Believe me when I say, princess, I make no harsh assumptions or thoughts of ill deeds, but I need to know why she was in there."

Malady wiped away misty strands of pure onyx bangs, perplexed. "The Royal Treasury? How can you be sure? Do you trust this source?"

"Aye, he said he heard her before he saw her. She thought she was alone as she made her way to the catacombs and thus was cursing up a right storm. Yelling and carrying on. He hid as she approached and watched her enter. You know her well. And I know the coffers hold many things . . ."

The procession continued. They strode side by side as Malady grew lost in thought. This was supposed to be a solemn time. A time to reflect and mourn. A time to cry and laugh. But as usual, one of her sisters had to derail things. Instead of embracing the legacy of their mother, they now had a mystery to solve.

"The coffers have centuries of important things. Documents, scrolls, deeds, spells. But most of the family's artifacts, the big pieces, are out near Nohope. In the Crystal Reliquary" Malady said.

"Which confuses me all the more" Nicodemus returned.

"I will let you know if I discover anything."

"I thank you. And I thank you for your discretion on the matter. Best if it stays between us," the big soldier said.

"If what you say is true, then we need to be on the watch. Heresy has never done anything that didn't yield disastrous consequences. Be them benign or malevolent," Malady said.

Nicodemus grumbled, "So mote it be."

She could smell the incense before she could see the grim cathedral. Rose and thyme mixed with a bit of musk. It brought Malady back to her childhood. The night of the Harvest Solstice when she was fourteen. There were so many lanterns and ghost effigies everywhere. Lots of food carts offering smoked meat skewers and honey wine. This terrible place was almost bearable that night, but never again, and especially not tonight.

The procession turned west at the intersection of Oud and Odd, and there, at the end of the street, it stood in all its dreaded splendor. The Cathedral of Set. The Shadow Keep was home to many ancient buildings and structures, and the cathedral was among the oldest. It was standing before the Chaos Opus—history tomes say it was standing even before the Age of Plagues. It has been a sacred place since time immemorial, even if its real purpose is known only to dead gods. Torches, candles, braziers, and floating phantom lights give life to this giant corpse of the past. Malady looked away from the towering monstrosity. It wanted her to look; it wanted her to behold it.

"I never get used to the sight of it," the soldier said.

Malady noticed her friend was staring up at the cathedral's steeple, lost somewhere high in the clouds.

"I pray this won't take long," Malady returned.

"You'll be back in the palace soon. Until then, we all have a role to play, my lady."

"That's exactly what I fear. Our future seems so uncertain. Not even Entropy can see what will happen."

"Diana knew what she was doing. Have faith."

The hundred doors of the Cathedral of Set opened at once as the mourners crested the stone steps leading into the ancient house of ritual. Inside, the massive structure was oppressive and stifling yet filled with void. There were no higher floors or rooms to fill the sprawling open box of stone, nor seats for weeping mourners or weary travelers. The gigantic stone building was round and lined with statues hundreds of feet tall. Some so tall they couldn't be seen from the ground floor. The names of every statute lost in time, not uttered for centuries. If it were not already a solemn occasion, Malady would weep for this wretched place like she has done many times before. But tonight, she weeps for someone she knew well.

Every person, spirit, and beast took up only half the building, still giving it the ability to be cold and unforgiving. A low thunder rolled and soft lightning cracked high inside the dome of the temple, where a perpetual storm has been simmering for eons, and for just a moment, Malady could see a stone face staring back at her. One of the many forgotten gods that filled the cathedral. She looked away, not desiring any unwanted attention. Her sisters gathered near her as four guards carried in her mother's remains. Lifted by the four guards, the simple pine box was set upon a table, and with bowed heads, they walked to the center of the cathedral.

"Such an obnoxious way to go. Give me a gilded coffin filled with sapphires," Fallacy muttered, "That's what a true ruler would do."

"Mother wasn't one for pageantry, especially when it came to personal matters," Entropy said.

The four guards rested the remains in the middle of a massive stone sigil. The elegant stone masonry incorporated numerous types of stone and thick colored glass to make a detailed and complex map of lines and angles. The shapes and signs and symbols precise, a working testament to the sacred geometry it was meant to harness. The doors to the cathedral closed. Around Malady and her sisters, the crowd formed and settled in for the ceremony.

It was time.

From the shadows of the far side of the building, a small man in fine robes came forth, followed by the templars of Set, the last of a long line of Clergy for the deceased god. The priest, censor swinging from one hand, gestured with the other, carving symbols into the air as the templars began to chant. The choir guttural and deep, like glaciers moving across a silent sea. The templars spread out, forming a semi-circle around the temple. The chants grew more intense as they came to a stop, arms out and palms up.

Malady gripped her robes and pulled them tight. She watched as the mourners did their best to appear comfortable amidst the ritual playing out in front of them. Even in a land haunted by beautiful tragedies, this scene was too unnerving. She shook as she witnessed the magic at work. The ornate floor started to move. The fine-crafted stonework shifted. Malady felt her friend step next to her. Normally, the presence of Commander Nicodemus comforted her, but this situation was beyond resolution.

Smoke bellowed from between the sigil stones, swirling and encircling the altar where Diana lay. Malady wrapped her arms around her stomach and clinched her cloak tight. In the realms of sorcery, there were few subjects that a practitioner would consider truly off limits, and this rare display of things inconceivable was the most terrifying; Cosmic Magic.

The baritone chanting rolled through the unhallowed hall. The sound echoed off itself, repeating into oblivion. The energy caused the hair on Malady's arms to stand on end. From the tips of her pointed ears down her spine, through her heels and into the cobblestone where she stood, a dreadful melancholy swept over her. The massive sigil her mother rested on began to glow and smolder. Deep reds and purples enveloping each other. Overhead, in the black magic clouds, thunder rolled. In the emptiness above, a strong gust brewed, swirling and grabbing at cloaks and hair alike.

The guests did their best to maintain composer. The glowing sigil and grave chanting made Malady fidget in her boots, fighting the urge to be sick. Magic so deep and powerful often had trickling side effects. Sickness and fever and often mania could be felt by those witnessing it. Summoning a dominating presence made for treacherous work. Black smoke swirled around the remains of the goddess. The onyx cyclone gathered speed as people and creatures backed away from the edge of the floor sigil, shielding their eyes from the storm of dust. Candles flickered, and the clouds high above in the enclosed dome writhed. Malady felt the bricks beneath her feet convulse, and the sigil opened.

Charon was here.

Bigger than the frost giants of the north, Charon floated up from the Underworld. Dried skin stretched over a massive skeleton that was almost transparent, revealing a hollow torso. An enormous skull filled with eyes looked all places at once. Massive and clawed hands rested on either side of the altar, and it spoke.

"Who offers this soul to the Underworld?"

Malady had only seen Charon once. She was a little girl attending the funeral of Nebuchadnezzar the Great. He had been the last survivor of the Battle of the Fallen. She couldn't look at the phantasm and instead buried her face in her mother's cloak. But tonight, she had no choice. She pulled three coins from the folds of her green cloak. Her throat dry, her hands trembling. She could feel Nicodemus next to her, but he did little to instill bravery. Charon's massive head shifted towards her. Several watering eyes locked onto hers. She froze; coins gripped in her hand.

"I do," said Heresy.

Malady shook and almost dropped her tithe. Heresy had spoken. Slack jawed, Malady watched as her eldest sister stepped onto the sigil. Dozens of Charon's eyes watched her approach while several more still glared at Malady. Heresy's satin robe slid off her shoulders, and her dark red dress of fine spider silk made her a sight unfit for such a solemn occasion.

"I do. I offer the goddess Diana to the Underlife," Heresy said.

"And who are you to do this?" Charon's voice boomed.

"I am Heresy, eldest of Diana's brood. It is my charge to deliver her to you," she said, stepping closer.

Charon leaned forward, his massive and hollow frame creaking.

"The price for a god is high. How do you intend to pay?"

Heresy smiled and walked up to the giant clawed hand of Charon and turned to face the congregation.

"O'Charon, gatekeeper to the Underlife! Hear my words!"

Malady clinched at her stomach. Her skin turned pale. She reached for Nicodemus's arm to steady herself. Three precious metal coins were still in her grasp. The crowd murmured and shifted.

"Take this as my offering so my dear mother may pass on to the Underlife."

She opened her hand, revealing a small amulet with a green gem. Malady screamed.

"Blasphemer!" Malady cried, dropping her own coins.

Nicodemus grabbed her by the shoulders and fought to keep her back. "Princess, don't. I can't protect you from that," he pleaded.

Fallacy clung to Malady and leaned in close, whispering, "Hells bells, is that what I think it is? Where did she get that?"

Malady turned to her sisters, hoping for help. Hoping for a way out of this. Past Fallacy, she saw Entropy leaving. She, of all the people in the realm, knew the magnitude of this offering to Charon.

Fallacy turned and noticed their sister's departure. "What a shit, things are just getting good," she whispered to Malady, suddenly realizing her youngest sister was in tears. Fallacy dropped her grin and tried to right her face.

The gathered guests began to panic, what was supposed to be a somber affair had turned into something sinister. Valkurl, the great frost giant, pulled his massive war hammer into both hands. Throng, from the third layer of Hell and the city of Dis, drew a sword of tarnished gold that dripped with green fire. Even Nicodemus drew his broadsword with his free hand. His other kept Malady at bay. Some ran for the doors, others opened portals and fled to places safer. Some flew to the windows. The curious and the strong stayed put. Nearby, Malady and Fallacy watched.

Heresy smiled and held her hand out for the world to see. Malady ceased her struggling and stared. She held an ornate and polished silver amulet, a small charm fitted with a dazzling emerald.

"Fallacy, please, what do we do?" Malady whispered.

Her sister leaned in close. The harsh winds and rumbling chanting making the temple awash with sound. "I know not but this isn't good," she said.

"She stole it. The Amulet of the Covetous. From our own coffers she stole from us," Malady said.

"O'Charon, take my offering. See well that my mother finds her way through the strange eons that lie beyond this world. See her well to sit with our ancestors and to drink of their eternal ambrosia." She leaned to place the object into the outreached palm of the god of the dead but stopped. Turning back to the stunned crowd, she addressed them once more.

"And let my dear mother Diana rest knowing the Shadow Realm is in good hands."

She looked into the eyes of each of her sisters.

"No!" Malady screamed.

"My Hands." Heresy dropped the amulet into Charon's palm.

The old and magical piece vanished as soon as it touched Charon. Above, the rolling thunder and clouds lit the cathedral right before the rain poured down.

"With the sacred Amulet of the Covetous, I offer my mother's soul so that I may rule! I am now the Queen! I will rule these lands! They are mine! Gods and men be damned!" Heresy howled.

The bells rang, and Malady ran.

3

Malice Like a Scythe

And so, Malady fled.

A tempest rolled in, sweeping across the Shadow Keep. Paupers and nobles alike ran for shelter. Residents pulled shutters closed, visitors rushed into taverns to order warm honey wine and whiskey, merchants did their best to keep their beasts of burden from running wild. And through the crowd, Malady ran. She fled down a stone walk next to the wall of the palace to a secret entrance to the grand kitchen the staff often used. Sobbing and wiping her eyes, she muttered the secret words. The stone shifted open, and she slipped in.

Servants and spirits paused to watch as the youngest princess ran, her flowing gown of gossamer black and silver floating behind her. If her sisters could abandon their duties, then so could she. If they can act as children and neglect their birth rite then she would as well. Wiping away tears, she ran to the grand kitchen; it was the quickest route to her chambers. Inside, a bevy of bakers, pie makers, and stewards paused their labors and watched. They whispered as Malady passed. Seeing the princess in the grand kitchen was no surprise; she had used the shortcut since she learned to walk. She could even be found in the pantries after hours, foraging for frost berry cakes or whatever kind of cheese she could get her hands on. Gustav, the head chef, looked up from his hushed conversation to see the princess running by. The old man choked up and raised a hand as if to reach out to comfort the girl, but she was gone before he could.

Malady dashed through the west hallway. Ashen marble floors covered with burgundy rugs. Countless portraits on either side, paintings, and glass etchings of ancient kin and important moments from the realm's long and tumultuous history. She knew them all by heart, as did her siblings. Soon, another portrait would grace the walls of history. She sobbed as she thought of the royal painter, Simtteen, putting oil to canvas and the image of her mother being captured.

The west hall ended near Malady's personal chambers, where she slid in and closed the heavy oak doors behind her. In her own private space, she fell to her knees and cried. Sobbing, she grabbed a silver candelabra and threw it against the wall. Lit candles crashed to the floor. It was all over now. They had no warning, no sign of Heresy's intentions. This was all so sudden, and now Malady was alone. Her family divided—split over matters she cared not for. Let Heresy take the Cold Throne, let Entropy manage the Crown's affairs, or let Fallacy deal with the denizens. She wanted only to sequester herself in the labyrinthian library deep under the palace. She wanted to creep into the grand kitchen late at night to steal cheeses and fruits. She wanted solstice getaways to Tyr and the Emerald Plateau, long carriage rides with plenty of scenery, and good books. She knew she wasn't a ruler. She was not a figure of authority or someone to look up to. She was a sickly girl who would never amount to anything. If she wasn't born of royal and holy blood, she would surely be dead by now. Left stranded in the orphanage deep under Nohope to be forgotten or used as a barge hand in the coastal town of Nevermore until she collapsed of exhaustion and slipped into the icy and unforgiving current.

But she was made from Diana, and because of this, she received the best attention and medicines and care. Yet she was still a frail and delicate thing. Far too delicate to govern a nation of souls. A sharp knocking jolted her back to the present.

"Go away!" She gasped and covered her mouth. She had never used such an aggressive tone before, and she immediately regretted it. "I'm sorry!" she shouted.

"Lady Malady. It's me," Nicodemus uttered.

She didn't need to say more, instead, she slumped to the floor at the foot of her bed as the door creaked open. Nicodemus, rain-soaked, stepped in and closed the chamber door.

He walked across the room and sat on a wooden chair near the bent candelabra. He snapped the clasp on his soaked cloak, and it slid off, letting it thump to the floor. Taking a deep sigh, he rubbed his tired eyes.

"I can't believe she acquired it," Malady finally said, not looking up.

Nicodemus adjusted in his chair, resting his hand on the pommel of his sword. "I didn't even know it existed to be acquired. That bit of jewelry was supposed to be a tall-tale and nothing more."

Both soldier and princess sat, slumped and exhausted. Malady snapped her fingers and a small fire formed in the corner fireplace. She watched Nicodemus as he pulled a bronze flask from his hip pouch. The old soldier opened it and took a long draw. Closing it, he tossed it to Malady, who took her own swig. It was good fruit brandy all the way from Omon-ka.

"She betrayed us. She betrayed all of us," she said, tossing the flask back.

"So now we regroup. Formulate a plan," Nicodemus said.

"That was the Amulet of the Covetous. In one grand gesture, she banished my mother to the Underlife and gave herself the Cold Throne. All while smiling."

"What of your sisters? Surely they will have some protest?"

"They know they can't beat Heresy at this game. She's got Hellfire in her blood."

"But there's three of you. What of Diana's last wishes? Do her words mean nothing?"

"She did not make her desires known publicly. As far as the realm is concerned, Heresy is the rightful heir."

Nicodemus stared out the window. The night cold and black. Shivering, he took another swig. Malady gathered a blanket from her bed and sat before the fire.

"What will Heresy do? Why would she go to such lengths? This explains why she was seen in the coffers late last night. Seems as if she knew it was there. Did you?" Nicodemus asked.

Malady thought of the Royal Depository. The palace was huge and held many rooms and corridors and hallways. Over the eons, more and more had been added. And now the palace was a maze of rooms, new and old. Some wings and hallways have been unused for decades. Somewhere midst the tangle of weblike corridors was the coffers; the Royal Depository. Another memory from the back of her mind.

Years ago, during a brutal winter, deep into the Cruelest Solstice, the long nights and unforgiving weather meant Malady and her sisters were sequestered to roam the palace fueled by abject boredom. Malady was young, thirteen. Which meant her sisters were of the age for complex hijinks and nefarious doings. The four of them had managed to get themselves banned from the state rooms after Fallacy dared Heresy to steal from a magistrate's coin purse. A feat that Heresy was all too eager to achieve. A handful of palladium pieces later, the sisters were running to hide deep and away from any adults looking to ruin the good times. Midst their travels, the four found themselves deep inside the maze of the palace.

"What's that room?" Fallacy asked. Pointing to the far end of a cobwebbed hallway.

Entropy closed her eyes and concentrated. "Antiquity. Parchment . . . money."

"I think my purse could be a little fuller," Heresy said, walking down the long hall.

"Mother said to stay out of the southern passages," Malady protested.

"Mother says a great and many thing. Nary a one we listen to, so why start now?" Fallacy said, following Heresy.

Entropy followed, leaving Malady alone in the dusty and unwelcoming hallway. Turning, she glanced back the way they had come. It was dark now that her sisters had moved on with the candles; each had a candlestick except for Malady, who was still nervous about wielding one. She sighed and followed.

It took one of them uttering the family name to open the enchanted lock, but they managed to enter the old stronghold.

"Hells Bells, this place is amazing! Why haven't we been down here sooner!" Fallacy exclaimed.

The sisters lit the candelabras wherever they found them; old tapered candles waiting to be useful. One by one revealing the cavernous room.

"Because, gods forbid, we disturb all this old junk. We keep everything. Every scrap of paper, every bauble and tincture and coin and trinket that comes along. Magical or not," Heresy said, lighting more candles.

"When the Chaos Opus occurred, the family hid most of our heirlooms out west. In a crystal cavern. I would love to go there. Such an amazing feat of nature and oh so quiet," Entropy said.

"Go there for the antiques or the solitude?" Fallacy asked.

Entropy shrugged and continued to light candles.

Soon the massive room glowed with warmth. Aisles of shelves stretched out into the shadows and beyond. Centuries worth of curating accumulated in one place. Each sister explored the family's collection. Fallacy fumbled with forgotten phylactery. Entropy examined elegant examples of extravagance. Heresy handled heavy hardbacks while Malady manipulated many manuscripts. Such a rich collection of anything and everything lost and forgotten. Things loved and forlorn.

"Listen to this!" Fallacy declared as she lifted a scroll. "According to this decree, the last full moon of every season is Royal Jam Day. We are supposed to celebrate with toasted breads, butter, and a fruit spread gifted from a farm, stronghold, or keep!"

"And to think we have been depriving ourselves all this time," Entropy said, picking at a waist high mechanical knight, complete with sword and shield.

"What's that?" asked Malady.

"A clockwork sentry. Keeps used these as guards centuries ago. But it involves a now outlawed incantation: the living spell. I can sense that this one has been here since the palace was built," Entropy said.

"I've read about that. Magic that can imbue life into lifeless things," Malady said.

"But that was all before the great war. After, many magics were outlawed," Entropy added.

"Sweet buttery Beelzebub! Finders keepers!" Fallacy shouted.

This got everyone's attention. Fallacy was always dramatic, but it didn't lessen her ability to discover the best ways to be mischievous. The trio made their way deeper into the yawning room.

"Look at this!" Fallacy quipped, ushering her sisters closer.

There stood a six-foot-high glass enclosed display. A perfect cube of glass molded onto a beautiful wooden pedestal. Each sister gathered, bringing more light to the sleeping artifact. Together, they surrounded the pedestal and lit it from all sides.

". . . strange," Entropy uttered. "I can't read this object. There's no trace of a past and no shadow of a future."

"For a seer, you're really terrible at it." Heresy jabbed.

Entropy, as usual, was deaf when it came to her eldest sister. She continued. "Maybe it's never been used . . ."

"It hasn't," Diana said.

All four girls jumped. Fallacy leaped into the air and hovered there as Heresy growled and glowed red.

"Mother!" Malady cried.

"You were all warned to stay out of the southern corridors," Diana said.

All the girls relaxed but for Malady. Fallacy lowered to the ground, and Heresy fizzled out, but Malady grew tense, holding her breath and trying to keep tears at bay. Ignoring the accusation, Entropy pressed on. "What is this?" she asked.

Diana glided forward deeper into the hall. Her ease with elegance made her seem as if she were floating liquid; a beautiful specter joining them.

"On occasion you'll find things you cannot read," Diana said, eyeing Entropy.

"But why?" Entropy asked. Ever seeking the answers to every mystery. She stared into the glass display. Inside a satin pillow held a silver amulet reflecting her prismatic gaze.

"This amulet is a fulcrum. A means to machinate. By itself, it's simply a beautiful piece." Diana leaned forward to examine the artifact. "But under the right circumstances, it becomes something much more commanding. This item allows you to make a wish."

All four girls stared in awe. Such a declaration for something so small. Even Heresy was impressed and, for once, was struck speechless.

"That seems dangerous. Why is something so powerful merely protected by glass? This should be locked away," Malady said, barely a whisper.

"By itself, it's merely jewelry. This piece requires more—much more—to be useful," Diana said.

"Pray tell, what price would a wish cost?" Entropy asked, enthralled.

"As with most magic, the cost is equal to the prize. In this case we needn't lock it away. No one will use it." Diana stood tall, her brood turning to watch her, hanging on her every word. "The price is your soul."

All four girls were lost in thought. Mulling over the concept.

"Indeed, a steep price. So this device has never been used?" Asked Entropy.

It was a rare occasion that all four girls were so focused on a singular thing. A rare reprieve from the never-ending sibling rivalry.

"Never. Many have had the chance. But to part with one's soul . . . I can't fathom anything that could be worth it. The legend goes that once a bargain is struck, you have two days to contact the Unpious to complete the deal. Those fallen gods deep in the Underlife."

"What if you give it someone else's soul?" Heresy asked. Staring into Diana's eyes.

Diana didn't flinch. The question silenced the room.

"While I appreciate my daughters enjoying the antiquity and history of our realm, I'm afraid it is bedtime," Diana said.

The girls snapped out of the odd tension and began to protest as Diana led them out of the coffers.

"Oh, Heresy." Diana turned and locked eyes with her eldest. Once again, the girls fell silent.

"Magistrate Jeffery would like his coins back."

***

Malady drifted back to the present moment. Such an innocent encounter. Kids at play, exploring this palace they called a home. And somehow that day's experience stuck with Heresy. Years later she saw the opportunity and sold away their mother's soul. Malady stiffened and looked Nicodemus in the eye. "We have two days."

This perked up the old knight. "Why do you say this?"

"Her tithe. That damned piece of jewelry. She has two days to complete the spell," Malady said.

"You're sure of this? I know nothing of the piece save for its promise of a wish being granted."

Malady adjusted and motioned for the flask again. Nicodemus tossed it to her. She took a small swig and continued, "It's a tool to make a deal with the Impious. Simple but effective, and somehow Heresy managed to pay the cost with my mother's soul instead of hers."

"That's . . . dark, even for her," Nicodemus uttered.

The brandy wasn't doing much to keep the tears back, like Malady had hoped. "We must do something." Her words were forced.

"Go to your sisters. Make Fallacy and Entropy understand that they must work with you."

"Suggesting to usurp the Cold Throne is punishable by a millennium in the Pits," Malady said.

"To Hell with the Cold Throne. We both know Heresy will burn it all down, regardless! You must find a way to bring her to kneel!" Nicodemus raised his voice. Like a bass drum and gravel.

"I cannot! She has been my personal tyrant my whole life! This is not who I am!" Malady screamed.

"Then become who you need to be!" Nicodemus roared.

"I can't!"

"Then we succumb to Heresy," the big man uttered, defeated.

The bedchamber was crypt quiet. The patter of rain on the stained glass windows the only clue to the outside world. The world has shifted. Townsfolk would gossip and talk, and the peace that Diana had held for so long would fall to pieces. Everyone knew of Heresy—her temper, her rage.

Nicodemus stood, his back popping in the process. He sighed and fetched his soaked cloak off the floor and walked to the door. He reached for the handle and stopped.

"She will bring this palace to its knees. Not tomorrow. Not overmorrow. But it will burn," Nicodemus whispered and left.

Wiping away tears, Malady watched as her friend and confidant left. She knew he was right. Heresy was wild and unpredictable. Yet cunning enough to somehow sell their mother's soul for control of the empire.

She jumped as another knock came at her door. She hopped to her feet and answered it. In the hall was a maid holding a box. The young girl curtsied as best she could whilst holding the package.

"My lady. Another condolence package has arrived. I know it's late but I figured you were still awake," the maid said.

"Thank you, Wendy." Malady took the heavy box.

"I can carry it in for you, princess."

"Rubbish, my arms aren't broken. Least not yet."

Wendy followed Malady in and watched as she placed the parcel on an oak table near the fireplace.

"My lady, I wanted to say I'm very sorry for your loss," Wendy said, staring at the ground.

Malady smiled and wiped away a tear as she hugged the maid.

"Thank you, Wendy."

"She was always nice to me. And my mother. Such a nice lady."

Malady smiled and squeezed Wendy's hand.

"That's because we love you and your mother," Malady said.

This made Wendy smile. "My lady, would you like me to bring you some honey cakes and some of that fresh sage brie?"

Malady rubbed her eyes but still smiled. "Yes, Wendy, that does sound nice. And maybe a bottle of cherry mead."

Wendy, full of purpose, threw back her shoulders and sought after the task at hand. Before she was out the door, she paused and turned back to Malady.

"My lady . . ."

"Yes?"

Wendy looked down both ends of the hall, not a ghost in sight, and turned back to Malady and continued, "Is the rumor true?"

"What rumor?"

"That your sister will take the throne?"

Malady let out a small sigh. "It seems as such."

Wendy contemplated the news and slowly backed out the door. "Oh my. This is certainly not good."

Malady bit her lip as the door closed. This was too much. She wanted sleep. Maybe tomorrow she would awaken and all this nonsense would be sorted out. Someone will set it all right, and she could go about her days in peace and solitude. But that was unlikely to be the case. Tomorrow she will hear about whispers of Heresy and her plans for the Queendom. The townspeople will talk, and the peace that her mother cultivated for an eon will be lost. How incredibly fragile an empire could be. A sudden change of power. A shift of intentions. Heresy hasn't done anything yet, and the wheels were already turning.

She threw a fresh log onto the fire and then remembered the parcel. It was in poor shape, battered and chipped. It was easy to open and inside was a sealed parchment tube. She fumbled with the container and soon pried the lid off one end. Inside, she found a rolled scroll. She spread the paper across the table and pulled a lit candle near. She gasped. Atop the parchment was a crest. An ancient one that shouldn't be. A heart pierced top to bottom by a sword with an inflamed pommel pointing up. It was the crest of Hellheart.

Ages had passed since word or glance from the bony empire of Hellheart. So long, in fact, the lore of Hellheart had become legend; and legend nothing more than crumbled heaps of something once mighty and formidable. For so long had the spiny spires of Hellheart been dormant that Malady stood dumbfounded. *More things that shouldn't be.* She studied the brittle scroll; the script was of a tongue unknown. She could speak and spell numerous languages, from Elven, Fay, Gnomish, and even some Draconic and Infernal, but even with her learned past, she was lost, *who was left in Hellheart?* And why did it take the death of a goddess for them to make their presence known? Malady reached into the dark of her sleeve as arcane words slipped from her lips. From somewhere else, she pulled forth a few small bones. As she studied the parchment, she cast the remains upon it. She acted out small delicate gestures with her hands as her eyes closed and the evocation continued. The sharp lettering slowly liquified on the parchment as the black ink shifted this way and that across the rough-hewn paper as if looking for something lost. Slowly, the thin liquid found its new home. Malady lifted her eyes as her spell came to an end. Her gaze swept across the new script, and she read:

"The Heart of the world has grown still. Your tears are ours. And in the dark days, our steel is yours."

As the last words escaped her lips, the parchment erupted in a plume of black fire; this was old magic. She watched as the flames of the void vanished. In its place lay a dull, black coffin.

In awe, she brushed her thin fingertips across the lid. It had been hastily constructed from what smelled like Dire Oak. It was simple and anonymous, lacking the ornate and regal dressings befitting one empire's gift to another. It was simple and focused in its purpose. She caressed the black metal latch and then quickly withdrew. Should she open it? What if it wasn't meant for her? There was no name or indication after all. She stared at the oblong box; it was almost three feet long and looked heavy. *Well, it didn't say that it wasn't for her*, she mused as she gingerly flipped the latch.

Carefully, she opened the coffin. Cool air traced across her pale skin, inducing a chill. Inside blood red silks cloaked something. She slid her hand into the folds where a warm pommel found her grasp. Holding her breath, she lifted the gift. As the silks unfurled and fell to the coffin, she was awestruck. The blade was dull black and completely smooth, as if forged from smoke; the pommel felt at home in her hand. She traded it to her left hand and then back to the right. The stiffness in her fingers and wrists melted away, and the more it glided from hand to hand, the lighter the blade became. She had seen many swords in her life but nothing like this. She strode across her bedchamber, spinning with the sword outstretched. It was almost weightless.

A rap at her chamber door made her jump again. She stopped and, without warning, the sword was gone. It merely vanished from her grasp as if she never held it to begin with. As she stepped towards the door, she paused and focused. She could feel the sword somewhere near, as if watching her. *What devilry was this?*

"My lady?"

It was another guard. One of Nicodemus's men.

"Yes. Enter, please."

She stood there glancing from side to side.

"Princess, are you okay?" the guard asked. His hand found his sword.

"Yes. Sorry. What may I do for you?"

"It's your sister, Fallacy. She was seen passing through the Slave Gates along the north wall of the city," he stated.

"No."

"I'm afraid so, my lady. Two guards tried to assist her, but she put them to sleep. She used some sort of spell," the guard said.

Malady felt the sword nearby. The black blade's warm pommel echoed in her palm. The words her mother whispered into her ears stirred in her soul. She was not a fighter like Heresy. She was not a cunning trickster like Fallacy. She was not omniscient like Entropy. She was nobody. But they left her no choice.

"Would you please send a message to Commander Nicodemus?"

The guard snapped to attention, back straight. "Yes, my liege."

"Tell him we ride to find my sister tomorrow."

———

4

Thanks to Those Who Brought the Madness

Malady tossed and turned the whole night. Night terrors and visions haunted her. She witnessed her dear mother being torn asunder by wicked things deep in the Underlife. She cried as she watched the Shadow Keep burn. Its stately towers collapsing. The wails and screams of her people filled the night like a forsaken choir. She awoke gasping. It was early morning, the sun obscured by a deep gray fog. The stained-glass window in her room barely illuminated. She dressed herself; riding trousers and a long-sleeved tunic, knee-high boots, and a simple cloak. An image of the armory flashed through her mind. Would she need armor? What about a weapon? In a flash, the gifted sword from Hellheart was in her hand. Just as suddenly her chamber door swung open, she turned, blade in hand. It was Wendy with a tray for her morning meal. It smelled and looked divine. A rash of bacon, hard-boiled eggs, and thick buttered toast slathered with fig jam.

Wendy beamed a happy smile. "Good morning."

Malady expected a look from the girl; the blade was unusual and imposing, but the maid said nothing.

"Here's your morning break, my princess. Commander Nicodemus said you are wanted in the royal stables, but I told him you're not going anywhere without a proper meal."

Malady stepped closer; sword extended.

"Enjoy, love." She smiled and left.

Then it dawned on her; Wendy couldn't see the sword. As if responding to the thought, the sword vanished. Shocked, Malady stared at her empty hand, still warm from the pommel. Who was in Hellheart and why did they gift such an intriguing thing? More and more questions were piling up with no time to answer them. She reached for her pen and jotted down a quick thought in an open journal on the large table. *Inquire about living weapons.* Despite her curiosity, the matter would have to wait. She crossed her heart, said a prayer for the damned, and ate.

Gloom hung over the Shadow Keep. Malady made her way through the palace. Servants and maids glancing away. Some quickly moved on to other duties elsewhere upon seeing her. In less than a day, the peace was already challenged. She could feel the spirit of the land shifting. She had to hurry. If there was any hope of restoring order and obeying her mother's wishes and saving her very soul, she would have to bring her siblings together and demand a peaceful reign.

The Vanguard was waiting outside the stable.

"My lady," Nicodemus said.

Behind him stood an order of black knights, each standing at attention next to their horses. Her own favorite mare, Haste, was saddled and ready.

"We are only going to find Fallacy and talk some sense into her. Do we need armed knights? I would rather them here seeing to the order of the palace."

Nicodemus held Haste's saddle while Malady climbed atop. "There are scores of sentries here. I only wish for us to return her quickly and safely."

"Great way to skirt around the question." Malady settled into her saddle.

"I learned it from Fallacy. Knights of the Shadow Keep. Mount," Nicodemus ordered.

In unison, the knights mounted and readied themselves.

Adjusting her riding gloves and reins, Malady said, "We head north. I believe I know where Fallacy fled to."

Nicodemus mounted his steed as well. The big man settling into a saddle made for one wearing armor. "And what of Entropy? She left the ceremony in a hurry. None of my soldiers have seen her."

"One sister at a time. We ride north to the Hanging Gardens. She's most certainly ran there to sulk and pout."

The Vanguard departed. A lone priest met them at the Slave Gates; a crumbling wrought iron fortitude from the old days. A point of entry used by servants. There the priest, cloaked and face hidden, said a prayer of protection over the Vanguard. Malady atop her Nightmare, Nicodemus at her side. Six black knights behind.

"Blessed be thy stride and journey. May your path be true and your Darkstar guide you. Go forth to the end times and the end of time with the black flames of Hastur lighting your path," the priest said, pale hands tracing a sacred seal in the air.

"So mote it be," Malady whispered.

The group slipped away, heading north for a hard day's ride. If they were fast, they would be at the Hanging Gardens by late day. The road north, The Queens Way, took the small group through the steep valleys that nestled the Shadow Keep on all sides. A thin cobbled path that twisted and turned like a river through the jagged cliffs and mountains. Malady thought of Fallacy. The second oldest of Diana's brood. Born under the waning gibbous moon of Beltane; a season of passion and mischief. A season of perplexing contradictions and fever dreams as the realm awakens from a fraught hibernation. Fallacy was Diana's second daughter and the first to set Heresy down a wanton path of jealousy. Heresy was all too happy being the only child and the primary princess of the Shadow Keep. The attention and adoration were enough to make any young woman drunk with pride.

The sun was past early evening when the Vanguard arrived. Their steeds breathing heavily but still plenty of fire in their bellies. They crested a low peak and looked out across the Emerald Plateau, a sea of grass from horizon to horizon. A place of simple beauty if not for the island of suspended stone hanging above it. The platform was massive, the biggest gods-made structure the world had ever seen. Titan chains reached skywards, disappearing into the clouds above, suspending the monstrosity above the green ocean.

"I never get used to the sight. Just doesn't sit right with me," Nicodemus said. His horse huffed in agreement.

"I think that's the point," Malady replied.

"The point is, it shouldn't exist. Such a toxic place. Full of bitter regrets. Countless souls suspended, waiting for judgment that never comes."

"And amidst the damned is my sister. Shall we?"

Nicodemus gave a command, and the Shadow Knights led the way down the peak to the green plains below.

"We shall."

The Vanguard galloped across the bright ocean of waving green. Such a sight to behold. A heavy contrast from the Shadow Keep tucked down into the Valley of Shahrazad, a place of perpetual fog. Here the sky was open, and from left to right, all Malady could see were rolling hills of green. It was refreshing until she looked onward and upward to see the rocky suspended platform. It was said to be a gift from the gods. She pondered what gods would consider this place worthy as a gift. Only Hastur knows.

"Might be wise to set up camp here," Malady said.

They stood near the only means of accessing the suspended island, a massive wrought iron stairwell that zig-zagged along the structure's stony side. The knights were busy seeing to the mounts as Nicodemus surveyed the stairwell.

"You think it will take that long to find her?"

"It will take me an hour just to reach the top," Malady said. Looking out towards the sea of green grass.

"*Me*? The whole point of us coming was to protect you."

"And you are doing that well. But my sister is unpredictable on the best of days. I know she will be in dire straits after all the chaos that has ensued. Set up camp and wait for me."

"I don't like this."

"Nor do I. If I'm not back by dawn, you can assume I'm dead." Malady didn't look back. She didn't want her knights or the dear friend, the commander, to see her wipe away her tears.

How long ago did a team of ironworkers set out to build the thousands of steps that allowed travelers to this place? Had the Hanging Gardens always been a place of sadness? A place of unrest? Perhaps it was something else long ago. Maybe as far back as the Age of Plagues or even further back into the mists of time, this place had a better purpose. Otherwise, it seemed like a monumental waste just to remind people the end is always near.

Step after step, Malady traversed. She had been so fixated on not falling she hadn't realized how high she was until a flock of sparrows passed by. The birds startled her as she fell forward onto the stairs. Gasping, she braced herself against the stone cliff and watched as the chaotic swarm of birds make their way by. That's when the view caught her eye. She had been climbing for at least half an hour, enough time to put a meaningful amount of distance between her and the ground, more than she was accustomed to. Slowly, she rose to her feet and held the banister with clenched fists and stared out. The palace of Shadow Keep was certainly tall and provided a scenic view of the valley, but this was beyond anything Malady could have envisioned. Soft clouds floated by, and birds made their way to and fro. If not for the nature of her visit, she may have been far more humbled by the sight of her world. She certainly didn't imagine that the death of her mother would prompt her to see the world from this angle.

She was breathless when she reached the summit. Her legs quivered and ached, and her swollen feet were numb. The thought of having to walk back down made her nauseous. Might be easier just to jump. That's if she had the pleasure of leaving this place. The Hanging Gardens were even bigger up close, and the name certainly served no justice for the sight she had to behold. Everywhere she looked, there were gallows of every sort. Some artisan made, fine woodwork and proper built. Some were dead trees; others, simple stakes rising from the stone below. But every structure shared the same purpose: all were suspending corpses. Malady drew her hood down and pulled her cloak closed. This was too much. Was she shivering from exhaustion or because she was now witness to thousands of dead bodies swaying in the wind? Again, Malady thought of the palace library. Of warm fireplaces and soothing spiced tea.

"I'm getting a new family after this," she muttered.

There was no path, at least from where she was standing. It was almost dusk, so she made her way cutting between and around the gallows on shaky legs. It made sense to head inward, so she made her own path. She tried her best to keep her eyes down; thankfully the bodies were all above her, hanging from their final resting places. The ground was a tapestry of weeds, dead leaves, and dried tree roots. Here and there she could make out posts buried deep in the ground. Pulling her hood around her face, she relied on these to navigate. Quickly she walked, studying the ground, thinking of the biggest slice of mutton pie the palace kitchen could muster. Lots of mustard and a glass—no, a flagon of wine to wash it all down. She weaved to the right, avoiding another hanging post. A foot brushed her arm. Without thought she ran. Her shoulder shuddered, and with a gloved hand, she brushed at it frantically. Wanting no part of the dead on her. Suddenly another post came into view. She stepped left, still running. Another post, she swept right, not daring to look upward. Another one. She sidestepped it and fell. Throwing her hands out, she tried in vain to catch herself, slamming into the cold ground chest first, she quickly fought to turn over, fighting for her breath. Lungs empty, she gasped, clawing at her throat. Tears rolled from her eyes as her body finally cooperated. Like a thirsty hound, she inhaled hard, stars and glitter clouding her view. Struggling to her feet, cloak and hood disheveled, she glanced from side to side. That's when she saw them.

Every way she looked, the hanging dead stared back. Somehow, they were all facing her. Hundreds and more as far as she could see. Dried and angry faces. Bloated and warped gazes. Hollow sockets and bare skulls all staring. She spun in place, unable to look away. Unable to flee. There was no path, no escape, only the hateful gaze of the damned and the forgotten. Backing away, she felt something stiff and dry press against her cloak. She spun, coming face to face with a fresh corpse. Eyes as white as fresh snow. Malady was lost, dumbstruck by the depth she was staring into. Unable to move, frozen in her steps, she stared. Her spine relaxed, and her legs went limp, but she was still suspended. The gaze of the damned had her. A thousand strong peered into her soul. It was warm and hollow. Infinite and tight. She floated as her brain screamed for help. Her soul was being ripped apart. It started in her toes and fingertips. A tingling numbing that sent shocks up her limbs. Her heart missed beats, and her brain boiled. She wanted to scream, to cry out, to fight back, but it was too late.

"Whatever you do, don't look them in the eye," Fallacy said.

Malady crashed to the ground. The pain of soul rendering being replaced with cracking her elbows onto hard stone.

"Calm down," Fallacy said. Coming to a soft landing near Malady.

Wide-eyed and confused, Malady looked up at her sister. Golden dusk setting her flaxen curls ablaze. Her flowing hair framing her angelic face. Silks of blues and greens wrapping her as if the dress had its own motives. Fallacy was always considered the pretty one, and despite the world crumbling around her, Malady couldn't help but be in awe.

"Did you just save me?" Malady whispered.

"Yes. You're an idiot. I expected better from you. Aren't you supposed to be the smart one? Come this way so I might kill you proper," Fallacy said, spinning on her heels and walking away.

Malady shuffled to her feet, knees shaky, brushing her ebony hair away from her face. She was covered in sweat but shivering with cold. Fumbling, she followed, making sure not to look up.

Further inward, the hanging posts and gallows stopped, and a clearing began. Great black and white marble slabs making a massive game board. It looked akin to the board game they played as children. In the center sat a stone table. If there had been chairs, they were long gone. The marble courtyard was huge, but the line of the hanging bodies butted right up to the marble platform as if this could be a safe place even for a moment. Malady dared not look to the edge, but she could feel them looking at her. The sisters approached the table where a modest bag of fruits lay. Near that were two empty bottles of wine, and near that, leaning against the table, was Fallacy's scythe.

Fallacy yawned and turned to face her sister as she leaned against the large stone table.

"How'd you find me?"

Malady glanced towards the scythe and then quickly away. "You were seen leaving through the Slave Gates. So north. There are very few reasons to head north."

Fallacy bit into a ripe plum. "So astute. Maybe I was finally going north to Tyr. See what all the fuss is about."

Malady studied the game board. It was a much larger version of the game board for Destroy, a childhood favorite. A game of deceit. "Too cold for your liking. You're trying to make a statement, not adjourning to an icy wasteland."

"The frost giants are such a bore. Okay. What do you want? Why are you here?" Fallacy crossed her arms.

"I need you to return to the palace and rule the Shadow Keep and the realm with me and our sisters."

Fallacy choked on laughter. "Oh, piss off. What do we know about ruling a civilization?!"

The scythe gleamed in the dying light. Polished Vithium, an unbreakable alloy. Sacred sigils etched along the blade's face and its five-foot-long red handle made from the bone of a behemoth that terrorized the Shadow Keep centuries ago. A dramatic yet foreboding piece of family keepsake. The scythe chose Fallacy around her sixteenth natal day and has been hers ever since.

"Nothing. We know nothing. Which is why we need each other. The realm needs us."

"It's not going to happen. Even Emmy abandoned us. She's probably at that silly crystal cave crying about the end of all things, and don't get me started about Hellish Heresy! She used that damned trinket to do the unthinkable! She traded our mother for power! You don't come back from something like that!" Fallacy screamed. She reached into the bag atop the table and pulled out another bottle of wine. "What would you have me do? Sit in the shadows as you rule? I think not! Or do you wish to put me atop the Cold Throne? I couldn't possibly be queen, no more than you could."

Fallacy opened the bottle and took a long swig.

"So you'll sit atop the Hanging Gardens and watch the realm burn? You won't even try to help your people or your own kin? The first sign of turmoil, you just turn tail and run?! That's childish even for you!" Malady's cold cheeks reddened.

Fallacy placed the bottle on the table and drew closer to her scythe. "Best watch your tone, weakling, lest the gallows find use for you." Fallacy reached for her scythe.

Malady bit her lip and braced to sprint into the gallows, gods be damned, but as she turned on her heels, her right hand suddenly bared weight. It was the black sword.

Fallacy's hand dropped away from her attuned weapon and stared at Malady. "What is that?"

The onyx blade felt good in her hand. Her shoulders dropped, and her pulse slowed. Malady recalled how her maid, Wendy, couldn't see the weapon.

"This?" She held the sword up.

"Yes, you fool. That ridiculous sword. Where'd it come from? You mean to strike me down with it? Not sure Mother would approve of that," Fallacy said.

Despite the edges of exhaustion and collapse surrounding her mind, a spark lit up her thoughts like hellfire. There was no way of leaving the Hanging Gardens without convincing Fallacy to do the right thing. She couldn't force it either. She had to make Fallacy believe it was her own idea, nay, duty to do the right thing. The spark of an idea quickly brightened, revealing a path. It had to work.

Malady bit her lip. "That's incredible. So the arcana was right," she lied.

Fallacy stepped away from her scythe and grabbed the wine. "What is this dribble coming out of your mouth?"

The trap was set. It was time to act. "This sword is magical. It's prophesized that queens and kings are the only beings that can lay eye or hand upon it," Malady continued her lie.

Fallacy drew another mouth full of wine and strode towards her sister, leaving that damnable scythe behind.

"I've never heard of such a weapon. How did it come to you?"

Malady bit her lip, mentally leaping steps ahead. "Hellheart. It arrived last night . . . It's the reason Heresy left . . ."

It was a leap. A bold lie. Shooting an arrow into the abyss. She held her breath.

Fallacy stepped closer. She was now within slaughtering distance of Malady.

"Hellheart is in ruins. Who would have sent this?" Fallacy asked, eyeing the blade.

"It's unknown. Heresy destroyed the scroll before I could read it. She was devil mad and threw it into the fire, declaring the parcel was empty. After she stormed out, I found this sword in its box. It took me all night but I descended to the library and spent hours researching to figure it out. And that's why I'm here. To test you."

This was it. The point of no return. This had to work. Fallacy eyed the sword and took another swig.

"I always knew Heresy was incapable. This all makes sense now! She can still hang out with us; she will just be our servant or maybe my personal boot cleaner!" Fallacy laughed.

Malady exhaled the breath she was holding and unclenched her jaw; it worked. It was working. Just a bit more, and it would be done. The tension lifted as Fallacy ate the lie with a grin. She liked the idea of putting Heresy in her place.

"I agree; she will serve the realm in some suitable capacity," Malady said.

Fallacy took a final swig and tossed the bottle onto the tiles below, shattering it. "Well, you better get to her fast. She's already putting together an army to overthrow us—or at least that's the vicious rumor," Fallacy said, pulling her satchel across her shoulder and grabbing her scythe.

"What? Where? Are you sure of such treason?" Malady fumbled over her words.

Fallacy lifted off the ground, loose straw and dead leaves swirling in a vortex around her.

"She's the dramatic one, remember? She has to find the Unpious and whore herself to them. May I have the sword?" She reached out.

Malady bit her lip. This gesture should solidify her sister's dedication. ". . . fine. Here."

Fallacy grinned as she grabbed the pommel, immediately swinging it in wild arches as she danced in the air. Malady backed away. "And what of Entropy?"

"Damnation if I know. She's probably at that silly cave."

It made sense now. All of her sisters were reacting in their own ways.

"Please. What of Heresy?"

Sword and scythe in hand, Fallacy rose into the darkening skies.

"Go find Emmy. She sees all. I'm going back to the Keep. I have a coronation party to plan! Find our sisters!" Fallacy shouted.

Malady watched as her sister circled above her. There was so much to do. If Fallacy was right, then Entropy would be at the Crystal Reliquary. From the Emerald Plateau, it was almost a hundred leagues. It would mean leaving immediately.

"Oh! And you might want to run! They come alive at night! I'll see you at the party!" Fallacy shouted as she flew away.

Malady glanced around, doing her best to avoid any lingering stares from the dead hanging in their resting places. She looked back to the twilight sky, and her horrible sister was nowhere in sight. The last wisps of daylight etched away. The ancient game board now rested in darkness. Malady spun around in place, looking, searching. For what, she didn't know, but the chills running up her neck and across her scalp said something was there. That is when she noticed the quiet. No chirping of insects, no cawing of birds, and no wind to stir the blanket of dead leaves. It was now crypt quiet as if Gaia herself had turned away from this forsaken place. She was horribly, terrifyingly alone.

Making the creak of rope moving all the louder.

Ropes and chains and old wood shifting. A sour taste crept up her throat, stifling a scream. Shaking, she strained and glared into the night, pitch black in every direction. With a trembling hand, she signed an ancient sigil and uttered a simple spell. In front of her, a soft glowing sprite appeared, giving off a soft white light. The darkness was pushed back long enough for Malady to see the dead shambling towards her. Faltering her concentration, the spell broke, and she was once again alone in the dark. She ran.

———————

5

Bat Out of Hell

At the base of the Hanging Garden, the Vanguard made a simple camp. Sir Dakken Hexling, a knight of the Shadow Keep, made a fire after watering his mount. The other five knights slept as he and Commander Nicodemus watched as sentry. Both men nibbled on dried oxen and sipped cold water from a nearby stream.

"Commander?" Dakken spoke softly.

"Yes?"

"How long do we wait?"

Sir Dakken Hexling was the last knight to be ordained under the rule of Diana. It was a simple ritual. A personal ceremony. Held in the courtyard of the palace. Nicodemus was there, as was Malady and the holy pontiff. Surrounded by busts and statues of knights before him, he swore his life to the Keep and the royal family in this life and the next and the next. He had risked his life when a wild mammoth rampaged through a nearby farm, destroying everything in its path. Sir Dakken charged the beast and slew it with a single arrow between its eyes. For a week, they feasted on the kill.

"We wait till dawn. You know this," Nicodemus said.

Dakken chewed on a strip of ox, staring into the fire.

"What will come of the Shadow Keep? What if the sisters can't come to terms?" Dakken asked.

Nicodemus pulled a pipe from his satchel. "There's the real question you wanted to ask."

"Yes, sir," Dakken said.

"Do you remember the night of your ordination? 'Twasn't that long ago."

"Yes, sir. I do," Dakken said.

"You swore to protect the Shadow Keep, the Royal Family, and all the denizens that make us who we are. Our beliefs and our way of life."

"Yes, sir."

"I took that same oath. Yes, these are uncertain times, but we have a role to play. Now tell me, Hexling, what's bothering you."

Sir Dakken chewed his lip and stared into the fire, not wanting to look his commander in the eye. "I fear what's to come."

Nicodemus lit his pipe. A sweet plum of tobacco smoke swirled upwards, dancing with the haze from the fire. "Then you are doing your job. Yes, the denizens are worried. That's to be expected. But short of Minerva strolling into the throne room, we will be fine. Malady will serve her mother's dying wish."

"Minerva? The late Queen's sister?" Dakken asked.

"Aye. She's thankfully far away . . ."

A body slammed into the soft earth a few feet from the campsite and exploded violently on impact. Both men sprang to their feet, swords and daggers at the ready. Nearby, the other knights scrambled for their armaments.

Another body collided with the ground from on high, dried bone shattering and launching haphazardly, chipping Dakken's leather armor. Two more bodies exploded on impact.

"It's raining dead!" Nicodemus cried. "Quick, take cover!"

The tiny Vanguard, half-dressed and two-thirds asleep, grabbed at hilted swords as they scrambled to take cover under the gargantuan suspended island. Another cadaver landed feet first and disintegrated into bone dust as it collided with the ground. In an instant, the body was reduced to nothing more than a skull on a pile of remains. Nearby, a fleshy and ripe body fell onto the campfire, sending cinder and ash everywhere. Dakken watched, eyes wide, as the body, slowly catching fire, stood. A walking immolation. The engulfed zombie turned, raised its flaming arms, and staggered towards the knights. More corpses were falling, and some were getting up.

"Weapons ready! Hold the phalanx!" Nicodemus cried, pulling his sword.

The Shadow Keep was a hallmark of civil ingenuity. Diana had fashioned the realm into a place of equality and prosperity. In the valley of Shahrazad, every man, woman, and beast was free to do as thou wilt. Every servant was such by their choice. Every stone smith, cobbler, and ditch digger had free will. This was important to Diana. But so was a well-trained military. Despite the rude awakening, the knights were ready. The inflamed undead lunged for the small cluster and was taken down with a clean sword swing. Its flaming head rolling away.

"Remember! The undead least like it when their heads are removed!" Nicodemus shouted.

More poured off the edge of the Hanging Garden. Some moved towards the knights, who made quick work dispatching them.

"For such clear skies, the weather has certainly taken a turn for the worst," Dakken said, driving the end of his sword into the skull of an encroaching corpse.

Nicodemus struck down a zombie, its head leaving its shoulders forever. "We must head up to the summit. Princess Malady is surely in peril! Knights, to the—"

"Commander! Look!" Dakken cut him off, pointing towards the night sky above the fire.

Nicodemus lowered his sword in awe. There in the night, floating like a dream, was Malady slowly drifting downward. Her arms stretched out as if to keep her precarious balance. Nicodemus smiled. "Knights! To your princess!

Acting as one, they flanked and enclosed the fire. A horde of undead was engaging from all sides. Above, Malady was doing her best to maintain control of her slow descent.

"Princess! What would you have of us?!" Nicodemus yelled.

He glanced skyward and could just barely make out Malady mouthing silent words, and then it dawned on him; she was invoking magic. One by one, the knights fought back the falling dead as Malady drifted into the safety of the inner circle. She softly landed on wobbly legs. Stumbling, she fell to the ground.

Sir Dakken ran to her side. The other knights fell in tighter, closing the gap.

She looked like death warmed over. Bloody and bruised, her eyes smoldering with arcane magic. Her lips moved, but her words were too small to hear over the attacking horde. He leaned in and finally heard the words.

———

6

A Road to Nohope

If one were to head westward from the Emerald Plateau early before dawn, one would enjoy the calm and serene landscape till just before high noon. Soon the Plateau would give way to the sharp rocky hills that make up the home of Necropolis. The burial grounds for the times before the Chaos Opus. A time left forgotten and cursed. A time before man. One would find it best to avoid this place. Thick forests and winding trails can make it difficult to navigate.

It's said that after every pregnant moon, the paths and trails change, rendering maps useless. But if one were to figure out the way into the city of the dead, they would likely never be seen again. It would be wise for one to take Razor Back, the northern path, and skip this dreadful place entirely.

That's precisely where Vanguard was riding hard and fast. The dirt road north of Necropolis and west of the Emerald Plateau would lead them to Nohope, a small settlement near the Shrine Sea. A simple place of commerce and good food. If one enjoyed a good chowder and a dark ale after a long day of fishing, then there would be hope for you after all. And near Nohope stands the stronghold of The Crystal Reliquary.

It was past half day when Malady awakened. Her head throbbed, and her hands tingled with shock. The taste of iron tinged her tongue. Thankfully, there were low hanging storm clouds, otherwise, the shining rays of the day would surely wreak havoc on her swollen eyes.

"She wakens," Dakken uttered.

"Princess. We are arriving at Nohope." Nicodemus leveled his horse with Dakkens. Malady had been asleep in his arms.

"What? Why? Where's Haste?"

"Your mount is with us. What do you remember of the Emerald Plateau?" Nicodemus asked.

It was hard to even recall her own birth name at this moment. "Please. My satchel," she said.

Nicodemus guided his horse next to Haste and fetched the Princess's travel bag, and brought it to her. She opened it and waved her hand above the dark opening before reaching into the abyss. Dakken, having a premier view of magic in action, tried his best not to be awestruck, lest his self-control be questioned. From somewhere else, she pulled forth a clump of Burgundy Root, thick and deep in color. She chewed on the plant, and immediately her brain fog began to clear.

"Better?" Nicodemus asked.

"Gods, yes. But I would kill a sister for some strong black tea."

"Soon, my princess. We will be at the reliquary in a short interval."

It was beginning to come back to her. Dealing with Fallacy—convincing, *manipulating* her into joining forces. Then her escape from the plateau . . . running, screaming, bones tearing at her flesh. She felt her limbs, looking for signs of injury. Other than copious scrapes and bruises, she was fine. She had run until her lungs gave out, and that was when she made it to the edge. Below, she could make out the Vanguard's fire, and behind her the dead rushed upon her. With nothing more than the impulse to flee, she jumped; the dead followed. As she fell, she recited a spell from her childhood, and thankfully, it worked.

"My lady," Dakken uttered.

She had forgotten she was sharing a saddle and was jolted back to the present moment.

"Yes, Sir Dakken?"

"Last night, before you passed out, you instructed us to the Crystal Reliquary, post haste. Hence why we are here. I don't mean to undermine you."

It all came back now. The weight of responsibility came crashing down. Her shoulders slumped and her mouth went dry.

"Thank you, Sir Dakken. Sometimes these spells can leave me forgetful. May I go to my mount?"

"Company halt!" Dakken instructed.

The Vanguard did as commanded, and Dakken helped a stiff and sore Malady down from his steed.

Nicodemus, peering through a looking glass, held the reins of the nightmare Haste. Malady shouldered her bag and grabbed the water canteen fixed to her saddle, gulping down the cold liquid in eager mouthfuls. For Malady, it was proof of firmament made flesh. Pure bliss. She splashed what remained on her face and hands, godless grime coming clean.

"What do you see?" she asked, tying back her dirty ebony locks.

"NoHope. We need to ride hard. Only Throng knows what Entropy has in store for us."

Malady mounted Haste. "Nothing, Emmy doesn't believe in violence."

"But does she believe in our cause?"

"She believes in nothing. And everything."

The Vanguard rode fast, Nicodemus taking the lead and Sir Dakken taking the rear. More storm clouds rolled in. Massive gray mountains in the sky, illuminated here and there by lightning, giving life to the infinite forms. The hour was growing late.

———

"This is it?" Asked Dakken.

The Vanguard dismounted at a simple cave opening with a stone wall and heavy iron door closing it off.

"What did you expect?" Nicodemus asked, helping Malady off her steed.

The knights gathered, hands on swords.

"Isn't this a chamber of heirlooms and treasure from the Shadow Keep?"

"'Tis," Malady said. "So discretion is key. No fanfare here. But there are a vast number of magical death traps and lethal pitfalls just beyond that door."

Nicodemus smiled. "So those who do know of it tend to stay away."

"Smart," Dakken said.

Nicodemus ordered the knights to start a fire and tend to the horses. Malady took a moment and stared down into the valley where NoHope rested. On the other side, she could make out the Shrine Sea. Beautiful blues and greens overlapping. Once this was all over, maybe she would put her toes in the waters.

"Sir Dakken?" Nicodemus said.

Dakken stopped his chores and went to his commander.

"Sir?"

"Head into town. Quickly. Go to the council chamber. Tell them to send their reserves to the Shadow Keep."

"Sir . . ." Dakken said.

"I must plan for all contingencies. Even the most dire. If the Keep falls into chaos..."

"Yes, Sir," Dakken said.

He mounted, dawned his helm and rode off.

Nicodemus watched as his knight left. Then, his attention went to the princess.

"Princess. The weather is turning. This needs to be done."

"I'm aware, commander," she snapped.

Nicodemus bit his tongue, bowed and left her to be. She sighed and stretched her neck and walked to the ancient iron door. There was no knob or even hinges. It looked as if an iron slab was held up by a stone wall. She took a deep breath and reached her hand out, touching the door. She could feel its energy ready to strike, but it hesitated, sensing her blood, her spirit. She whispered a long list of sacred words, each actuating hidden levers and locks. Slowly, the door opened. Nicodemus and the remaining knights stopped and watched. Soft blue tinted white light poured from the entrance. It felt clean and infinite and engulfed Malady. The Vanguard had to look away, shielding their eyes, and in an instant, the light was gone. The door was closed, and Malady vanished.

———

7

Echoes of an Echo

The cavern was massive, its ceiling twice as high as the Temple of Set. It stretched out before Malady, easily double the length of the Shadow Keep. Crystal shards the size of beasts of burden jutted out of the cavern walls and ceiling at random angles. Some the size of cottages and all glowing with an angelic hue. This way and that, chests and wooden crates and statues covered with tarps made makeshift paths, mostly leading to nowhere. When the Royal Family stashed the Keep's antiquities here, organization was their last concern. There was a war going on after all, and afterward the family decided to keep the treasures here. So here they sit. Paintings, statues, busts, objects of curiosity. All waiting. Malady meandered through the collection. Peeking into chests and peering under tarps. Most of it meant nothing to her, but some of it she could identify. Under a beige and dusty tarp was a wall sized painting of the infamous Kraken, Gilgoloklok, destroying fishing barges. A decaying chest was filled with silver coins bearing the likeness of Shahrazad. She couldn't help herself; history had always been a fascinating topic. But the reliquary would have to wait.

"Emmy?" Malady said.

She didn't need to shout. The cavern carried her voice. Her thin words echoed deep into the hollow. She went deeper.

"Emmy. I think you're here. I hope you're here."

The path in front split left and right. She went right.

"I need help. I need you."

Nearby, a rack of rose gold swords caught her eye. They looked forge fresh and ready for war.

"You don't need me," came a voice. It was solid and unwavering. The words echoed off themselves and reached every angle of the cavern all at once.

Malady turned left, then right, and then around. Entropy was nowhere.

"You know Mother's last wish," Malady said, tired and defeated as she sat on a nearby iron chest.

"And you know how this will play out which, I assume, is why you're in hiding," she added.

From behind a nearby armoire stepped Entropy. A silken tunic, dark blue. A heavy gray cloak and simple britches cinched with a belt.

"I'm not hiding. I came here for my own purpose," Entropy said. She strolled forward, studying her sister. Those haunting prismatic eyes that Malady has never gotten used to.

"It's a fine time to catalog the family heirlooms," Malady muttered.

"It's unnecessary," Entropy said.

Malady held her head. "I'm joking Emmy, this has been a difficult time, and I'm just trying to do what's right."

Entropy looked out across the cavern. Lights here and there dancing together like moonlight across a rippling pond. It was peaceful here. Such a departure from the chaos outside. The sudden turmoil that had consumed them all. Entropy crossed her arms and stared at the floor as she spoke. "I miss Mother."

The notion stopped Malady in her tracks. This has been such a whirling dervish of events that she forgot they were all supposed to be together mourning. As a family. Tears flooded her eyes, and she ran to hug her sister.

"Emmy, I'm so sorry. I miss her too. I'm so saddened by all of this."

Entropy did not hug her sister back, instead, she simply endured the affection, letting Malady do what she needed to do.

"I know we haven't been the closest as of late, and I'm sorry for that. I feel like I try, I really do, but it's perplexingly difficult to carry on talks with someone who is omniscient." She felt dumb for pointing out the obvious. Entropy had known this her whole life.

"Do you know why I came here?" Entropy asked.

"No."

"It's quiet. Peacefully quiet. This place has been the same for millions of years and will be here for millions more. Far beyond what I can witness. These antiques, these keepsakes, they are all forgotten about. When I look upon them all I see are ashes. I see no strife, no suffering, no chaos, or malice here. It's quiet here."

Malady pondered the confession. Of all her siblings, Entropy was blessed with the grandest ability and at the same time the darkest curse.

"This is a refuge for you, a safe haven the palace cannot be," Malady uttered.

"Indeed. The domain is in such turmoil that everywhere I look, I see nothing but death and destruction. It's truly overwhelming, even maddening. It's all I can do to keep from clawing out my own eyes."

Malady went to a nearby wine cask and tapped on it. It was full.

"Have you seen any mugs?" Malady asked.

"Fantastic idea."

For the first time in a long time, Entropy and Malady conversed. There were no distractions from their duties or siblings or, unfortunately, their mother. They drank wine from the Hellheart vineyard, Bao-khan-ra. Smooth and silky. They talked about the guests at Mother's funeral. So many faces from every domain. They talked of the upcoming solstice and what foods they were looking forward to. Entropy longed for a good mushroom and leek pie, while Malady pined for a spicy pepper stew. In a forgotten pit of the world, they were sisters again.

"I get it now," Malady said.

Entropy sipped her wine. "Get what?"

"Why you came here. This is the first time since Mother fell ill that I've felt like myself."

Entropy stared out past the priceless antiques and up the crystalline walls and ceiling.

"And soon we will argue and fight over what we shall do for the realm."

Malady set her mug aside and observed her sister. "No."

"You want me to rule with you and our sisters. I will agree. I've seen it all. I've even seen what you'll do to Heresy. Morbid but necessary."

"Then why hide? Why fight it?"

"Because somewhere inside, I'm still human, if only a fraction. And the torment I see is truly crushing me. It's more than I can stand," Entropy said, wiping away tears.

"Then help me."

"And how would I do that?"

"Of all of us, you understand the frailty of life the most. You understand how precious and temporary all this is. You can't change the world, but you can change the world for the people we protect," Malady said.

Entropy stood and crossed her arms, biting her lip.

Malady continued, "I believe there's a reason Mother asked for us to protect the lands as one. We each bring a unique perspective to rulership. I know the human side of you gets lost in the chaos and death, but you have the most unique perspective to offer. Everything dies, it's true. We will both perish as well. But that's what makes life special. Because it ends. With what abilities and time we have, we can make our people's lives special. I need your humanity to see that."

Entropy took a few steps, her head hung low, hands clasped behind her back. Malady picked up her mug of dark red wine and saw her reflection looking back. Was this all for naught? The wine grew bitter on her tongue. Enjoying the nectar during a time of upheaval didn't seem right suddenly. She sat her mug aside and rose to her feet.

"I have to go. I still have to track down Heresy." Malady turned to leave.

"That won't be hard." Entropy turned to her sister. "For you, I'll do it. I'll return to the palace and assist Fallacy. I'll see to the order of things. For our people."

Malady hugged her sister.

8
The Chapel at the End

Nohope was a ghost town. Sir Dakken Hexling cantered into the village proper. A fountain in the middle. A statue of the ancient sea wyrm, Cobaal, in the center. He has yet to see another person, despite traversing half the town. Wearily he dismounted.

Forming a broad circle around the fountain were all the normal staples of small-town life. A couple of saloons, a general store, all the facades Dakken would have expected even though he had never been this far west of the Shadow Keep. Beyond Nohope was the Shrine Sea, so here he stood near the edge of the world. He took off his gauntlets and kneeled at the fountain, plunging his sore hands into the frigid spring water.

It was soothing and numbing on his leather hard hands. Splashing his face, he gasped as he washed away a layer of dirt. It felt good, better than his morning cup of bitter root. His mount joined in and took a healthy swig from the fountain. Nohope was known across the lands as a seaport. A hub of commerce between the seas and the domains inland. Yet not a soul was here. Dakken cupped a hand and took a sip from the fountain while eyeing a nearby saloon; the well-made sign on the second floor designated this business as The Lost Dog Saloon. He gripped the pommel of his sword at his hip and walked to the shop front. Cresting the high set front porch, he eyed the boarded up windows. Rubbing a nail hole revealed freshly splintered wood. The wood was still bright and new. This was just done. He tried to peer through the smokey glass, but the inside was pitch black. He glanced across to the business next door, a stationary shop and mail service. Its facade hastefully boarded up as well.

"Won't find yaself a drink in 'er."

Dakken turned. Near the fountain stood a squat, barrel chested man. His back strapped with a large travel trunk.

"Good day, sir," Dakken said.

"Ain't much goo 'bout it," the old man said as he started walking.

Dakken hesitated but finally spoke up. "Sir, I'm looking for the constable of Nohope." He glanced around as he stepped off the porch of the saloon and approached the elder. "Or anyone for that matter."

The old man eyed the bat and crescent moon sigil embossed on the knight's armor. The elder simply raised and pointed a stubby finger to the far horizon. Dakken followed and squinted towards the hazy sea. There on the far side was the island shrine, an old and beautiful monument to the oceans and seas. Even from such a distance, it looked massive and formidable.

"The Shrine of the Seas? What of it?" Dakken asked.

"That's where ye will fin' tha constable," the man said and continued forward.

Dakken, confused, gave chase. "Sir. Excuse me. Is that why Nohope is barren? Are you going there too?"

"Aye, an you would do well to head there."

"Sir, why?" Dakken asked.

The old man turned. "Yer from tha keep! Ye of all should know!"

"No, sir, I do not. We've been on a mission and away from the keep for two days now. Please, sir, the commander of the keep sent me. I require Nohope's infantry reserves and some supplies."

"Then you'll need to board with me. As the constable and Nohopes fightin' men are already at tha shrine. Let's go." He turned and kept walking.

Dakken followed. "Sir? Why?"

"Heresy. She's makin' a move for the Cold Throne. And she's bringing Hell with 'er."

"Heresy? Where is she? What have you heard?"

The old man turned one last time and eyed Dakken. "The Chapel at the End. She's there summoning one of the Impious. Trading 'er own mothers' soul for the wager."

"How do you know this? How can you be certain?"

"Cause she tol tha whole world! She wants ery one ta know! Tomorrow at sunup!"

The old man left. Dakken mounted and stampeded away. Leaving the ghost of Nohope in his wake.

9

A Path Forgotten

"I see Dakken. He approaches." Commander Nicodemus collapsed his spyglass.

"Is he alone?" Malady asked. The knights and the two sisters stood near the fire. It was hastily growing dark, and the cold was setting in.

"Yes."

Entropy studied her sister, those brilliant shifting eyes looking into every aspect of Malady's life. "Mother is proud of you."

The simple words made Malady blush. Her pallid complexion became almost rosy. "That's fine, but I want her to be proud of *us*."

"She is a complicated woman. Sometimes contradictory, sometimes cantankerous and even sometimes unruly, but she's always proud of us."

"Here he comes!" a Shadow Knight shouted as he ran up to greet Dakken.

Dakken dismounted before his steed had time to stop and ran to the small group.

"Commander, my ladies." He bowed his head and tried to look Entropy in the eye but shied away.

"Sir Hexling, I'm so happy for your safe return. Come, warm yourself," Malady said. One of Dakken's fellow knights handed him a bowl of simple stew. He gulped it down.

"Dakken, did you find the constable of Nohope?" Nicodemus inquired.

Dakken swallowed hard and caught his breath. And realized everyone was eyeing him. His shoulders tensed, and he spoke, "No, Commander, the town has been abandoned, boarded up. Its citizens have fled to the Shrine of the Seas for safe haven, including their soldiers."

The small group fell quiet.

"Is there any other news?" Malady asked.

Dakken held his breath. He didn't care for being the center of attention. "Yes."

"Well, tell us." Nicodemus crossed his arms.

Dakken, wide eyed, tried to avoid Malady and Entropy. "It's Heresy. She means to complete the pact with the Impious. Rumors are spreading. They say she seeks the Chapel at the End. There she will complete the ritual she started."

Malady grasped her stomach. Entropy looked through the knight.

"How can you be sure?" Malady asked.

"There was one man left in Nohope. He said Heresy has made her intentions known well and wide. She's at the Chapel at the End, completing the pact."

Nicodemus began to pace.

Malady covered her mouth and tried her best to conceal her tears. Dakken, feeling even more out of place, backed away, feeling much like paying the penance of his message.

Nicodemus paced, chewing his lip. The other knights found things to do elsewhere, gathering wood and tending to the horses. "Entropy. Is this true? Can you tell us?" the commander asked.

"I think you know Heresy well enough. She's rageful, impulsive. This course of action would yield the fastest, albeit, most extreme, results."

"I was really hoping for a different answer," Nicodemus uttered.

"I know," Entropy said.

"The Chapel is two days' ride from the Keep," Dakken uttered.

"She must have fled for it as soon as the funeral ceremony was over," Nicodemus added.

"No." Malady was staring at her Nightmare, Haste.

Nicodemus and Dakken followed her gaze. Entropy sat on a nearby boulder, biting into an apple.

"No. No, this is not an option." Nicodemus crossed his arms once again.

"It's our only option," Malady said.

"Aren't Nightmares fickle about flying?" Dakken asked.

Nearby, the mare's ears perked. She was busy eating grass but looked up at her rider.

"Incredibly. Which is why you shouldn't. Haste has never taken to flying with a rider," Nicodemus said.

"Commander Nicodemus, Sir Dakken Hexling, please see my sister back to the Shadow Keep. Ride all night. You'll make it there before dawn," Malady said, still watching Haste.

Dakken stood quiet. Nicodemus looked to Entropy as if asking for help. Entropy returned the glance in kind and continued eating her apple.

"My princess. Please. Let's return to the Shadow Keep. Surely Heresy will come to her senses and return in a few days. We can put all this behind us." Nicodemus knew that wasn't true.

All three of them turned to look at the Commander. "Ok. I know that's not going to happen. But neither is our getting to the Chapel in time to intervene."

"Commander, I mean no disrespect, but my sister gave you an order," Entropy said.

Nicodemus glanced across the fire and locked eyes with Entropy. "I am sworn to protect this family, and I will not allow Malady to take flight on an untrained mare to one of the most dangerous places in all the lands!"

Malady turned on her heels, locking eyes with the commander. "And you shall do that. Fallacy is already there. Travel with Emmy. Go to the keep and prepare for my arrival . . . and Heresy's."

The commander bit his tongue and stared into Malady's dark sunken eyes. Wet and red with exhaustion. "So mote it be," he muttered. "Sir Dakken, ready the Vanguard." He turned and walked away.

Dakken lingered for a moment, feeling Entropy stare into him. He started to step towards Malady but stopped and bit his lip. Blushing, he finally spoke up. "Good luck my princess."

Malady smiled, and he walked away as well.

"I know this is hard," Entropy said, tossing her apple core to the wilderness.

"It's going to be a lot harder if Heresy comes to the Keep in the morning instead of me."

Emmy smiled, brushed her hands against her britches and stood. "And that's why Mother is proud of you. Not one word for your own safety. Not one word of doubt for the cause."

Malady crossed the fire pit and neared her sister. "What choice do I have? No one else is doing what needs to be done." She wiped her eyes.

"We all have choices. I see them all. Infinite possibilities intertwining and overlapping. But when I look at you . . . I see clearly. This is my curse to bear. And you have yours."

Malady held back. Her body ached. She wanted to scream. But instead she let loose quiet tears.

"Fine. Return to the Keep. With any luck or fortune, maybe Hastur will keep me in the saddle. Did I mention I hate the idea of flying?"

"Don't tell Haste."

Within minutes, the campfire was doused and mounts readied. The knights and commander of the Shadow Keep left, escorting Lady Entropy. They would ride hard from the Crystal Reliquary, past Necropolis, taking the Scribes Road southeast directly into the Shadow Keep. With luck, they will avoid any Grumblemutts or Thin Whips. Both of which are mere nuances unless they stumble across a pack of them.

Malady watched as the Vanguard rode from sight, disappearing into the rocky outter crest of the city of the dead. She was alone. Pulling her cloak tight, she adjusted her hood and tugged at her copper trimmed riding gloves, eyeing Haste. The nightmare stood near, nibbling at a patch of green bitterroot. She and Haste had years of training together. She learned to ride with her at a young age and formed a strong bond from the beginning. The stable master, Dodson, spent months making sure Malady understood how to feel the animal, to understand her. Dodson said that when the time was right, they could try to fly. To let Haste do what she was born to do. To take to the night skies and soar amongst the clouds.

Malady stroked Haste's mane. A mane she's brushed for nary a decade. Haste had a brother, Torrent, a fearsome nightsteed. Torrent took instantly to Heresy. The bawdy and big steed only let Heresy atop him, despite Dodson's attempts to break him. The other two sisters had no interest in equestrian matters. For Fallacy, it was obvious; she could fly. But Entropy simply avoided animals altogether. She said it was because she loved them too much. She went as far as to abstain from eating them as well. But Heresy loved her brash beast of a horse. And as far as Malady could figure, Torrent was the only way Heresy could have made it to the Chapel at the End so quickly.

"What a lovely night—a lovely night for a sprint across the clouds," Malady said.

The thought of flying turned Malady's stomach. Her head spun at the notion of leaving the solid ground below her feet. Haste stopped her grazing, lifted her head and seemed to eye Malady. She knew nightmares were smart, and the more time a person spent with one, the more they shared the ghost of empathy. Was Haste feeling her hesitancy? Malady was never convincing at hiding her feelings, so instead she was used to just hiding herself. But here she was. Leagues from home. Her domain on the verge of chaos and upheaval. The time for flirting with pleasantries was gone. The time to hide herself away was gone.

"My beauty. I need to ask something of you."

Haste lifted her head again and regarded Malady.

"Take me to my sister. Take me to your brother."

The mare looked away and went back to nibbling on the ample green fauna. Malady pinched her eyes shut and turned away, walking a few paces to the extinguished fire pit. She kicked a rock and cursed at the spirits of frost and night.

"Hastur!" she screamed into the dark.

"O' Hastur! O' Lamashtu! O' Lilith and all the Impious! May the ruin of the domains of man fall upon your souls!" She tried to rage, to fight, but her voice cracked and she began to cry. Sitting on a rock near the dead fire, she sobbed into her gloved hands. "This isn't fair!" she screamed at the clouds, which didn't seem to care.

"I swear I will wage a Holy War upon Heresy if she forsakes our mother!" She stood again and began pacing. "We are so close. I just . . . I need you." She looked at Haste.

"Please."

Malady mounted the mare. Soft and ancient words slipping from her lips. Jagged and icy. Above Haste's head she drew a semicircle, thin wisps of light left in her tracks. Her words and motions became more elaborate and detailed. Haste seemed tranced and stood still. Malady finished her incantation as a thin rivulet of blood dripped from her ear. Her head swam as a part of her escaped and powered the magic summoned. She and Haste were now as one. With this intricate magic, she could speak into her mare's soul. *My beautiful girl, take me to Heresy*, she whispered into Haste's mind. The Nightmare gave no hesitation; she knew it was Malady speaking to her.

Malady grabbed the horn of the saddle with one hand and the reins with the other. With fluid grace, the nightmare trotted across the soft hills and away from the Crystal Reliquary, her speed gradually gaining. Malady tried to recall her training and her hours of riding practice, but spells and riding don't align well. Her head was lost in fog, and just staying atop the saddle was a miracle. The mare was at full gallop. Ahead was a Wisp Bog, a swampy, frigid lowland full of foul gasses and mud. It was time. Now or never. Malady wiped away tears and strained to see into the darkness ahead. Gritting her teeth, she once again eased into Haste's mind.

Fly.

The rhythmic jolting of the steady gallop suddenly seized. She gripped the saddle horn as she leaned back. Pinching her eyes shut, she buried her chin into her chest and squeezed her legs around the body of the mare. The cool wind pulled her hood back, her onyx-black hair flowing in the cold night air. Eyes still closed, she noticed the lack of sound. The lack of hoofs smacking hard ground, the sound of the saddle, and reins working against the animal. It was quiet and effortless to sit atop Haste. Slowly she opened her eyes.

It was beautiful. Within moments, the pair were above the clouds. A dark sky full of diamonds glittered before them. It was enough for Malady to put away her fear of heights. This was a rare event and an even more rare sight. This was what the gods saw when they contemplated making man. More tears flew off her cheeks, freezing mid-air and falling to the ground below. Her lips were dry, but she was smiling. She was even laughing. If she survived the night, she would certainly do this again. Her fears melted away with the ease that Haste had over the situation. The nightmare was truly meant for this. But the revelry would have to wait. The excitement of seeing the world from on high would have to wait. It was time to face Heresy.

10
The Chapel at the End

Throughout the Shadow Realm, there were many chapels; churches, many altars, shrines, sanctuaries, oratories, and even a tabernacle. Many places of worship and reverence. Places built by creatures in service of a higher power. Countless deities, gods, and demigods have made a most complex and astonishing pantheon. All made by those seeking to appease their gods. But for all the holy places throughout these rolling hills, jagged mountains, sea-swept beaches, and dark woods, there was one place that served as the opposite. All these places served a specific purpose: to praise, except one. A lone chapel at the end of a lonesome road. A place meant to mock and ridicule. A blasphemous place. The Chapel at the End.

High above the Lim-dul mountain, a lithe figure atop a stunning beast of burden traversed the clouds. *I think I see it. There, in that narrow valley,* Malady whispered into the mind of her nightmare.

Malady pointed into the mist. A small stark building with a steeple, surrounded by blazing braziers. Haste fixed her equine eyes on the forsaken sight and began a gentle descent into the shallow valley. With ease and grace, the nightmare landed as if the beast were just a normal creature. She began nibbling at the sparse and tall grass growing between gray rocks and boulders. Malady slipped off her mount. The separation severed the spell; the link between animal and human broken. A sad pang held in Malady's chest as she watched her mare casually graze.

It was cold here. And the darkness was oppressive. She glanced behind her. The narrow trail headed north towards the Shadow Keep. Turning, she faced south, which led to a dead end and the chapel. And her possible demise. She sighed and adjusted her cloak. The chapel wasn't far. The path would weave here and there, but there was no deviation.

"Stay here, my love. You've done more than enough. Your quest isn't over yet, but this fight is mine alone." Malady brushed Haste's shimmering black mane. The horse nuzzled Malady.

"I just wish I had brought something bigger than my dagger. Not that I want to use any weapon."

Her gloved hand dropped as a weight occupied it out of nowhere. She gasped and grabbed at the pommel suddenly in her hand, not wanting to drop it. It was the blade Fallacy took. The one gifted from the abandoned empire of Hellheart. How was this possible? Not only was the weapon invisible, but it could travel beyond the vale? She felt a tug in her stomach, like seeing a long-lost friend. Had this weapon bonded with her? Maybe it was cursed? Didn't feel cursed. But a good curse never does. So many questions. All that was clear in the present moment was the weapon came to her at the mere thought of it and when she needed it the most.

"Truly stunning . . ." Malady said, holding the sword up, admiring it. "Well, this will come in handy. But I'm sure Fallacy is very mad right now."

Malady kissed her companion. "She will get over it. Stay here Haste. If I don't come back"—a lump formed in her throat—"go free. Fly and live a life far away from here."

Malady gripped her sword and followed the path.

The thin trail threaded through the terrain, tethered together, twining and after some time and traversal, Diana's youngest stumbled upon a clearing, a natural circular area surrounded by steep cliffs. In front of her, a chaotic graveyard of unmarked headstones, all facing random directions. To be buried here was to have been a person of vile reproach. A person unloved and unadmired by all. This was the final resting place of the hated. At the back of the clearing sat the small and simple white church. Such an unassuming building to carry such weight. In front of the church was a witch's pyre. Alive with dancing flames and fire engulfing the piled-up refuse. Embers floated skyward, dancing with tendrils of white smoke.

Malady heard Heresy before she saw her. Spicy laughter floated to her from near the fire. Sharp words—old words. Spellcraft. The words of arcane power. Heresy spun into sight. She was dancing around the fire; her artisan-crafted dress of burgundy silk and lace was shredded to ribbons. Her wavy copper hair was down and dancing with her. Malady ducked behind a gravestone, jumping as something brushed by her. An animated corpse was lugging rotted wood. She watched as the undead servant shambled toward the fire and pushed the wood into the pit. It turned and shambled away, looking for more, obeying one final command. Even in death, there was no peace here.

Here and there, more corpses and skeletons drudged to and fro, busy fulfilling the spell cast upon them. Heresy kicked an empty bottle of wine, it shattered against a headstone. She looked like chaos incarnate. A wild and dangerous creature on the verge of lashing out. That's when it dawned on Malady. She's casting a summoning spell. She wasn't dancing for reverie; she was moving for incantation. This aligned with the rumors Dakken had heard in Nohope. It all made sense now. The Impious were heathens even in the Nine Hells. So cunning and diabolical, the Kings of Hell cast them to The Pit, the deepest place in all the lands of the underlife. So this was her sister's plan. To forsake kith and kin alike because she didn't get what she wanted. Instead of acquiescing and coming to terms, she was asking for ruin. She was demanding vengeance.

Nearby, two zombies ripped open a mausoleum's steel door. The wood of the coffins inside would be used for the fire. She watched as Heresy continued her circling of the large and roaring pit. Close counterclockwise laps, sipping dark wine from an unmarked bottle. Malady crept closer. Staying tucked behind the tombs, she made her way to the freshly opened mausoleum.

Heresy was deep in spell, and Malady knew how distracting that state of mind could be. Spellcraft of any sort required intense concentration and adherence to exacting details. The chances of her sister seeing her were slim, but she treaded lightly. Near the above-ground tomb, she peered in. It must have been a large family; dozens of smashed and desecrated corpses lay strewn across the tomb's dusty marble floor. The soulless slaves drug the coffins out, slowly feeding the fire. When the last one left, Malady ducked into the tomb.

It was hot, dark and musty. The dead smelled of spicy musk, almost sickly sweet. From the tomb, Malady could better see her sister's trance-like dance. She was reaching the spell's zenith. She didn't have long. The exact spell was unknown to her, but she assumed Heresy had been at this for hours; spells of this magnitude were difficult for a reason, lest someone accidentally summon Nyarlathotep himself. She had to act now.

She was no stranger to magic herself. Spending countless hours pouring over the tomes and books in the Royal Library, specifically Necromancy. It was an alluring subject for her, full of taboo and forbidden spells. She studied the strewn corpses. There was one spell that came to mind. It would take time. More time than she had. But she had no other options. Reaching into the dark recesses of the cloak, she pulled out several components. Glancing out the door, she hurried; it was time to take a stand against Heresy.

"That should do it," she said. Finishing the last few passes of emoting sacred symbols with her hands. The bodies that were resting just a short time ago were now letting off a soft green glow as her spell took hold. "But now . . . I need time."

She stepped out of the tomb immediately spotting Heresy. She had stopped her dance of invocation and was now praying in front of the pyre. The fire itself began to blacken. Onyx and purple flames seamlessly transformed from the rich red fire. A chill shot through Malady. Clouds circled the steeple of the lost church. All the zombies and skeletons stopped in their tracks, staring up at the hypnotic flames. It was happening.

A rift slowly tore open above the black flames. Malady fought to not stare into the abyss. The opening inhaled, drawing the dark flame inward, even the swirling clouds above broke formation as the vacuum continued. She drew her hands up in front of her face, shielding her eyes from the chaos but, despite herself, she peeked between two fingers. She wished she hadn't.

Her heart stopped as she glimpsed the dark side of Hell. Nebulous forms created faces and landscapes of torture and terror. A dreamscape of shifting worlds colliding, eating each other, and forming new terrors. A never-ending amalgam of suffering and tears. Each new image made her soul scream and her breath quiver. This was not meant for her. This was not meant for anyone. But here it was, eating her from the inside out. In front of her, Heresy screamed commands foreign to even Malady. It sounded as if she was trying to get the attention of this gargantuan life force. This presence, seeming infinite in all directions and bigger than Malady could fathom, suddenly took notice, heeding the call of her sister. The air stood still, the world holding its breath. Malady, tear-stricken and as pale as a phantom, dropped her hands and walked forward, the ghost sword suddenly in her hand again.

"O'Impious! O'Forsaken of the pit! Heed my summon! I have paid a tithe in soul and spirit! I have fulfilled your wants! Your Desires! Take my own mother and give me my desires! I will have the Shadow Keep and all the realms that serve her! Be it done now, I say! What say you?!" Heresy cried.

Something heard her.

A visage of shifting faces paused on the other side of the rift and came forward. Eyes, so many eyes, all staring. All exquisite in their detail and all dream-like at the same time. Every emotion Malady ever experienced was summoned into the front of her mind. Her soul tried to keep up, but she had never been in the presence of a cosmic being. The spirit beholden was too much. She fell to her knees. Trying to catch herself, she pushed over a fragile headstone. Heresy spun on her heels.

"What are you doing here?!" Heresy screeched.

Malady didn't feel the need to reply even if she could. The being beyond the rift shifted closer, thousands of little burned and blackened arms reached out along the edge of the rift as if trying to hold it open. Heresy spun back to the rift above her. The shifting face of damnation drew closer, eyeing the eldest of Diana's brood. Heresy stepped forward, stretching her arms out and up, stepping into the edges of the witch's pyre, what fabric was left of her delicate dress immolated instantly. Stepping up the burning logs and wood like an infernal stairway, she reached up, seeking to embrace the infinite being, her skin left blackened by the soot of the flames but unmarred, unharmed. The divinity in her blood protecting her from the chaos of the element. Her hair too, unburnt, the flames enveloping her and crowning her head.

Malady shook off a deep chill and stood despite her useless legs. This was all too much. The shifting face of the Impious and her sister's exaltation made her numb. From her tingling scalp to her numb toes. It was over. She tried. No one could deny her that. Wrangling two of her three sisters was a feat in itself. But what of her people? What of those she stood for? Those she sought to protect and provide for? Heresy would bring doom to the realm. Somehow, she managed to stumble forward.

Heresy crested the witch's pyre, the rift within reach. Both arms reaching for the infinite deafening void of another world. From the rift, something slender extended, viscous and slick and dripping with grime and saliva. The appendage slowly lowered and caressed the hands of Heresy, tasting her.

"No," Malady whispered, stumbling closer. "No."

She neared the pyre, looking up to the rift. If Heresy heard her plea, she did not respond. Instead, her arms entangled with the pulsing appendage.

"No," she whispered to herself, lifting the sword and pointing it to the center of the portal. She wiped away tears and gripped the blade with both trembling hands. The sword hummed with a faint vibration. The crownless king on the other side began to lift Heresy with its tentacles. She was laughing and gyrating in the thing's grasp. It looked like spasms of pain and joy, her mind and body unable to decide.

The sword felt hot in her hand. She wanted this to be done or over, or both. Much like the mind meld she experienced with Haste, she felt the tug of thought from the sword. Like it was trying to reach out to her. "Do it . . . please . . ."

With unnatural speed, the blade shot from her hands and impaled itself into the ever-face of the abomination. Malady fell back as the horror on the other side dropped Heresy, tumbling down the fire, her concentration shattered. The creature screamed as the delicate hands holding the rift open receded back to the other world. The portal snapped closed with a deafening clap. Headstones shattered from the sound wave, and some of the nearby zombies exploded. Malady covered her ears as she cried out.

Heresy tumbled off the pyre, her body smoldering and black, passed out.

Malady made it to her knees. The world was spinning, her vision blurry, and all she could hear was her muffled heartbeat, pounding in her chest. She fought to reach into a small pouch tied to her belt and pulled out a tiny silver vial. With quivering hands, she pawed at the stopper until she managed to open it. She poured the black liquid into her mouth and swallowed hard. Almost instantly her symptoms lessened, but she was still very far from anything resembling normal. Nearby she sensed movement, and before she could decipher it, Heresy kicked her in the face.

"Bitch!" Heresy, covered in chaos, stood over her. She grabbed a handful of Malady's black hair and pulled her back to her knees, slapping her across the face.

Malady tried to stand, tried to fight back, but Heresy was mad. Devil mad. Tittering on the threshold of insanity. "How dare you!" She hit her again. "I should have killed you when you were a baby." Another strike. "The audacity to stand between me and the Cold Throne."

A low moan emanated from the crypt Malady was in. Heresy let go of Malady's hair and turned towards the tomb. If not for the potion Malady had taken, she would be dead right now, but the magic was taking hold and she sprang to her feet and ran. Heresy turned back. "Hey! I'm far from done with you! Your corpse will hang from the walls of the palace!"

Malady passed the pyre, weaving between and around headstones, making her way to the chapel. She didn't dare look back; the thought of tripping made her throat constrict. Within a breath, she was at the base of the stairs. Running up, she slammed into the flakey white door of The Chapel at the End. It opened easily. She spun and bolted the lock. Inside a single brazier burned, casting the small one room chapel in dull oily light. Heavy wooden pews scattered throughout the square room, and at the far end stood a meager podium. Behind it a blank and barren wall. There was no holy symbol of effigy. The chapel of nothingness.

Glancing around, Malady realized this may have been a mistake. There was no other door to escape and painfully nowhere to hide. A violent bang on the door made her jump. Heresy was mad. The most enraged Malady had ever seen. Another heavy attack made the door shudder in its frame. Slowly she backed away, drawing her small silver dagger from her belt. Wherever the phantom sword ended up, it seemed to be stuck there because if the weapon had been attuned to her, it seemed to no longer be so. Her panicked urges to summon it failed. Another heavy hit knocked loose a hinge. She neared the back of the building when the explosion happened. A fury of fire and rage destroyed the simple door, sending deadly shards across Malady. The old oak pieces stabbing into her, piercing her flesh, others beating her. The fireball instantly caused the pews to erupt in flames. Malady struggled as she pulled a small plank from her stomach. She heaved; black bile poured from her throat, burning the roof of her mouth. Bloody tears streamed from her bruised eyes. Her head was spinning. She could tell her collarbone and left shoulder were shattered. The pain was almost too much. The previous potion, while lifesaving, had already worn off. With a trembling and strained hand, she reached into the folds of her cloak and pulled forth a small skull. She began chanting in a strange tongue as she crumbled it into dust; it gave little resistance, quickly becoming a fine powder. She needed to buy just a bit more time. The Chapel was now open as Heresy stepped in.

In the realms of magic, there are many ways to gain an edge. But this method was more akin to the illicit drugs and compounds made in secret and in shadows behind closed doors by bards, alchemists, and assassins alike. In this moment, Malady needed might. Without hesitation, she dropped her face into the handful of powder, inhaling hard. The enchanted drug crashed through her blood as she breathed in; her heart began to hammer. Whatever blinding pain that had her on the verge of passing out suddenly flickered away. Her soul clung to her spine as her brain exploded; she was filled with Hellfire. The dark fuel coursing through her body, the only thing keeping her up right. Knife in hand, she gritted her teeth and lunged at her sister.

Heresy blocked the jab and punched her sister in the jaw. Knuckle to bone that should have knocked out Malady. Instead, she slapped Heresy with her free hand.

"You little twit!" Heresy shouted, seeming more shocked than hurt.

Malady swung the dagger back around and shoved it into Hersey's arm. Both sisters, stunned, stared at each other. The flames of the burning chapel grew.

Malady let go of the dagger and backed away. Heresy grabbed the handle and pulled it out as she bellowed in pain. She threw the blade, and it landed in Malady's thigh, all the way to the hilt. She fell, screaming.

Heresy shambled forward as Malady struggled to pull the dagger out. The tip was in her bone. Every touch made the blade thrum inside her, and she vomited from the pain. Heresy leaned over and withdrew the weapon in a single yank.

The pain was too much, and Heresy was far from gentle, opening the wound more as she pulled it free. The flames were touching the wood and thatch roof. The whole place was going to Hell in mere minutes. Heresy stooped and pressed the dagger into Malady's other leg, giving matching wounds as Malady attempted in vain to slap her again. The magic she had ingested was already wearing off. She knew she would be dead soon. Her eyes fluttered as she fought to stay awake, her limbs going numb.

"All you had to do was go hide. None of this involved you. Stay in the Royal Library. Get fat off the cheese stores. Stay drunk off all the red you can pour down your gullet." She jerked the dagger free then plunged it into her stomach. Malady shuddered, too weak to fight back. "But you chose this path. This is all on you. Good riddance," Heresy hissed, bringing the knife up to Malady's neck.

From the door came a deep guttural growl. Heresy wiped around, knife at the ready, but stood, shocked, staring at the creature stooping to fit into the chapel.

"A golem," she whispered.

The golem was a ghastly sight. Bit and pieces of corpses both new and old held together by the blackest of magics. It towered high in the chapel, and although its pieces were never meant to be joined as they were, it still seemed as solid as anything natural. It cried an infant's wail and stretched a number of limbs out; newly appointed joints and unions getting accustomed.

"When did you have the time to summon this?! Really?! This is your champion? This is how you will save the Queendom? This is how you will reconcile your sweet sisters?! And to believe Mother would have you rule as my equal? I would have it all burn with Hellfire before I let you or anyone else take the Cold Throne," Heresy said.

The giant crypt golem shifted its weight from one foot to the other. What could be considered its face glanced around the burning chapel. All the while keeping eyes on Malady.

Her spell worked. Praise be to Bacchus. Malady struggled to open her eyes, her life force pumping out of her body from more places than she could count. But she managed to catch a glimpse; her incantation held. There was one potion left in her pouch. If she could get to it, she might just beat death this night. She rolled to her side and fumbled with her small satchel; her sister too distracted to notice. Malady pawed at the bottle and drank it quickly. Instantly she was alert, her wounds clotting. She hobbled to her feet.

"Why?" Malady asked.

Heresy spun and faced Malady, her back to the monstrosity.

"Why must you choose this path? All Mother wanted was for us to cherish each other. To share our talents, help each other, and with all our hands, protect this sacred realm," Malady asked.

"Because it's mine. It's all mine! What could you idiots bring to rulership? The three of you couldn't even decide on a cake for Samhain! So, I'm taking what's rightfully mine by birth!"

Malady studied the crypt golem behind Heresy. Entropy was right. Morbid but necessary.

Heresy followed her sister's gaze and turned back to the golem.

"And as for this monstrosity. You can't kill me. At least if you're following Mother's precious rules. What? You gonna beat me into submission with this thing?"

"I would never kill, but . . ." Malady trailed off. Heresy turned back to Malady.

"Please forgive me," Malady whispered.

Her sister's glowing eyes widened with sudden realization. The crypt golem took her head in its fleshy grip and twisted. With little effort, the magical creature pulled Heresy's head from her body. In wild spasms, her limbs flailed and whipped in all directions. With its free hand, the golem grasped her body to steady it as it pulled. Heresy's mouth tried to scream, but she never would again. Like opening a bottle, the golem easily twisted her head and pulled, her spinal cord followed. There was no time to be repulsed by the sight of her actions, nor could she mourn, there would be time for that later. She could feel the fuzz of unconsciousness approaching. She needed to act quickly if she was to fulfill her mother's dying request.

Sacred words slipped from Malady's lips, commanding the crypt golem. The chest of the abomination split in the middle and opened. Ribs and bones cracking at hinge points, revealing an empty cavity. The spell worked. It actually worked. If the stakes were not so dire, Malady may have even been proud of her accomplishments. Inside the chest of the magic made monster was a glass canister filled with green liquid, oily and thick. Carefully the golem eased the detached head and spine into the phylactery. The liquid brightened and gently bubbled as the head found its new forever home. Smoothly the creature's rib cage shut. Its flesh scaling at the scams.

Malady fell to her knees and passed out.

11
So Mote it Be

"Oy. Yer shift is done." A tall guard spoke to a short guard atop the south gates. A small point of entry for the Shadow Keep from the mountains to the south. The guards out here don't see much or keep anyone or anything from entering the valley of Shahrazad because there isn't anything out this way to keep out. Due west from the gates was Hellheart, a day's ride away. But no one was coming or going from that dreadful place. To the south was the Lim-dul mountains and The Chapel at the End. Another place no sane person would travel to. But this was still a point of entry to the Shadow Keep and thus needed to be guarded by some very bored guards.

"Fine. I could use an ale. Is there any bacon left?" The short guard was referring to the small living quarters built into the stone building of the gate house.

"Aye. Eat up. Any action last night?" the tall guard asked.

"What the Hells you think?" the short guard said.

Both men looked equal parts tired and dreadfully bored.

"I thought there might have been something, what with the rumors going around about the daughters fightin' n' fussin'," the tall guard said.

"Weren't nothing lest you woulda heard me sound tha horn. I'm going down ta drink, eat, and sleep." The short guard took his leave. Leaving the other guard atop the watchtower. Dawn's rays were waking up the chilled forest surrounding the gatehouse.

Inside the small space were a couple cots, a potbelly stove, and a table covered with dried goods. The guard grabbed a rash of bacon off the stove and took a bite as he filled a flagon from a small wooden keg. The bacon was salty and the beer was good. But before he could make his way to the cot, the horn blew.

"What in blue Hells!" The short guard dropped his flagon, grabbed his bow, and ran.

The horn sounded again as the guard made his way up the circular stony staircase to the top of the watchtower. "Stop that racket! I'm the only one around to hear it, and I damn well heard it!"

The tall guard dropped the horn and pointed down the southern path. "Golem!" he shouted.

The short guard turned and strained to see through the early morning mist. In the distance, far down the winding path, a slow figure shambled into view. It was massive and lumbering. "Sweet Lucifuge that *is* a golem!"

"That's what I said!"

"Light the beacon!"

Both guards fumbled to light the beacon brazier atop the watchtower.

"Should I blow the horn more?" asked the tall guard.

"No! You wanna piss it off?" said the short one, lighting the oil soaked kindling. The flames quickly engulfed the wood and lint, spewing out a steady cloud of black smoke.

Both men watched as the signal smoke rose.

"What do we do now?" asked the tall guard.

"Don't be a fool, nock an arrow! We ready for battle!"

The enthusiasm was lost on the tall guard. "Battle? Yer a retired farmer and imma tailor. They put us out here because we don't know how to battle."

"To Hell with ye then. I'll defend the Keep!"

"Hey!" a voice called.

Both men stopped and stared at each other.

"Did ye hear that?" tall asked the short.

"Aye."

"Guards!" The voice called again.

Both men turned and looked out to the southern path. The golem had stopped, and now there was a small figure in front of it waving its arms.

"Hells bells! It has a captive!" the short guard said. "I didn't know they did that!"

"What do you know of golems?!" the tall guard shouted.

A horn sounded faintly in the distance. They both turned northward to where the next watchtower lay. A thin plume of smoke rose on the horizon. Help was coming.

The guards turned back to the southern trail. The waving captive was closer to the closed gates now, the golem following.

"We are coming! Fear not! We will banish that creature to Hell!" he said, running for the stairwell.

"We will?" asked the tall guard, reluctantly he followed.

Both guards ran the length of the stairs and met the captive at the gate.

"You poor thing!" the short guard shouted.

The girl was an abysmal sight. Covered in dried gore, black bile, and bruised with wounds and injuries.

"How are you alive?" the tall guard asked, slack jawed.

"Magic. Please! Extinguish the beacon! There's no need for it!" Malady pleaded.

"Sweet Lucifuge it's Princess Malady!" the other guard shouted.

The short one staggered back and quickly took off his helmet to bow, dropping it.

"Please! Open the gate! I need to reach the Keep!"

Confused, the tall guard eyed the golem now closing the gap between it and the gate.

"But, my lady! Watch out! The monster is upon you, run!" The short guard nocked an arrow and tried to draw the bow. His hands shook, and the arrow fell to the ground.

"You tit! I'll slay the beast!" the tall guard shouted, running to the nearby iron door, adjacent to the gates proper.

"No! She's with me!" Malady yelled.

The tall guard exited the door, sword drawn, running to the golem, who towered over the tailor. "She?!" he cried. The tall guard knew he was no match the closer he got. The thing was massive and heavy looking. A mess of limbs and legs and more heads than he was comfortable with.

"Yes! Do not harm her!" Malady threw herself between the guard and the golem.

The tall guard lowered his sword. It was better this way. The guards had only attacked straw stuffed dummies, and they rarely fought back. But this ten-foot-tall abomination would most certainly fight back. And win. Instead, he put his attention on Malady.

"My Lady. Are you in peril? Please stay away from that thing," he pleaded.

The golem seemed to take offense and grumbled from a few mouths.

"What's your name, noble guard of the south?"

"Me? I'm Watson, my lady. At your service," he said, eyeing the golem. "And that's Roddy." He shot a thumb behind him, not looking away from the golem.

"Watson. Roddy. Thank you for your service to the Shadow Keep. This will sound absurd, but I need passage to the Keep for myself and" —she glanced over her shoulder—"my new bodyguard."

"My lady, are you sure that thing can be trusted?"

"Yes, I am in complete control of her."

Every once in a great while, the steady cascade of gray and white clouds that hang over the valley of Shahrazad will find purpose elsewhere and gently float away, letting the sun drench the Shadow Keep. This early morning was such a day. The word spread easily across the land of the sisters reconciling. Fallacy spoke to any and all about her brave sister Malady and her quest to best Heresy. The Shadow Keep was abuzz with celebration spirit. Town folks and dignitaries alike had taken to the streets and allies decorating for the feast at midnight. The reverie so thick that even the sight of a crypt golem lumbering down the streets with Malady perched atop its shoulders did little to sway the mood. Although the sight certainly raised questions.

"Malady . . . would you please explain?" Nicodemus stood in the grand hall of the palace. Fresh tunic and britches and freshly shaven. His normal plate mail was absent, and instead, he was clad in respectable leather armor emblazoned with the Shadow Keep's crest. An indication that the need for drastic measures had come to an end. This made Malady happy. She also stood in the grand hall, bustling maids and servants preparing for the coronation and the feast to follow but giving a wide berth around the golem.

"She did what she had to do," Entropy said. Strolling up to the conversation. Her thistledown dress seemed to float around her body, somehow modest and provocative at the same time. A dream of a green dress caressing her.

"Lady Entropy." Nicodemus bowed. "I'm sure she did. I suppose there will be time enough for explanations."

"Emmy, you look gorgeous." Malady looked down at her war-torn body. Between her and the golem, she was sure they made quite the visage.

"Hells bells, you look like shit!" Fallacy yelled as she floated down from a high set balcony, joining the fray in the massive grand hall. She too was of proper attire, an elegant bodice and voluminous silhouettes of sheer silk dancing about her.

They were all together now.

"I'm afraid I need a proper bath and a change of clothes," Malady said as Fallacy landed near Nicodemus.

"Lady Fallacy," Commander Nicodemus said. "Ladies, if you'll excuse me, I need to attend to the planning of tonight's coronation." He gave Malady a slight smile and left.

"A bath? You need a preacher!" Fallacy quipped. Even Entropy laughed.

Fallacy eyed the massive golem. The hulking creature stood there with an intimidating presence. Some ten foot tall and almost as wide. The spell Malady set forth was complete now. A potent display of what the end results of necromancy and being pushed too far can create. Fallacy edged closer, leaning towards Malady, and whispered, "Is Heresy really in there?"

The reverie had been a welcome distraction to the dark truths Malady had made whole a matter of hours ago. But the question hit her in the heart. "Yes. Some of her. She will outlive all of us as long as the magic holds. I don't know if she can hear or see us. But she's here."

Emmy leaned a little closer and whispered, "By any means necessary," and walked away.

The words felt like an explosion. Malady, stunned, watched Entropy leave.

"Malady? Are you ok?" Fallacy asked, also watching Emmy leave.

"No. And I may never be again."

The coronation was held on a hastily constructed stage near the statue of Helen. Once again, the royalty of the realm gathered with all the townsfolk far and wide. Incense and candles filled every ledge and window once more. Wine and mead poured. The threat of Heresy was over. The turmoil of uncertainty halted. The realm would continue to know peace.

After the coronation, Fallacy declared the midnight feast official, and they danced.

Fallacy, wine in hand, danced with every boy from here to Tyr, leaving each one wanting more. She stopped to nibble on a cherry when she saw Malady sitting alone, sipping mead, and picking at a plate of fresh cheese. "I won't judge you for what you did. But I will wonder how you did it. Heresy was so full of rage it was only a matter of time till it would be her undoing. Creatures like her don't last long. But I will miss her," Fallacy said, leaning against the table Malady sat at.

Malady stared at the happy people roaming the streets, celebrating the night. Celebrating their new queens.

"I need to know it was worth it," Malady said.

"Look around you. You think Heresy would have allowed such merriment? Such reverie? I loved her and still do, but let's be truthful with ourselves, she needed to be dealt with."

"Did you come over here to cheer me up?"

"No. Because I don't need to. You're a queen now, and so am I. Do what thou wilt is the whole of the law. But please don't kill me next. I will actually work with you," Fallacy said.

"That's rude even for you," Malady said, standing.

"Relax. I'm joking. You're Queen for a few hours and you're already stuck up just like mother. I wanted to tell you, a scroll came for you. No one can decipher who it's from. I thought you'd enjoy a challenge tonight. I, on the other hand, will find a cute boy to occupy my night." Fallacy smiled and danced away.

The night carried on. And slowly people retired to their homes. This included Malady, who eventually sought the comforts of her chambers. Sir Dakken escorted her. He opened her door as she entered. "Sir Dakken, thank you for everything you've done for this house. Please go enjoy the rest of the night."

"Would you like me to stoke a fire for you?"

"Hells bells, no. You've done more than enough. Far beyond the call of duty."

"It's my honor, Your Grace."

Malady took off her cloak and tossed it upon her bed. "That will take getting used to."

"It suits you."

"You're too kind, Sir Dakken." Malady smiled but suddenly noticed the scroll upon her table. She approached and rolled it from side to side. It was the scroll Fallacy had mentioned.

"What is it, Your Grace?"

"I'm unsure. But let's find out."

Sir Dakken, interest peaked, stepped further into Malady's chambers as she lit the silver candelabra atop her small table.

Malady crafted a familiar spell as Dakken Hexling watched in awe. After a few gestures, the sharp letters and piercing tapestry on the scroll turned to liquid and reformed the same words anew. Both the new queen and her loyal knight read the new words.

The mouths of the cosmos once again open.

They hunger for our end.

Send help.

Hellheart.

Both the Queen and knight stared at the parchment. Slowly the letters faded and returned to their native tongue. Dakken broke the long silence first.

"Can this be real? Maybe a hoax?" he asked.

Malady walked the room, contemplating the weight of the words. "It matters not. Such a message shouldn't go unheeded."

"Then we shall investigate," Dakken said.

Malady stopped in her tracks. Suddenly she was beside her dying mother once again. Listening to the frail words she whispered into her ear. She turned to Dakken.

"By any means necessary."

AFTERWORD

I love to write. You are holding evidence of that declaration right now.

My first book was The Warriors of Time. A heart stopping eleven-page fantasy/adventure with zero narrative structure, pointless characters, and no coherent ending. I was nine when I wrote it. A couple years later, I tried my hand at the world of superheroes with the thrilling first appearance of The Terror. I'm forlorn to admit his crime fighting adventures only lasted a few pages.

Fast forward to high school. I discovered screenplays and screenwriting. This was still the dark ages of the pre-internet world. Before endless resources and nifty screenwriting software. So instead, I filled a spiral notebook with a crude facsimile. My script was called Bathory. Based on the titular character, Elizabeth Bathory. My take of the blood countess involved a modern-day reincarnation with plenty of shenanigans. I still have that spiral notebook, right next to the only copy of The Warriors of Time.

Early adulthood found me surrounded by creative types, thanks to my brief career as a special effects makeup artist. This period provided huge artistic growth for which I will be forever grateful. During this time, I co-wrote a script with a friend, Sacrilecious. An odd comedy through space and time. This time we had a computer but no screenwriting software. I still have the only copy of Sacrilecious. Around this time, I helped a good friend develop a script idea into a feature length film. By the grace of the gods, we managed to get the movie made. A mockumentary about vampires called Night Life. And yes, it predates a certain movie and TV with very similar themes, but that's a conversation for another time.

Despite all this and much more, I never considered myself a writer. Sure, I was an active artist and working within the confines of storytelling, but the idea of being an actual writer would not hit me until I was 30.

I had the idea for an hour-long drama TV series called Magician Syndrome. I quickly fell in love with it. Down and out characters with lots of flaws living on the fringe of society. People so interesting and complicated that the audience forgets the characters have lethal special powers. I ended up writing a 10-part season one, complete with lots of intrigue and subplots. I even had a computer and screenwriting software this time around. I even came up with the perfect logline: magic is real and it's a deadly disease.

Despite the insane amount of research and development I invested and all the love I held for the project, I eventually had to come back to reality: I am a nobody. There wasn't a snow cone's chance in Hell that this thing would ever get made. My mild success in film didn't garner any connections that could benefit Magician Syndrome. No matter my conviction, this project was dead in the water. So I moved on. Life happened, and I continued forward. I would poke at the project sometimes. Working on scenes and dialog. Having conversations with the characters in my head. Wishing and hoping for more.

One day I was commiserating with a good friend. Discussing the misery of acquiescing, when he made a suggestion: Why not make Magician Syndrome a book? This simple idea changed me. In an instant, my excitement was rekindled and bursting at the seams. This was the exact prospect I needed. It was so obvious it was invisible. Such a simple thought awoke something in me. I was a writer. Not just an artist helping others create their visions. I could make my own and actually put them out into the world. I had been writing for decades, but I wasn't a writer until that day.

My creative floodgates were open.

So many ideas I had envisioned for the small and big screen alike could now live on in narrative form. So I started writing. I started reading, and I started learning everything I could about the craft of writing. And I loved it. I bought tons of books across many genres. And I wrote. I would challenge myself as a means of development. Once I challenged myself to write about a deaf character; Don't Tell the Snow was born. One time I decided an entire conversation around a single conversation. From that came A Carol After Midnight.

Not everything in this book was a writing exercise, but everything here is a product of that faithful conversation and finally realizing what I was.

The story you are about to read was left for dead on the editing room floor. It comes from my novel, Magician Syndrome. In the book, a character named PJ writes a book. Super meta, I know. Too meta, actually. After years of editing and beta reads, I realized the book within a book idea wasn't working. It was too much of a departure from the main narrative. It was meant to be a visceral example of how powerful another character was. Maybe a better writer could have pulled it off, but I couldn't quite get there. I wanted PJ to experience extreme isolation in the form of decades in the same space. An experience so real that the perceived decades passing seemed authentic when, in fact, only a few minutes had passed in the actual story. The scene still exists, but the display of power changed. But I loved the little story within a story, I decided to share it with you.

So I'm very proud to introduce Far Beyond the Fall. I'm proud and honored to share all these with you. There will be more. But for now, I will close this book and add it to my shelf.

Bonus Story: Far Beyond the Fall

J ordi walked along the sunken railroad, one foot in front of the other. He hadn't bothered to stop and rest since escaping from Metacity. He was past running on fumes or even a second wind, for that matter. He would go down soon and not get back up. His feet were cold and numb from what seemed like days of walking along the barely submerged train tracks. It was the wet season, and there was nothing but still water from horizon to horizon. Not even a hill or little mountain in the far off to break up the endless, still ocean. This flat land would normally be lush and grassy plains rolling on forever, but now the high tides owned it all. His mother (or maybe someone else; his head was foggy) had told him it was bad luck to look over his shoulder if he was trying to get away from somewhere or something. A lifetime ago he would have laughed off such superstition, but nowadays things were different. After Metacity, everything was different. He reckoned that if he had looked over his shoulder, there would be nothing but more still, mirror-like water, with Metacity out of sight.

His palms brushed against the sandalwood grips of his twin revolvers bouncing softly at his hips, his hands dry and chalky, completely opposite of his waterlogged and swollen feet. Dried blood still caked on the front of his ragged button-down traveler's shirt. Only some of it was his. He reached into the knapsack slung across his shoulder as he walked, pulling out an old, dented canteen. His stride faltered as he tried to unscrew the top with trembling hands. Slowly he managed to open the container as the chained top dropped to the side. He brought the container to his lips but tasted nothing; it was completely empty. Unfazed either from exhaustion or shock, he recapped the canteen and put it back in his knapsack. He kept walking.

Hours passed.

Jordi's knees were on fire; every step exploded a deep throb of pain in his hips. The blue water across the tracks was only a few inches deep, but between that and blurred, battered eyes, he didn't notice the raised rail spike. The toe of his boot caught the spike, and he fell hard to his knees. A shot of pain coursed through his legs and up his spine to his skull. He shifted forward as he threw his hands down to catch himself. The thick blue water splashed and lapped around his hands. The fall sent round ripples across the still glass of the water's surface. Jordie couldn't help but let out a deep howl. He quickly pulled his hands out of the water and shook them hard; the heavy salt was burning all the fresh cuts and scrapes on his hands and upper arms. His hands ached; he brushed them on his stained shirt. The liquid woke up the dried blood and made it glisten once again. Slowly he made it to his feet, holding the slick train track for leverage. He was done for. His swollen and dry tongue could barely fit inside his mouth anymore; he was starting to shut down. But despite it all, his feet kept moving. One foot after the other.

Would it have been worth it to take his chances in Metacity? They say hindsight is 20/20, and at this point they would be right. He was too far down the tracks to turn back and take his chances with the refugees, the mutants, or even the Council. Metacity was done with him. Too many old ghosts and demons to ever be normal there again. So down the tracks he went. One foot after another.

Overhead the sun was a few hours from setting; night would follow, and he knew that if he didn't find shelter the Water Razors would be enjoying a midnight snack tonight. They were quick and deadly, but for the time being, he was grateful that they only came out at night. It had been well over an hour since he took his stumble, and now, he walked with his eyes closed. He no longer had control over most of his body; his legs were in auto mode as his head fought against falling asleep. A slight cool breeze across his sun-reddened face caused him to momentarily open an eye, and that's when he saw it. Far down the track he saw the twinkle of something waiting. He rubbed his eyes and squinted. Was his head finally given in and seeing things he wanted to see? Without a single pause in his stride, he pulled his knapsack up to his chest and withdrew a small looking glass; it was old and fragile looking and in need of a good cleaning. With both hands, he extended the apparatus. Jordi held the small end up to his right eye and peered through it. If this was his head playing a trick, it was a damn solid one. The eyepiece showed him the source of the shimmer, and he supposed it would make sense that he would run into one eventually. He saw a massive structure. A train station.

He ran the last mile. The sun was finally setting, and he could hear the hum of the Water Razors in the distance. It was breakfast time, and anything that hadn't managed to find dry land was sure to meet them. Dusk was darkening as the whole building came into focus. It was built with the wet season in mind and appeared like a floating fortress in the middle of nowhere. Panting hard, he sprinted towards the master staircase along the right side of the complex. Which meant he had to get off the railroad track that had kept the salt-heavy water at bay and only about ankle deep.   From a sprint, he threw himself off the tracks and towards the entrance that was still about four hundred paces away. He splashed hard into the still water; it was deeper than it looked, coming up to his chest. Any time he had gained with speed he now lost. The master stairwell faced east, opposite the setting sun. In the depths of the horizon's darkness, Jordi could see the water was starting to foam. The Razors were awakening. He lurched against the water, half hopping, half trotting, the hundreds of cuts, scrapes, and fresh wounds across his body sang in unison in a song of pain. The agony made him move faster, and any tiredness he was feeling vanished. Under his feet he suddenly felt the smooth, hard surface of a sidewalk; this would help, it gave his feet courage to move faster. The bubbling foam in the distance was getting closer and more furious, like boiling water left unattended. Two winged maidens crowned the marble staircase, one on either side, their outstretched fingertips nearly touching above the ascent. Their eyes locked together forever. He was two hundred feet away. Surely there was a story or some forgotten folklore that at one time gave purpose and cause to the statues. But there was no one left who could share the tale. Another pointless relic from a time no one would ever ask about.

Stumbling forward, his footing discovered the bitter end of the sidewalk. He fell hard; his whole body dunked into the thick water. Grabbing wildly, he frantically continued forward at all costs. On his hands and knees, he fumbled down what would have been a grassy knoll in the dry season, the loose dirt and dead grass gave little friction for his efforts. Somewhere near, the sound of the water breaking gave an echo across the flatness, the first sound he had heard other than his own heartbeat in hours. He glanced over his shoulder, still fighting to get to his feet, only to see a low quake of foam heading his way. He was sixty feet from the grand stairway when he finally gained footing on the cement path that led up to the station. He sprinted. The stairs were partially submerged, something that may have occurred to him in less frantic situations, and he once again tripped and fell as his foot caught the first step. His palms and knees hit the edges of the underwater steps. Clawing and kicking, he crawled up the massive steps. The frothy chaos was close enough that he could feel the ripples from the hundreds of predators under the water, despite his own wave making. He grabbed the handrail, using it to steady his climb. His feet found the rhythm to the underwater steps. The smooth marble became easier to navigate as he began to finally rise out of the water; his right foot landed on the first dry step as his left exploded with white hot pain. Screaming, he yanked his foot out of the water and hobbled up a few more steps away from the things trying to eat him. His foot felt worse than it looked—the salt dense water merely helped amplify things. Just a few steps downward, hundreds of thin silver snakes thrashed wildly in the blood he had left in the water. They were looking for something that, as far as they were concerned, had suddenly disappeared. Jordi watched as he caught his breath. These little things with only one narrow purpose had no idea of the world above water. His existence and theirs would always be separate, worlds apart.

He hobbled up the stairs, holding fast to the handrail. The image of losing his footing and tumbling back into the water wasn't a pleasant one. It was full black by the time he reached the top. So black he couldn't see where the water met the stairs below him. Somewhere in the darkness he could still hear the water razors looking for him; they still had a taste for his blood. The building in front of him was nothing short of massive. Its size could rival most of the giant, sprawling complexes back in Metacity, and here it sat sticking out like a sore thumb. During the dry season, this place would have been alive with farmers, ranchers, and craftsmen from all the nearby villages. This used to be a place where goods were shipped out and distributed for thousands of miles and to more cities and towns than he could name. But that was a long time ago. Now the place sat, a tomb for a lost way of life. He had heard things were quite different back then. The old folk in Metacity would sometimes talk about the stories they heard from their great grand folk before them. The old stories had been passed down so much that he doubted if half of them were even close to true. But here he stood at the mouth of an ancient relic that was proving some of the legends. He was both nervous and awestruck. He remained silent on the massive landing, waiting for the moon to finally find its place in the sky and offer its own brilliance to the darkened place around him. Slowly, his ever present exhaustion took over. He collapsed in a heap succumbing to sleep; one he hadn't felt since escaping Metacity.

Dry and crusted eyelids peeled apart slowly as Jordi found awareness. As he had hoped, the lonely moon was full and hanging above him, giving a pale alertness to the quiet and useless train station. Some time had passed; the water below was once again still as the Water Razors had gone elsewhere to find food. Feeling a small sense of safety, he turned to the station's grand entrance, seeing it illuminated for the first time. From left to right the huge building sprawled, and leftward the building rose and arched over the train track, leaving plenty of room below. He felt a twinge of panic as he surveyed the building; it was in perfect condition. There were no signs of war, famine, or violence of any kind. It was as if everyone decided it was best to leave, and if the stories he had heard were true, that could very well have been the case. He was more surprised by his reaction than anything. Maybe it was his regained and freshened alertness, but he didn't like it, not a bit. The grand staircase he had climbed a few hours ago led to a large marble landing where hundreds of massive glass doors that he assumed led into the station's grand halls. He had heard enough stories and had seen enough similar buildings in Metacity to get the gist of how this one might lay out. He took a moment to relieve himself over the tall ledge into the salty brine below. The splashing sound echoed across the endless ocean. Thanks to the pale moon, the wave looked like shimmering mist. He thought briefly of Metacity, then pushed it out of his head and walked to the entry doors. The steel pull bars of the doors were as ornate as they were big, but failed in comparison to the door itself. None of the detail was visible at first in such poor lighting, but now that he was inches away, he could take it in. Slowly he reached for the handle, mostly expecting it not to budge a bit, but the door opened smoothly and with little effort. Jordi entered the building.

Inside the giant complex, the dusty skylights gave some light to the building's innards, for which Jordi was thankful. Endless rows of empty benches spread out before him. Their uniformity occasionally broke up by a forgotten blanket or a box of goods that had been deemed useless or unnecessary during the escape. Maybe it was the safety of a roof over his head, or the ignored hunger pangs brought on by hours of walking, but Jordi thoroughly felt the emptiness of his stomach finally. He didn't have the luxury of scavenging for food before escaping from Metacity for the last time; he only left with a half full canteen. He scanned the outer perimeters of the building where shops may have existed so many moons before The Fall. Across from the resting pews, he saw shuttered storefronts. After a moment of hesitation, listening for possible company, and hearing nothing, he made his way to the stores.

Previous looters had already ransacked the first store. It was barren save for the shelves that would have held goods during better times. He made his way to the next store and found its steel shutter closed fully. Out of curiosity, he pulled upward on the steel and, much to his surprise, they easily slid up. After the metal shutters found their home above, he pried at the glass doors ,and they also slid open with ease. Pausing briefly to glance over shoulder, he made sure the giant causeway was still and silent. Once assured, he entered the store front. The small store smelled rich and aromatic, and he couldn't help but grin. Despite the aching quake in his stomach, the rich aroma gave him a sudden happiness. He gazed into the darkness, suddenly realizing he hadn't accounted for the lack of moonlight from no windows. He fiddled in his knapsack until he found what he was looking for. With a quick thumb flick, his lighter flashed to life. To his amazement, the store hadn't been tampered with at all. There was no sign of pillaging; the shelves were pristine and virginal, just the way some store hand had left them some two hundred years before. There was a trash can nearby. He grabbed it and stuck it into the glass door way that led back into the common floor. Then he noticed a stack of brittle papers and tossed them into the can before he lit the whole set ablaze. It was enough to give purpose to his cause; he himself would loot this treasure trove. He studied the small store and quickly realized that most of the shelves were fully pregnant with liquor bottles. An ironic grin found his dry lips. He thought about Metacity and all the bridges he burned by fleeing; this bounty of unsullied liquor would buy him a handsome fortune back in the city. There were hundreds of untouched bottles of booze aged at least two hundred years. A simple bottle of whiskey would have bought him a house with a view of the wasteland back in Metacity, and now he stood in front of close to a thousand bottles of perfectly aged hooch. Despite his glamour, he meandered towards the back of the store near the cashier's desk, where he found a glassed-in closet of tobacco. In Metacity, as a younger man, he partook in the tobacco grown in the hydroponics of the basements of the skyscrapers—it was harsh but satisfying. But here were boxes of aged pure leaf smoke from the old world, the kind that was grown in the ground over a season's worth of rain. Despite the age, his first thought was sampling the leaves. He looked down kindly into one of the display boxes of cigars. There was a fine crystalline sheen on many of them, a mark of quality; the tobacco oils had naturally crystallized over time. Unable to help himself, he gingerly picked one up. It felt heavy and well made. He sucked on the tip, moistening it for smoking, and it made his lips tingle from the vigor of the leaf. He wouldn't smoke it in here, but he would soon.

He barely registered the dull sound from the grand room because of the overwhelming time capsule he'd found. But his instincts took over once it finally registered. Dropping the cigar on the counter, he pulled steel. No use in hiding, the trash fire gave up his presence all too easily. It was probably a wild cat or maybe a nest of irradiated rats—at least that's what he hoped it would end up being. He palmed the butts of the twin pistols on either side of his hips, painfully wishing for more ammo. In that moment he involuntarily recalled spending the last round right outside Metacity, where the train tracks left the city walls and headed to nowhere. He remembered the final foot soldier who had been chasing him, eager to claim the bounty on his head. It was just outside the walls that Jordi pulled iron and blew off the jaw of his would-be captor. With his eyes looking in opposite directions, he had stumbled forward and collapsed on the submerged tracks. That was Jordi's cue to run. It would be the last time he would ever be in Metacity alive, and the last bullet he would have for a very long time. And right now, he was praying to all the oracles that whatever was making such a noise didn't share the water razors lust for warm flesh.

The trash fire made the already dismal lighting worse with smoke as he peered into the moonlit grand room. He held his breath and waited. Sure enough, another muffled clang rang out. This time he was able to pinpoint it. Across the massive waiting area was another wall of shops like the one he was staring out of. He could barely make out the store front straight across from him, but the bent steel bars of the store gate gleamed dully in the moonlight. Another low shuffle came from somewhere in the store itself, behind the pried open bars. This second burst of noise made Jordi relax just a thumb's width, it wasn't the shuffle of a predator; predators don't make shuffles. This was the sign of a scavenger. Something, just like himself, looking for a dry place and a clean meal. He relaxed his shoulders but kept his wits about him. Eyes wide, he departed the liquor store, crouched low. Shifting around long benches he stayed out of sight as he closed the gap. Maybe it's a wild dog that lost its pack, then he paused for a second; what if the pack was nearby? Stopping briefly behind a rotted out long bench, he pondered the idea. If this were   a den, he would have already been attacked. This was something else. Brazenly, and before he could stop himself, he stood erect. Surprisingly, his fear had left him. His normally cautious demeanor was nowhere to be found. The fact that he was suddenly on display did nothing to settle the rustling in the store front. Perhaps thc thing was just oblivious, but it clearly didn't care if Jordi was there or not. Then it dawned on him; the thing didn't know he was there.

Smoothly and almost eagerly he clipped a mossy pile of burgundy bricks near his left foot. The little tower tottered over and produced a thudded clap that echoed off the old walls. Sure enough, the thing now realized it wasn't alone. Whatever it was, it suddenly fell silent. Jordi stood flat-footed, waiting. Half expecting to turn and flee to the grand entrance to escape and the other half of him was ready to fight. There was a sudden shift. Some empty bottles from the blackness inside the store slowly rolled out into the dim moonlight. Jordi held his breath, feeling the atmosphere around him. He stood still, waiting. Gently, a simple, small frame stepped into the moonlight. Jordi's tense shooting hand loosened, and his clenched jaw slacked. The figure didn't make any sign of aggression; her empty dirty hands showed their small palms face up as they dangled by her hips. She came to a halt once the moonbeams found her face, averting her eyes but keeping him easily in sight, waiting for him to make the next move. She was dirty and shaking from the cold. It looked as though she had lost her shoes some time ago. Her soles and toes blackened and crusted. He stood there, observing her. Her eyes were big and round, unlike the womenfolk back in Metacity who had dark almond ones. Her hair would have been a simple sandy color if it were clean. But now it was far from it. She refused to look him in the eyes, and the tense, ropey muscles under her thin, tattered clothes suggested she was ready to sprint at a moment's notice. He knew he shouldn't move too quickly and spook her; wouldn't spook her. A curious compassion filled Jordi, something he hadn't felt in many years. He couldn't help but grin a little at the thought of this girl considering him a threat. But when he paused to consider his own appearance, it suddenly made sense; he looked rough, if not at least a little dangerous. With caution, he raised his   hands up into the moonlight, revealing his empty palms, wanting to show her he had nothing to hide, his own hands matching hers in filth. The gesture did little to settle her; she remained still, watching him with big, unblinking eyes, her head tilted down just enough to prevent any accidental eye contact. She didn't move. Jordi wasn't sure where to go with this. He mulled over a few options that he quickly tossed to the side. Flustered, he finally just parted his salt cracked lips and offered a dry whisper. "Hi."

It must have been the way he said it because as soon as he broke the silence her eyes locked onto his. Suddenly she didn't feel so meek, and as if roles had changed, he found himself wearing the uncertainty that she had just so quickly shed. He felt like her equal. As he pondered what to say or ask next, she cut him off.

"Whhs nofas dishhwou nofff," she stated with clear certainty.

Jordi stared wide eyed in complete confusion. She didn't break her stare, so he could only imagine that she was waiting for a response. Jordi had never been one for diplomacy, or even civility, for that matter. She adjusted her stance, bending her knees slightly and crouching just a bit. *Was she getting ready to attack?* he asked himself, realizing that the option was fully possible. He didn't have the strength nor the vigor to defend himself. Quickly and smoothly, he raised his hands above his head and locked his fingers together.

"I'm assuming you don't use the common tongue?" he asked in a clear, non-aggressive tone, hoping his speech would show his true intention.

She held tense and unmoving. "Gsssch nawaba nossch ff icch." The words slipped sharply from her lips. She drew her hands into tight fists and stooped a fraction lower.

"Okay, that didn't sound friendly." He put out soft and cool.

He tried to swallow the lump in his throat, and before he could utter another word, she was hurdling towards him. She was fast; fast enough to catch Jordi off guard. But not fast enough to best him. Within the frame of an instance, she was within a foot of Jordi, delivering a hard right jab that was meant to split his jaw in half. She was fast, he would give her that, but that would be all the credit he would give her for the moment. He let his hands loose as he snapped his right one down, grabbing her wrist and side stepping, letting momentum do the hard work, leaving one leg in place she quickly found the floor. Her head smacked off the cracked tile and her breath knocked out as she hit the floor. He glided down on top of her, placing a hard knee onto her back, applying enough pressure to get her attention. With her wrist still anchored in his grip, he jerked it up behind her back. Despite the sudden and disorienting trauma, she let out a whimper of pain just enough to let him know that she hadn't lost consciousness. He watched as she fumbled for anything within reach of her free hand; still fighting for a life that was never in real mortal danger. Her dirty hand flapped hopelessly about the dusty tiles, finding nothing. She tried to push against the knee buried in her spine but was unable to gain leverage enough to do much more than squirm on the cracked sunbaked floor. After a few more moments of resistance, her feeble writhing came to a halt. His knee, so firmly planted into her back that he could feel the hard thumping of her heart, was slowly returning to normal; it was best to give her time. Her free hand, unable to find much more than dust and pebbles, eased to a stop, and softly thudded to the tiles in defeat. She lay still in surrender. For the moment he thought about offering more words but decided it would be a waste of energy. The thought of more struggle made his back and fresh wounds from the water razors ache. He was too tired for this.

With no warning, he rose to his feet and decidedly lost interest in his defeated foe. She lay still but staring wildly in confusion. Jordi took a deep breath and dropped himself onto one of the countless pews with a heavy thud. She didn't move, but he didn't care—he couldn't care anymore about anything. He let his heavy eyes slide shut as he eased back into the bench, his head resting against gently rotting wood.

She must have laid motionless for close to half an hour until she heard his soft breathing turn to a light snore. Without making a sound, she rose to her feet. She stared at the resting man, some ten feet from her. Slumped heavily onto the bench, his head tilted back, exposing his neck. She could have ended his life quickly from such a vantage point, but she didn't. She thought to herself in her own sharp worded language as ideas collided. She couldn't help but feel a bit upset by the sudden and cold dismissal. How dare this human simply cast her existence aside. Crossing her arms in disapproval, she stared impatiently at the sleeping man, waiting. Jordi snored softly, finding amazing comfort from such little accommodations. She fidgeted on her feet, biting her lip and thinking. Finally, she let out a stern sigh as she planted her hands on her hips. With a bare and dirty foot, she obtusely nudged Jordi's outstretched leg. The gaunt, dried out man didn't budge. The female was quickly losing what little patience she had. She jutted out her foot again, striking him again in the same spot, this time shaking his lower torso. He let slip a grunt of small disapproval.

Years ago, Jordi learned the necessity and benefits of being a light sleeper, and now that attribute brought him out of his much-welcomed sleep. One eye cracked open and peered in her direction. She was blurry, but he could see that she wasn't happy, and yet, it was profound how much he didn't care. He closed his eyes again. The action was followed by an aggressive huff and footsteps leading away from him. He was almost once again deep in slumber when he felt another sharp kick against his leg. That same eye cracked open, still blurry. The girl, or at least that's what she may have been, stood in front of him, arm outstretched. It took a second, but he finally realized that she was handing him something: a can of food.

A small fire burned in the middle of the monstrous causeway; they had pushed the benches away, making a clearing on the old tile. There was more than enough wood and kindling to fuel a bonfire, but it wasn't necessary. The cool winds blowing in through the cracked and crashed skylights were bearable, and there was no need to draw unwanted attention. The girl had wandered off somewhere after letting out a long spill of sharp words. All Jordi could do was nod and smile. She waved a dismissive hand and walked off into the darkness of the train station. He assumed she was looking for supplies. Which meant she was like him: new to the station and probably not looking to be found. He stoked the new fire till it was knee high and healthy. It didn't matter who she was, or where she came from, or even where she was headed. In the morning, he would be leaving.

With the fire set, Jordi sauntered back to the liquor store across the way. He lifted an aged root whiskey and a box of Mainsonne cigars. The humor and irony of such luxuries found in a place of such abandonment was not lost on him. Back next to the fire he settled into one of the benches and pulled his side bag onto his lap, digging inside he pulled out a brass disk that quickly expanded into a small cup with the press of a hidden button, he didn't bother admiring the label of the two-hundred-year-old booze. He could guess the usual flowery text that graced such high-end goods. Words meant to impress someone enough to justify buying it. Words meant for people from another time, another place.

He poured his brass cup half full and took a long sip, his eyes closing as the smooth burn of the liquid woke up his cheeks and filled his nostrils with fire. With an easy swallow, he took another sip of liquor he would never be able to afford. The wooden cigar box was also covered with beautiful labels and pretty words. He opened it and bit off the butt of one then spat the tip into the modest fire. Replacing the cigar in his mouth, he once again summoned his almost too-tattered side bag and withdrew a silver tube from one of the side pockets. A lighter with a strong green jet like flame. A moment later, bellows of opaque gray swirled up towards the fractured skylights. The smoke tasted sweet with an earthy tone of peat. He was on his second brass full of root whiskey and his head was starting to swim when he heard soppy footsteps in the distance in which the girl had wandered off to. Once she had made her way into the fire's dim glow, he understood why she sounded like she had taken a swim; and it was because she had taken a swim. Jordi stared in confusion at the soaking wet girl. She wore a broad and proud smile, teeth clenched tight despite heavy breaths caused by the labor of her prize and burden, the source of pride in her smile; a giant fish.

The root booze had made the otherwise amusing sight flat out laughable. The dirty girl plopped the very large and very freshly dead fish onto one of the benches. Taking a small knife from her makeshift shoulder bag, she began to clean the massive and ugly fish.

"That's a Rum Fish," he muttered mostly to himself from behind his curious grin. "It's damn ugly and tastes like mud, but I think it will cook up right."

The girl glanced up from her quick knife work and gave him a blank look, a look that said 'you talk too much'. Jordi took another short sip as his eyes suddenly flashed. He swallowed quickly and asked, "How did you deal with the Water Razors?"

For a moment Jordi could have sworn she understood him. She looked at him impatiently and gestured with her knife hand from the fish to the fire. "sssh nahanawana yuuotuto!"

He may have been on his way to a drunken stupor, but it was clear what she wanted. He was in charge of figuring out a way to cook the ugly as sin fish.

He was right, the Rum Fish tasted sins awful, but once the meat hit the hot metal and started to sizzle, the smell of cooking meat set his empty stomach on edge. He figured it had been close to a week since he had a hot meal, and despite the Rum Fish's gritty and terrible texture, he was glad to have it. Both he and the girl ate in silence. The dinner conversation never even had a chance to begin. After the girl's quick knife work she sat patiently next to a pile of fish cuts that she neatly stacked on the dead fish's flayed skin she'd stretched out on the dirty ground. It was clear she'd done this before, Jordi thought, probably a thousand and one times. He had a respectable cooking surface going in no time. The thin sheet metal propped up by bricks made a well enough cooking top for the ten some odd pounds she had managed to carve out of the hideous beast. They both sat crossed legged on either side of the fire. They had no way of showing it to each other, but they were both thankful for the temporary tranquility. They were warm and had a roof overhead. Their bellies filled with hot, blubbery meat. Neither one had any idea how much they had in common; at least right now they didn't. The circle of benches gave the camp a huddled feeling that was welcomed. Because the next day would be another long day of running. For both of them.

There were three Rum Fish steaks left. The girl wrapped them in paper from a nearby reading store. He reckoned at some point tomorrow he would be glad for the foresight. The thought struck him as funny. Somehow he had assumed that the girl would still be in his company the next day. He couldn't exactly ask what her itinerary was. Maybe it was the root talking, but he half hoped that maybe they were both headed the same way. Jordis head gently swam thanks to the dark and well-aged booze. He wasn't sure when he finally dozed off, but he was glad for the rest. The girl wasn't a worry. If she wanted him dead, they would have gone down that path hours ago. Who was she, though? Where did she come from? Where was she going? Why is she alone? He knew well enough that there were parts of the world you didn't go to unless you were meaning not to be found. And this ancient train station was very much one of those places. His heavy head sank into his traveler's bag which would serve as his pillow on that clear, starry night. The girl made her own nest on the other side of the fire. She was quick about it and efficient. She gathered old cushions from the countless benches as Jordi had and covered herself with a tattered green blanket that had been tied to an equally tattered backpack. He watched her as his eyelids grew heavy. He was helpless to the pull of sleep, and as he finally gave himself over to its ways, a single thought fluttered easily across his mind; what was her name?

They had both risen with the sun as it broke through the pyramid like skylights. What whole windowpanes that were left were yellowed and aged, giving the already warm rays an even more inviting quality. Jordi hadn't fully realized how big the station was in the darkness of night. But now that he was rested and the station fully lit, he could take in the awe of it. When he awoke, the girl was gone. But he located her quickly when he heard loud crashes from a nearby store. Surprisingly, the booze hadn't left him feeling groggy; an unknown side effect to liquor aged two hundred years. He gathered himself and walked towards the sound. It looked like a store that may have sold novelties and trinkets. The type of place that would have caught the attention of a child some five generations ago. *What could she want with this place*, he thought. He entered the store, where she instantly noticed him. Without so much as a gesture, she tossed him a full waterskin. He grabbed it with one hand and chugged the cool liquid, and then he decided that the first call to order was to discover her name.

It was far from easy, but after a few gentle attempts, he felt that she got the gist as she let out a long stream of sounds while tapping her head. "Qnnnatututwabba."

"Well, there's a name I'll never say the same twice," he joked, but she only stared back.

After a moment, he realized she was waiting for him to return the sentiment. He cleared his throat and tapped his head as he smoothly pronounced his own name.

She continued to stare, and he repeated the action, trying his best to sound just the same. She didn't look puzzled, but she didn't look sold on it either. He began to repeat himself for a third time, but as he made his way through the middle of his name, she cut him off.

"Yordi." She nodded and turned back to searching the old store.

The sun would soon be directly overhead in about two hours, and despite himself, Jordi was growing fidgety; it was time to move. For a moment he thought how Qnnn and himself could make this place into a home. There was plenty of Rum Fish, booze, water, and shelter. And when the dry season rolled in, they could till the fields and grow crops. He pictures them learning each other's languages over time. Hell, maybe he could even see himself falling for those clear blue eyes. But none of that was possible. He knew all too soon that word of his escape from Metacity would make it back to the Ragnarok clan. And they would chase him. They would follow him.

His neck hairs suddenly stood straight as all the sweet nothings brought on by the notion of a normal life shattered in front of him.

Jordi made his way back to the makeshift camp and now burned out fire pit in the middle of the causeway. Hastefully, he began shoveling his few belongings into his bag.

"Yordi?"

Her voice startled him. He had been fixed in his own head and hadn't heard her light footsteps approaching. He looked up into her eyes. He didn't need to speak her language to know what she was thinking. Her eyes said it all, she looked worried and confused. His sudden change in mood was easily noticed, and now she stood next to him, watching his actions. He sighed deeply as he tried thinking up a way to say that he was a dead man running. No easy task when they didn't even share one common word. But despite his impatience, he felt he owed his new friend an explanation. He gestured to himself with his right hand and slowly said his name. He watched her eyes, making sure she was following him.

"Jordi . . . go . . ." With his pointer and middle finger he mimicked a pair of legs walking away. Instantly her face lit up with a toothy smile.

"Queenawaq atuuu weqyy xcyio," she said almost in a shout as she grabbed his hand and pulled him to his feet.

Running with eagerness, she led him away from the causeway. She guided him towards one of the long hallways of terminals that connected to the main hub. He hadn't had time to explore any of the countless tentacles stretching off of the main common area, and he doubted he would today. The massiveness of the grand entrance wasn't lost on the vast hallway. Equal in stature, it was wide and capped with a long, arched dome that meandered the length of the hall as far as Jordi could see. Here and there were empty luggage racks that travelers would have used. A surprising amount of abandoned bags and suitcases littered the floor. *People dropped everything and ran when the great divide happened*, he thought as he stepped over a child's pink satchel. *Can't say I blame them.*

Finally, she veered to the right and entered one of the terminals. It was a small alcove with its own small seating area. Near the back wall stood a high-top desk covered in clutter. Behind the desk, Jordi spotted what he assumed Qnnn was so ecstatic about. There stood a large set of double doors with one of them slightly propped open by a shiv of rusted metal. She let go of his arm and shot him a big smile as she pulled and heaved the heavy door open. Sunlight and fresh air poured into the terminal as she swung it open. Outside felt warm and alive. She once again grabbed his arm and led him out into the dazzling sunlight.

It took a moment for his eyes to adjust, but then he found them both on a huge rusted metal platform. The wind caused the water rinsed plains to ripple, letting out the echoing sound of countless tiny waves. The strong winds were moist and cool despite the unclouded sun. He had almost forgotten about the hundreds of miles of barely submerged grasslands. He could see all the way to the horizon, and there wasn't anything out there, just clear waters and clear sky. The platform was two hundred feet wide and along the side of the building as far as he could see. He watched as the girl ran to the far side of the boardwalk, to where the submerged tracks sat. That's when it caught his eye. On one of the sunken tracks sat a hand trolley. He smiled with shock and followed the girl's quick stride.

It was old, but it worked. "Where did it come from?" he asked while at the same moment knowing she couldn't answer.

She smiled at him, oblivious to his inquiry. The trolley was made of mostly metal with a wood-metal alloy for its base to stand on. In the center was the pump action lever that would move it down the tracks. Jordi grabbed the horizontal pump and pressed down. To his surprise, the trolley glided easily across the underwater tracks. The girl smiled bigger when she saw Jordi's grin broaden across his face at the discovery.

"Yordi weereq suuuuufrww nu tu uu wu," she said, nodding as if proud of herself. She held up her right hand and mimicked his gesture of walking. Jordi smiled and nodded.

"Reeuouue sssuububu na nu tu fiiiuy nosss," she said, making her own gesture as she held up her pointer finger: Wait.

In an instant, the girl disappeared into the ancient train station. Jordi stood on the hand trolley, thinking. He should leave. Right now, without her. If Ragnarok did catch up with him, which was going to happen eventually, she would be dead too. But if he left her here, and the clan made it here, she would be as good as dead, anyway. The Ragnarok killed first and inquired later. He gripped the hand pump and thought for a long moment. He took a deep breath and adjusted his grip. Squeezing the old, cold metal in his hand, he sighed.

"Gahhhwee tetuutuutetu nu gu juuuu," she spat out, running across the platform.

Jordi snapped out of his thoughts. "Uh?" he muttered dumbly.

"Gahhhwee tetuutuutetu nu!!" she yelled, gesturing behind him as she let drop a heavy bag onto the trolley's deck. Jordi glanced over his shoulder. He didn't see it at first because of the water's glimmer, but far off on the horizon he finally saw it: a tiny plume of black smoke. It was coming from the same path he had walked just the day before. It was coming from Metacity. Puzzled, Jordi shielded his eyes for a moment to better study. White hot panic exploded in his chest. It was a train.

Jordi turned back to Qnnn. "We have to go." He gripped the hand pump again, and within seconds, the trolley was zooming along the tracks. Once they were clear of the massive train station, he glanced over shoulder. "You will probably never see that place again," he said, as much to himself as to the girl.

"Suu fewwehew," she replied softly as she watched the train station turn into a blur on the horizon.

As Jordi steadily operated the crank, the girl rummaged through the heavy bag she had brought and pulled out an old, folded map. She stepped next to him and took over the hand pump as she handed the map to him. It was worn and delicate, and he fought against the wind to keep it from ripping at the seams. It was a map of train stations, showing all the different places you could go. Jordi didn't recognize any of the dozens of names, but he did notice one. It was written by hand above a faintly drawn circle on a barren stretch of the map's railway. Whoever made the map hundreds of years ago either didn't know of this place or didn't intend for anyone to go there. Above the small, faded circle read the name Camp Town. He refolded the map and handed it back to the girl who let him take over operating the crank. She nodded and took a seat on the trolley's deck.

She squinted in the sunlight as she looked back at him. "Uuuewasss sss sxx fu tu lu," she stated with ease. As if to say that everything was going to be alright. He feigned a smile and returned to staring down the watery plains ahead. He knew it wasn't going to be alright. He knew it was going to get a whole lot worse from here.

Acknowledgements

I would like to thank Adam Solid for helping to bring this project to life. And Jessica at Desert Ink Editorial for making sense of my ramblings. I would like to say thanks to all my friends who put up with me and this pursuit. Including Bella, Mel, Paul, Nicodemus, and especially Blus.

About the Author

Marvin Day resides in eastern Pennsylvania.

www.marvindaywriter.com

ALSO BY

Coming Soon:
Magician Syndrome

www.ingramcontent.com/pod-product-compliance
Lightning Source LLC
Chambersburg PA
CBHW050507160726